DECEPTIONS OF THE HEART

Devilishly handsome, wickedly insatiable Martin Kestrel can have any woman he desires—and the one he's decided to marry is Abigail Perry, his longtime confidante. But the prim enchantress who's tempted him with respectability is actually Harriet MacLeod—a brazen deceiver... and a *spy*. So now, as punishment for trifling with Kestrel's heart, she must pay with her innocence.

Harriet's sole intention was to serve her Queen, not to fall in love. And now she's forced to use Martin yet again to infiltrate a house party. His insistence that she pose as his mistress worries her ... as much as it excites her. And when the masquerade turns all-too-deliciously real, will she and Martin be able to handle the consequences?

If You've Enjoyed This Book,
Be Sure to Read These Other
AVON ROMANTIC TREASURES

SUSAN SIZEMORE

Too Wicked to Marry

An Avon Romantic Treasure

AVON BOOKS

An Imprint of HarperCollinsPublishers

AVON BOOKS
An Imprint of HarperCollins*Publishers*
10 East 53rd Street
New York, New York 10022-5299

Copyright © 2002 by Susan Sizemore
ISBN: 0-380-81652-0
www.avonromance.com

First Avon Books paperback printing: January 2002

Avon Trademark Reg. U.S. Pat. Off. and in Other Countries, Marca Registrada, Hecho en U.S.A.
HarperCollins ® is a registered trademark of HarperCollins Publishers Inc.

Printed in the U.S.A.

10 9 8 7 6 5 4 3 2 1

For Elisa and Steve
in honor of March 9, 1998, and March 9, 2001

Chapter 1

1880

"Isn't the night *beautiful*?" the woman said soulfully.

"No." Martin's deep voice was as flat as the moonlit sea upon which he gazed.

Abigail would never have said something so banal. He was vaguely tempted to smile at the affronted look Lady Ellen Causely gave him at his answer. Vague emotions were about all he was up to this evening, about all he'd been up to for some time. This ennui and indifference *almost* annoyed him.

Lady Ellen tried again. "The sea air is so refreshing."

"It smells of salt and dead fish."

"The moonlight on the water sparkles like diamonds."

"You've always had a fondness for diamonds, my dear, but you won't get any from me."

Abigail would have tapped him on the arm and told him he wasn't getting into the spirit of the thing. Lady Ellen gave a furious gasp, whirled around in a froth of skirts, and marched back indoors, where music, laughter, and more genial prey beckoned. Abigail would have commented that the lady gave up too quickly if she'd really set her husband-hunting sights on Lord Martin Kestrel. Abigail had informed him on more than one occasion that when he was not with his daughter or performing his diplomatic duties, he was a wretched man with the tongue of an adder and the hide of a rhinoceros, and everyone knew it. People needed to be prepared for encounters with him.

"Lady Ellen has not done her lessons," he murmured, relieved to have the deck of the yacht to himself, as he had intended to have it all along when several people had followed him out of the party. He'd used his acerbic

2

tongue to send them back, one by one, among people who actually wanted to share company.

When Freddie had invited Martin for a fortnight holiday on the yacht and at Freddie's estate on the Isle of Wight, his old school chum had not mentioned how many other guests there would be. That many of them were unattached, eligible ladies had everything to do with Sir Frederick Hazlemoor's recent and still blissful wedded state. Freddie and his lady were of the opinion that *everyone* should be happily married.

"This will not do, old boy," Freddie said, coming up behind him.

Martin hid the fact that he was startled at his friend's sudden appearance. He'd spent some time staring at nothing, he supposed, with his mind as blank as blank could be. Better blank than thinking about marriage.

"I've been rude and ungracious to a flower of British femininity, and you've been sent by your wife to reprove me."

"I've been sent to express concern." Freddie clapped him on the shoulder. "You're not unsociable by nature, Martin, but you've been a bear with a toothache since coming on board. There's a movement growing among the ladies

3

to chuck you overboard, or at least to find a deserted island and put you off on it."

Martin rubbed a thumb along his jaw. "I rather like the deserted island scheme. Would I be allowed to pack a few books?"

"No. The point would be to punish your wretched behavior."

"Ah. So Lady Ellen's volunteered to accompany me. Or is it the whining Miss Greer?"

"Being in their company is not a punishment. Is it because they're respectable that you're not exhibiting your usual charm?"

Martin caught himself from saying that being in anyone's company at present felt like punishment, for that would be rude and ungrateful. He had accepted Freddie's well-meant invitation; he had no one to blame but himself. "My reputation is not that stained, surely."

"Hardly, old friend. But I'm relieved you chose to spend time in calmer company than with some of your recent friends."

"You've heard about the gambling and debauchery at Sir Anthony's parties?"

Freddie nodded.

"I did receive an invitation to that notorious

4

gentleman's house party," Martin admitted. "But I haven't been thinking I'd rather be there. Still, my mood's been ruining your party. I know it, and I am sorry."

Freddie eyed him critically. "Apology accepted, but is your behavior going to change?"

Martin was very tempted to say no. He gave himself a stern, swift, silent lecture, and said, "I will make an effort to be more amiable."

"Then come inside, where your expertise is wanted." Freddie draped an arm over Martin's shoulders, effectively trapping his guest as he guided him toward the main cabin.

"Expertise in what?" Martin asked. "Whatever do the ladies have in mind?"

"You needn't pretend to be scandalized, old man. My beloved bride has decided that we will entertain each other with amateur theatricals."

Martin groaned and glanced over his shoulder at the quiet sea. "Perhaps I'll throw myself overboard now."

"Oh, no, I'm not letting you off that easily."

"I'm a terrible actor."

"You're a premier diplomat."

"That's different. That's a game of bluff and bluster and figuring out who's the most dangerous liar in a room full of dangerous liars. It's not the same as spouting off poorly written doggerel."

"We shall be performing Shakespeare."

"Very well, spouting off *well*-written doggerel."

"It doesn't matter, Martin." They'd reached the door. "We aren't rehearsing dialogue this evening." Inside Martin saw that most of the furniture had been pushed aside, leaving a cleared space in the middle of the cabin. He also found himself standing in the center of this area with his host, all eyes—most of them female—turned attentively upon him. "Take off your coat, old man," Freddie advised. Someone tossed a pair of practice foils to Freddie, who turned on Martin with a smile. "Tonight you're going to teach us fencing."

When the lesson was finished an hour later and he asked for something to drink, Lady Ellen handed him a glass of champagne. Martin did not particularly like champagne, but he was thirsty, and the chilled wine went down in two long gulps. Vera Greer and Daphne Markham sidled up as he handed the glass back to Lady Ellen. Martin suddenly noticed that he'd somehow managed to get himself backed into a corner, and now he was trapped by a trio of females. He felt more than a little vulnerable, flushed as he was with exercise and stripped down to his white shirt, his hair disheveled and slightly damp with sweat. He was hardly in a fit state to hold conversation with well-bred young ladies, but they didn't seem to notice. He'd promised to be polite, and he never went back on his promises.

So he managed to smile without gritting his teeth, and said, "That was a pleasant beginning to rehearsals, wasn't it?"

"I've never seen anything like it," Daphne offered, fluttering her eyelashes in admiration. "I had not realized you were so athletic, Lord Martin."

She had pretty eyes, Martin conceded. In fact, she was quite an attractive girl. That was the problem: she was a *girl*, a charming innocent. Some men took a fancy to women half their age, but Martin found raising one daughter quite challenging enough without the complication of bestowing his hand on a lass he'd feel obligated to tuck into bed for a bedtime story rather than to make love to. The notion of bringing home a child bride was laughable, and he could imagine Abigail's sharp comments should he try.

"Fencing is merely a hobby with me," he told the girl. "I assure you that I am no expert with the foil."

"You look so dashing with a sword in your hand," Lady Ellen enthused. "So . . ." She blushed, and whispered, "Virile."

Vera and Daphne twittered like a pair of shocked but amused birds, while Lady Ellen eyed him with a more mature interest. Martin kept smiling at them, fighting the impulse to push through the gaggle and run for his life. *Someone please rescue me.*

Miraculously, it was Her Grace, the Duchess of Pyneham, who answered his prayer. Even in her mid-sixties, the tall woman towered over the trio of younger women as she came up behind them. "Put a sword in a handsome man's hand and watch the ladies swoon. At least I always have. I don't know about dashing, but if what I hear about the number and variety of Lord Martin's mistresses is even half true—"

"Oh, my!" Vera gasped before the duchess could finish.

"Your Grace!" Daphne exclaimed, equally in shock.

Martin noticed that Lady Ellen's lips curved in a faint smile, and that there was a far from innocent glint in her eyes. He was certain that Lady Ellen might not be averse to accepting the position of mistress if she could not find a way to get him to marry her.

"Come along, Kestrel," the duchess said, holding out an imperious hand. "I need some air. You have the privilege of escorting me on deck, since my dear husband has taken himself off to bed."

Martin didn't hesitate to make good his escape on the arm of the formidable old lady. Once they were on the deck, she led him to the stern railing of the becalmed vessel. The sea was still as glass, the moonlight bright. Martin could barely stifle a yawn at the lovely sight. It was as though he had done everything there was to do, seen everything, tasted every pleasure and pain, and was bored and irritated by turns.

"If Your Grace will excuse me, I fear I am in no fit state to—"

"Oh, leave off," she commanded. "Am I your godmother or am I not?"

Though it took him a moment to recall the connection, he answered, "Yes, dear lady, I believe you are."

"Good. Then I won't feel quite such a busybody for asking you what the devil is wrong with you? Why are you insisting on making everyone on the bloody boat miserable?"

"I—"

"Mind you, I see your point, with all the women tripping over you trying to get your attention. Subtlety does not appear to be this generation's strong point."

"Freddie and I have already had this talk, ma'am."

She smiled. "Look at you, all stiff and stern and officious. You look more like a bored butler than the most eligible widower in Britain. What's got you all broody, lad? I doubt it's grief for Sabine. She's been dead, what? Three years now? And ran home to Italy a year before that, without you bothering to follow to reclaim your absent bride. Mutual lust does not a successful marriage make, as you learned to your cost. No doubt you fear being burned

10

again, but it's time you married and had an heir."

"I have a daughter."

"And a fine little one she is, but your family's title and property cannot go to her. It's a pity, but it's the law; you need a son. You are in danger of becoming irredeemably dissolute, which I doubt suits you at all. Besides, your parents want more grandchildren, and your mother is one of my best friends. More importantly, my dear roving ambassador, you need a woman to make a home for you. The lasses being tossed your way by our hosts are the best we could assemble on such short notice; they'll all take well to the domestic life. I helped pick the Hazlemoors' guest list myself," she added. "Though I've got my doubts about Ellen Causely. She's worldly without being wise."

"She's rumored to run with a faster crowd than the rest of the pack you've set on me. She's not the marrying sort."

"And lives beyond her means, I hear. You don't want to have to take on her debts or any more gossip. All right, scratch Ellen. And Daphne's too young, I suppose. What's wrong with Vera, then? Too shy? Too romantic?"

Martin glared into the sparkling blue eyes of his blunt godmother. "Perhaps the answer to your questions lies in the fact that I am not currently interested in any woman."

Her expression turned from belligerently amused to downright skeptical. "Really? Then who is Abigail?"

"Who the devil are you?" The young woman's hand was raised to knock a second time. She showed no surprise at his yanking the door open and yelling at her. Nor did she hesitate when he barked, "Get in here!"

"The embassy sent me," she replied as Martin turned back to the man lying on the carpet. "He's been stabbed in the chest," the young woman said, matter-of-fact rather than shocked at the sight of the wounded man.

"That's right," Martin said. "Help me."

She did not ask why or how. She set about helping him bind the wound and clean up the mess in the most practical fashion imaginable. She did not ask foolish questions, but Martin eventually volunteered, "This idiot is my brother. He was wounded in a duel."

"I see." He looked up in surprise, and when their gazes met he saw that she understood a great deal.

12

"Dueling is against the law," she said. "No doubt the fight was over an important man's wife. Officers of the law are actively seeking to arrest the young man."

He nodded.

"We could take him back to the embassy," she suggested.

"No. Our presence in the country is unofficial. I won't involve Her Majesty's government in this sordid matter. He'll live." Martin stood. "We're near the Swiss border; we'll have him out of the country before morning."

Martin drove while the young woman tended to Daniel inside the carriage. It was a cold, snowy night, the drive treacherous, but the guards at the border crossing were amenable to a large bribe.

It was not until they'd safely left Daniel to be nursed by monks at the closest town over the border and were on their way back to the capital of the small Italian principality from which they'd fled, that Martin thought to ask, "Who are you and what were you doing at my door?"

"Abigail Perry," she answered, bundled up in a respectable cloak, gloves, and bonnet beside him on the driver's seat, the bloodstains not showing in the dark. "I'm your daughter's new governess."

* * *

"Abigail," he said to the duchess now, his brows drawn down in puzzlement. "Abigail is—" Martin gestured. "No one you know."

"She certainly seems to be occupying your thoughts."

"Is she?" Martin scratched his head. He couldn't recall having made mention of Abigail at any time in the last several days. One did not discuss one's paid employees with one's friends, it was rude to the servants and none of one's friends' business. He wanted to ask the duchess where she'd heard of Abigail, but he would not expose his daughter's governess to even the breath of a hint of scandal. He had his daughter to think of—and Abigail.

"Don't look outraged and shocked," the tall old lady told him. "You've been comparing every woman you meet to this Abigail person since you arrived."

"I have?"

"Yes. Muttered under your breath, usually, but I have excellent hearing for such an old harpy." She tapped him on the shoulder with a lace-gloved hand. "If she's such a paragon, why don't you marry this Abigail you're so fond of?"

What nonsense! What an incorrigible old ninny! Lord Martin Kestrel drew himself up haughtily. "If Your Grace will excuse me, the evening's exertion has fatigued me. I am going to retire."

"I most certainly do not excuse you," she said as he turned away.

"I'm going to bed anyway, Honoria," he answered, and walked stiffly away.

Martin banged into his cabin, filled with inarticulate anger. He sent his valet away with a sharp gesture and fell into bed half-dressed, certain that sleep was completely impossible. The logical part of him knew this response was all out of proportion to the duchess's words. The whole night had been a disaster! His life was a disaster, but for the shining joy brought to him by his child. The past was riddled with mistakes, the future bleak and dark. He was full of ennui, and yet the longing in him undefined, growing with every breath . . . He had no idea what the matter was.

"What am I doing here?" he questioned as he stared at the ceiling.

The yacht rocked gently on the calm water. The bed was soft and the night comfortably warm. It wasn't long before Martin's body began to relax, despite the restlessness of his spirit. He found himself talking to an absent green-eyed woman, one whose wide mouth curled in a sardonic smile. "What is the matter with me, Abigail?" he questioned the absent Abigail. He yawned, and almost reached out toward her in the dark. "Why am I so . . . ?"

Several hours later, Lord Martin Kestrel woke up in the depths of the night with a wide grin on his face. "Of course!" he laughed as he swung out of his bunk. "Why didn't I see it before?" Call it a revelation, the answer to his prayers, a dream come true. Whatever the reason, he suddenly knew what he must do. He had never felt so alive, so eager, so *happy* in his life.

"Cadwell!" he shouted, waking not only his valet, but probably everyone on the boat. "Cadwell! Pack up, man! I'm going back to London."

Chapter 2

❮──❮❮◦❯❯──❯

She was caught up on her correspondence, had plenty of time to herself, and had a stack of books to read. She'd considered spending all of her month-long holiday catching up with her large family. Most of the clan was gathered in one place for once, and perhaps she would take herself off for a visit in a week or so. But for now, she relished being alone for the first time in ages. Well, perhaps *relish* was not precisely correct. She had to admit that she didn't relish much of anything anymore. *Relish* was a bit too red-blooded a word.

She was entirely too comfortable here, she told herself as she settled on a bench in the garden. She was too fond of her charge; she certainly felt too much as though this were home. Such false contentment was a dangerous mistake for a woman in her situation. She looked around her, and smiled. The garden of Lord Kestrel's London house was in full bloom, the birds were singing, Patricia was on a visit with her grandparents, Kestrel was on a yachting holiday, and but for the skeleton staff, she had the house to herself. After several days of being alone a bit of restlessness was setting in, but for the most part she was able to convince herself that she didn't have a care in the world. All right, she had suffered from a bad dream last night, a recurring nightmare of horrible noise and bright blood and falling. But that was last night. Today she had a copy of *The Iliad* in her lap and the shining summer day stretching before her. She breathed in the scent of roses and opened the leather-bound volume.

She was barely more than a few lines into Achilles' temper tantrum over the possession of the captured Trojan woman when she realized that something was different, wrong. She wasn't sure what had caught her attention—some unexpected sound, perhaps, that had not consciously registered on her ears but had filtered into her awareness nonetheless. A door slamming, perhaps? Yes, that had been it. Who was likely to slam a door in Martin Kestrel's house?

She lifted her head and looked sharply around the empty garden, a small part of her automatically searching for escape routes. Senses acutely alert, she closed the book and rose to her feet. Trouble was coming, she knew it. She didn't know why or what, but she never doubted her visceral reactions. Woman's instinct, her father called it. He encouraged all his daughters to develop it.

She hefted the book under her arm and walked with a quick, wary step toward the entrance to the house. She was not surprised when Martin Kestrel stepped through the French door onto the terrace before she reached it. She had her usual appreciative reaction to the sight of his tall, dark figure, and put that reaction aside as she always did. She noticed instantly that he seemed somehow even more handsome and vital than she remembered. When he saw her he waved, and as he drew quickly closer, his long legs eating the distance between them, she was caught by the intense light in his usually stormy gray eyes. And was that a confident smile gracing his mouth?

"You are smiling," she said as he planted himself in front of her. She peered at him suspiciously. "What's wrong? You haven't smiled in months." This was not precisely true, as Kestrel frequently smiled in the presence of his ten-year-old daughter, but that gentle, paternal smile held nothing of the devilish joy she saw now.

"Suspicious woman." He grasped her hands, causing the leather-bound book to tumble to the ground. He kicked Homer away and drew her closer.

She was too distracted by the firm, warm touch to worry about the fate of the book. He was a large man, and his hands were strong, for all the gentleness with which he touched her. "Stop this at once," she commanded, and tugged against his firm grip. She hoped he did not notice that she trembled ever so slightly. She took pride in her self-control, and hated that he could shake it so easily. Obviously, four years in the quiet life of a governess had made her a bit soft. "Let me go."

"I have no intention of ever letting you go."

As soon as he spoke, he planted a kiss on her forehead.

"Are you drunk?"

"I love it when you look outraged."

"I am not outraged," she answered. "I am appalled." She glanced around. "What if someone sees us standing like this?" There had never before been this sort of intimacy about their nearness. Was the sun shining more brightly with him looking at her this way? And what an odd thought that was. She stiffened her spine and her resolve. "What will people think?"

His smile widened. "Who cares what I do in my own garden?"

"The world cares, as you very well know. I care. You care."

"I do indeed." He lifted her hands, kissing first one and then the other. "I care for you."

She ignored the jolt of pleasure that went through her. "Then have a care for my reputation and release me at once."

"I love your tart tongue." His eyes glittered with amusement, and a wild heat she'd never seen before. "Say something else priggish and governessish, Abigail."

"I *am* a prig, it goes with the post, and *governessish* is not a word."

He laughed. Blast the man! And why did his tone of wicked amusement sound so good to her ears? He looked good, he sounded good, he even smelled good this close up, and the effect was devilishly distracting.

"You are not drunk," she decided, though she felt intoxicated herself. "I can't smell a bit of alcohol on you. Have you gone mad, then?"

"No, love," he said. "I've gone sane."

Love? It was a short word, but probably the most frightening one in the English language. She tilted her head to one side and studied his face. He still held her hands, and she feared he might kiss them again at any moment. She feared that she wanted him to. His touch rattled her, even more than his expression and words. Calm, she told herself, stay calm. It was not as if he'd said he loved her, he had merely called her *love*. She sensed a disaster in the making, but surely there was still time to—

"I love you," he said.

"Oh, dear."

He pulled her into an encompassing embrace and, with his lips brushing her ear, said, "Marry me, my dear Miss Perry. Marry me, my love."

She discovered that it was possible to have

the heart soar and sink at the same time. She was left sick with the pain of being so torn. Her heart was hammering like a drum, yet being in his arms seemed quite natural. She had only to turn her head a little way to be able to meet his lips with hers and—

"What is the matter with me—you. I mean, what is the matter with you, my lord?"

"You generally call me Martin when we are alone."

Words tumbled out of her breathlessly, a paltry cover for her shattered emotions. "A presumption of familiarity on my part. I see that such a presumption was a grave mistake. I assure you that I will never again be so bold as to address my betters in such a—"

He silenced her with a kiss. She wasn't quite sure how he managed to shift their positions so that his mouth covered hers, and for a few moments she didn't care.

Kestrel smiled even though Abigail pushed him away with enough force to make him stumble back a step. The backs of his knees encountered the edge of a pot holding a small orange tree, and he abruptly found himself seated on the pot's rim, looking up at the glaring governess. "You enjoyed being kissed," he said, even as she made a point of wiping the back of her hand across her mouth.

"Of course I enjoyed it," she answered. "You, my lord, are a practiced seducer. You would not have such a reputation if you did not know how to make a woman enjoy being kissed."

Her cheeks glowed a very becoming pink. He crossed his arms and drank in the sight of Abigail Perry discomfited. "You should pick up that book and hurl it at me," he suggested as she looked around at anything but at him. "In defense of your virtue."

"I can defend my virtue without the assistance of a horde of ancient warriors, thank you very much." She finally met his gaze, her green eyes blazing. "What I should do is slap you."

"But you said you enjoyed it."

"Enjoyment is beside the point, my lord." She wiped her mouth again. "That should not have happened."

"It should have happened years ago," he countered.

"Really?" she said, the word coldly scathing. "Recall my place in your household, my lord. What of your daughter?"

Her dignified outrage made him wince. "Abigail, please!"

"What of your promise?" she continued relentlessly. "I trust you do recall that promise?"

He knew he should not have left the child's room so soon after kissing her good night, but he could not bear to answer the question Patricia never tired of asking in the last two months. "Where's Mama?" she asked over and over again. He did not blame her for her confusion, but he almost could not bring himself to lie to her anymore. Tonight he had nearly broken, had nearly told his darling baby that Mama had run off with another man and would never, ever be coming home.

Even if Sabine someday begged him to take her back, no matter how much his senses still craved the intoxication of making love to her, he would never allow a woman who abandoned her only child back into that child's life. Something stronger than fury seethed through his blood at the thought of what Sabine had done. He found himself with a longing for revenge. And unexpectedly, a longing for flesh, a frustrated need that surprised him with its intensity.

What did he have to lose when the marriage vow had been broken already? What business did he have

25

being faithful when adultery already stained his marriage bed?

Though he'd left Patricia to Miss Perry's care after kissing her good night, he still lingered in the drafty hall outside the child's bedroom. The hallway overlooked the dark main room of the small rented villa. He gripped the polished wood railing, looked down into the darkness, and listened while the young woman spoke gently to her new charge and read in a soothing tone until the child fell asleep. Her voice filled his head with a certain amount of peace, and he sighed when she closed the book, wishing that she would go on for at least one more page.

He turned when she came out of Patricia's room and eased the door closed. She held a lamp in one hand, illuminating her face and form in a soft pool of light. Kestrel caught his breath, realizing for the first time that Miss Abigail Perry was a lovely young woman indeed. He already knew from their adventure the night before that she was stalwart, sensible, competent, calm, and discreet. He knew that the British embassy had sent her in answer to his request to find him help after Patricia's last governess decided she could not stay, claiming the scandal surrounding the family would besmirch her good name. He knew that Miss Perry had excellent references, and that Patricia had taken to her instantly, but this was the first time he'd actually seen her. Abigail was a tall, lithe creature with dark brown hair and uptilted sea-green eyes that would have done justice to a mermaid.

"Good lord," he said. "You're lovely." He was not sure it would do to have such a beauty in his house, because instantly, and for the first time in years, he wanted someone other than the sumptuous, sensuous, fiery woman he'd taken as his wife. His faithless wife. He took a step toward Miss Perry, who gave him a withering look, put a finger to her lips that reminded him of his sleeping daughter, and walked swiftly down the hall and down the stairs. He could do nothing but follow, heedless desire raging through him.

Kestrel stood in the shadows and watched her until she finished lighting enough candles to chase most of the shadows away. She wore a simple high-necked brown dress decorated with a few bits of cream lace, and a cameo brooch at her throat. She looked prosaic, practical, respectable, and most of all, unapproachable. Sabine had looked cool and unapproachable when they first met—for all of twenty minutes. Then she had dragged him out into a moonlit garden.

27

"I trust you will not insult me by making such personal comments again, my lord. I came here to be your child's governess," Abigail Perry informed him before he could say a word. *"I did not come here to audition for the role of mistress. Keep that in mind, and we will deal quite well together."*

He was outraged at the chit's daring to address him in so bold a fashion. He was the master of this household! And knew quite well that a higher-handed, harder-to-please, worse-tempered employer than himself had never existed. He went through a lot of help, but the ones who stayed were well paid for what he made them put up with. *"Who are you to tell me how we will deal, Miss Perry?"* he demanded.

"The woman who is going to devote herself to looking after your child," she shot back. *"I do not know about you, my lord, but I will not allow a breath, not a hint, of scandal, old or new, near Patricia. I saw how you looked at me just now, and I also know it had nothing to do with me. So I am willing to ignore it this once."*

"Nothing to do with you? You were the one I was looking at." As angry as she made him, he still found looking at her more than pleasant.

"If you feel you must take revenge for your wife's behavior by indulging your carnal appetites, you

28

*will keep that behavior well outside the confines of
this household."*

*Martin seethed with outrage and stared at the
young woman until silence built up around them
like a heavy storm front. Their gazes were locked,
and furious fire and physical awareness crackled between them. But he was never at a loss for words for
very long.*

*"I see," he said at last, the fire in him banked, but
still burning. "You are instructing me on how to behave in my own home." He took a step forward. "If I
were to touch you now, what would you do?"*

"I would scream," she answered.

*"Scream? Would you really?" He was tempted to
see if she would. He was tempted to touch her, for
her skin looked so warm and inviting in the candlelight. Women wanted to be touched, didn't they?
Even when they professed to be honorable and pure.
"How very weak and feminine of you."*

*"I would scream very loudly. Loudly enough to
wake Patricia."*

*Like being hit in the face with icy water, these
words finally brought him back to his senses. He
blinked and saw his child's governess standing defi-
antly in front of him, instead of an object of seduction. He gave his head a sharp shake, took a long,*

deep breath, and said, "I apologize, Miss Perry." He gestured toward the villa's main door. "I would not be surprised if you chose to walk out right now."

"And leave Patricia alone in a foreign land? I think not."

Though she didn't say it, Martin had the distinct impression that she also had no intention of leaving a little girl alone in a household where the mother ran off, the uncle got into duels, and the father appeared to be at least half-mad. Good for you, Miss Perry, he thought, good for you.

"I take your point, Miss Perry," he told her. "And I make you a promise—never, ever, during your tenure as my daughter's governess, will I make any improper advances upon your person." He held out his hand. "To seal the bargain, will you shake on it?"

She did not hesitate for an instant; she boldly stepped forward and shook on the pact. "You will not regret this promise, my lord," she said.

But he did. Not then, or for years afterward, but he certainly regretted it now.

Chapter 3

~~~⌒◯◯⌒~~~

"**B**ut . . . I've changed," he said. "Things are different now!"

"In what way?" she inquired in that crisp, precise way she had.

Such skepticism was to be expected, he told himself. He'd misjudged how she'd react to such a sudden appearance, but he hadn't been able to stop the spontaneous declaration at the sight of her, sitting there as fresh and beautiful as the roses that surrounded her. There was so much that had gone unsaid between them for years that the floodgates were threatening to open—no, they already had, and he was babbling like a fool as he tried to express the deluge of feelings he'd pushed deep below the surface for so long. He had to remain calm, reasonable, to find a way to negotiate through the obstacles he knew she'd throw up. To get them where he was certain—hoped—they both wanted to be.

"You have become my dearest friend," he told her.

She was not prepared for the pain that shot through her when Martin spoke those words. Didn't the man understand what he was doing to her? How much this hurt? No, of course not. *You're my dearest enemy, more like*, she thought. *Though I truly have tried to be a friend.* "Friend, yes," she answered, having great trouble keeping her voice steady and her true emotions hidden.

"More than friend," he went on, his rich, sincere voice wounding her further. "We need not keep the memory of a no longer necessary pledge between us. I'm not asking you to do anything shameful. You should be flattered, you know, having a peer of the realm asking for your hand."

"You are not a peer, your father isn't dead yet."

"You know what I mean."

She knew he was joking about his deigning

to offer a commoner his hand, but it gave her a means to defend herself against the impossible situation. She lifted her head proudly and said, "Noblesse oblige, my lord? You're good at grand gestures, Martin, but I'd rather have a raise in wages than an offer of marriage if you're looking for some way of rewarding my services."

He chose to smile confidently rather than recognize the ridiculousness of it all. She'd always found his confidence both endearing and infuriating. The combination tended to charm her, but she could not afford to let him charm her now. This was no ordinary conversation, nor was it an ordinary dispute. She had to control her emotions and the situation. But that smile sent unreasonable hope through her, as well as a surge of heat—

"Blast you," she complained. "Stop looking at me like that."

"Like what? A man openly in love with the most wonderful woman in the world?"

"Like a man who has lost his mind."

"Like a man who has come to his senses."

"Shall I send for a physician, my lord?"

"Don't patronize me, Abigail Perry. And why is it, I wonder," he inquired of the world in general, "that I am standing here offering my heart and hand to a woman with a tongue like an adder?"

"I don't know," she answered. She turned her back on him as she asked, "Because you're bored, perhaps?"

"Other women bore me. Never you."

Life with Lord Martin Kestrel was certainly never boring, but she refused to confess to any shared sentiment. She knew too well to never give the man an opening; he was too good a negotiator for that. "If you weren't bored you would not be behaving like this. You were bored when you left," she reminded him.

"I was restless."

"Perhaps it's being back in England that's the problem."

"Perhaps I was struggling to come to my senses and didn't know it."

"Perhaps you miss Patricia."

"Of course I miss her. We shall go and tell her the good news together. She'll be delighted to have you as her stepmother, you know."

"Perhaps you need a new mistress." She swung around to face him once more. "That's your problem; you feel challenged. You need a new conquest."

"I want a wife."

"You once told me that was the last thing you wanted."

"If you recall, I made that statement only a few weeks after I discovered that I was a widower and on the day I received my father's letter saying he wanted me to marry the daughter of a neighbor for the sake of increasing the size of his estates."

She folded her hands to hide the fact that she was trembling with her effort to appear calm. She hated herself for having to argue with him. "You showed me the letter," she recalled. "In it your father said that you had followed your heart once and married a woman beneath your station. He also stated that it was time for you to do your duty with a biddable girl from a good family. I am not biddable, nor is Abigail Perry of a good family."

"Your father's a vicar."

"Well, he was when I met him," she whispered, and was so shocked at this lapse of discretion that she coughed.

"What? Are you all right?"

"Nothing." He came closer; she backed up. "I just recalled an old family joke. The point is"—she forced herself back on track—"while I may come from a decent, respectable family, you can't marry me."

"I can so. Just watch me."

"Your aged father would disown you."

"I don't need my family's wealth; I have quite enough of my own."

"Society would be scandalized. You would be ostracized."

"Not by anyone who matters to me."

"Her Majesty's government would also consider it a scandal. It would jeopardize your position."

"I do not officially work for Her Majesty's government, if you recall. I could retire. We could take Patricia along on a long honeymoon trip. We could spend several years exploring America. You'd like that, wouldn't you?"

"What I would like is not the point, Martin." Duty was the point, it always was. Duty and honor and loyalty and other abstract notions that didn't take personal feelings into account. "Take a mistress," she pleaded with him. "Run off and have a wild fling and forget about me."

He cocked a dark, arched eyebrow at her. "Is my daughter's prim governess urging me to set a bad example for my child? Shouldn't you counsel me to lead a quiet, moral life?"

"I suppose I should, but how can I ask you to give up something you're so good at? Seducing women is as much a hobby with you as fencing and boxing, marksmanship and riding to hounds."

"You make it sound as if I hang trophy heads on the wall!"

At another time his outrage would have amused her. "Well—"

"I have standards. There are rules to the game of love."

"Ah, but you do consider it a game."

"You twist my meaning. Love is not a game. Romantic liaisons with ladies of worldly sophistication are not the same as love, and you know it. It's not as if I've gone around seducing maidens and nuns."

"No. I concede you're no despoiler of virgins. The women you've been involved with have hardly been victims of your rapacious lust."

"I could teach you a great deal about rapacious lust if you like."

"I'm sure you could, but no thank you."

"Aren't you a little bit curious about the ways of the flesh?"

"Of course I—"

"Well, then." Suddenly she was in his arms again.

"This will not do," she declared, and found herself beating on his chest with her fists like a heroine in some melodramatic stage play.

When he laughed in the same dastardly way as the villain in one of those plays, she couldn't help but laugh with him. They knew each other too well on some levels. They thought so much alike that sometimes they seemed to share one mind. One soul?

Now who was being the melodramatic one? What they shared was on the surface; they could never share the basic, important things. The basic truths about who they were and where they came from could never be reconciled. Lord Martin Kestrel might think he loved Abigail Perry, but Abigail Perry could never love him. She would not even allow herself the pleasant fiction of thinking she could.

"You are a womanizer," she told him, hoping that shining a harsh light on his past would put a stop this. "How can I believe you love me? How could I believe you would be faithful?"

"Because I—"

"I will not be another fling, Martin." She was

far too aware of his arms around her, of the strong body so close to hers.

"Of course not!"

"Nor will I go to the bed of a man who has a rakehell's reputation. As you pointed out, I am a minister's daughter."

"Most men are less than pure, my dear. At least you know the worst of me."

But he did not know the worst of her. She sighed, and was unable to ignore the pain in his eyes. "You were hurt once, Martin, and—"

"I reacted badly to it, I know," he cut her off. "I really did want to try my hand at being a wicked seducer after Sabine betrayed me, but you know I got over that fool mood."

"Turned out you had too much conscience," she agreed. "But you have had a great many mistresses in the last several years."

"Not *that* many," he corrected. "A man has to work, eat, and sleep sometimes."

"Enough."

Martin hid a smile. Was that a hint of bitterness in her voice? Perhaps the faintest tinge of jealousy? He *had* been wild for a time; now it was catching up with him. He only prayed that the price was not losing the woman in his arms, for he knew with his heart and soul that she was the only woman he could ever truly love. "I have been circumspect," he offered, as though discretion were some form of virtue.

"Which does not change your behavior."

"I am not coming to you pure of body and soul," he admitted. "There is a disadvantage in your knowing me so well, but the heart I offer to you is clean. I've never loved another woman, Abigail, not even Sabine. She gave me a child I love, and I'm grateful, but what we had was not love. You, I love. I think I've loved you since the moment I opened the door and dragged you into my life. I've gotten over being angry at women, you may have noticed. I'm through with chasing them. I'm sick of them throwing themselves at me. I want only you. Marry me, Miss Perry, become Lady Martin."

She did not melt into his embrace and offer her lovely mouth for a kiss. "Is your proposal to me a way of laughing in the face of all those ladies who want you for your name and fortune? Are you using me to get revenge?"

This stung, and his answer was an angry shout, filling the gentle space of the walled garden. "I no longer blame every creature in skirts—"

"Including Angus MacTavish the ghillie," she interrupted.

"—for wounding my heart. Not breaking," he hastened on, before she made some other remark intended to throw him off course. Oh, he knew his Abigail, all right. He had her cornered and she was fighting dirty. He considered this progress, though her distrust stung. He supposed he couldn't blame her for being skeptical, nor could he blame an upright, moral woman for doubting that a man of his former habits could change. For the love of a good woman he could do it, wanted to do it, would do it. "Marry me," he said again. "That's all I'm asking."

"All?"

"We can spend the rest of our lives working out the rest."

She looked up at the sky, blue dotted with puffy white clouds. The air was fresh and sweet, freed for a time from London's usual sooty grit by a hard, windy rain the day before. The garden was a tame, pretty place, and she found herself longing for heather and gorse and the wild landscapes of home. She should have left a week ago, gone home to the people with whom she could truly be free. She had probably not gone because she knew that her family would have told her the same thing she now so disastrously faced: it was time to move on—her usefulness in the Kestrel household was at an end. It was over.

Control the situation, she told herself. *Deal with it later.*

Martin did not know exactly how she managed it, but one moment he held Abigail close; the next he was standing with empty arms, while she was several feet away from him. He sensed instantly that the distance was more than physical. She stood still as a statue, and the green eyes that surveyed him were hard chips of ice.

"Abigail."

She held up a hand when he would have come closer. "Enough."

This time she definitely meant it. He did not push his luck for the moment. Martin carefully clasped his hands behind his back. "Why don't we have a seat on the terrace. I'll ring for some tea and we—"

"The butler's on holiday," she reminded him. "So is Cook, and most of the maids. And I believe the ones that are left have started their weekly half day off by now. They have lives you know nothing about, Martin," she pointed out. "Especially since you are not supposed to be here."

"Are you telling me I can't get a cup of tea in my own house?"

"Not unless you plan to make it yourself."

He tilted his head to one side and looked her over from head to foot, wearing plain black and white, her rich brown hair twisted up in a simple knot. "This is where you remind me of our relative positions in this household, bob me a curtsy, and offer to fetch the tea for m'lord, isn't it?"

"That was next on the agenda, yes," she agreed.

He shook his head. "Too easy, Abigail."

Martin noticed Abigail's gaze shift over his shoulder just as he heard a footstep behind him. Martin turned to see his valet approaching. He was more than irritated at this interruption, but he also knew that circumspect Cadwell would not have disobeyed an order not to be disturbed unless it was absolutely necessary. "What?" Martin demanded.

Cadwell gingerly held out an envelope and backed away when Martin snatched it from him. "How the devil did the Turkish ambassador know where to find me?" he asked once he'd ripped open the envelope and read the message inside. Neither Abigail nor the valet ventured an answer. He folded the paper, waved Cadwell off, and turned back to Abigail. "Rather urgent business," he apologized. "You'll have to excuse me while I send off an answer."

She relaxed ever so slightly as she said, "I understand."

Oh, no, he thought. *This is no time to be smug, Miss Perry, I'm only giving you a momentary respite.* "This isn't over," he warned. "You and I are going to settle this today. Stay here. I'll be right back."

"Of course, Martin," she answered as he started back toward the house. "Where else would I go?"

Chapter 4

"Gone? She can't be gone!" But, of course, she was.

"I have searched the house and grounds, my lord," Cadwell answered.

"Search again," Martin ordered. He knew it was futile, though he tried to tell himself that it couldn't be.

It had taken no more than five minutes to go into his study, write out an answer, seal it, and entrust it to the messenger he found waiting in the front hall. When he rushed back out to the garden, she was not there. He'd searched the grounds and every room in the house, then called for Cadwell. They'd made separate sweeps of every nook and cranny before meeting back in the study. Cadwell hurried to carry out the useless order to search yet again, and Martin found himself staring at the top of his desk, his heart clutched in a grip of iron.

Five minutes, possibly less, and Abigail used that small space of time to walk out of the garden, out of the house, and out of his life. Or so she no doubt thought. He smiled mirthlessly. He hadn't thought she'd make it easy for him, but he had hoped—

That all he had to do was walk in and proclaim his undying devotion and she'd swoon with love and, yes, gratitude, at the offer of his hand. His smirk was a bit less mirthless as he admitted that deep down—barely under the surface, actually—he'd believed such arrogant tripe. When he'd awakened to the revelation of how he felt and what he must do, the vision of lifelong happiness with Abigail as his wife had been crystal clear. That clarity was a bit faded now, obscured by Abigail's arguments and actions. No, it was blocked by her stubborn adherence to class differences and the conventions of society!

"Maybe I should have tried seducing her, then talking to her," he muttered. No, that would have been unworthy—pleasurable, but unworthy. He was going to do right by this woman. He pounded his fist on the desktop. "Whether she wants to be done right by or not."

Martin climbed the stairs to the second floor, to the rooms that were Abigail's domain. There was the schoolroom, a cozy place with pale green walls, a deep window seat surrounded by lace curtains, cupboards and shelves, and a worktable and chairs set in front of a white-tiled fireplace. He had spent much happy time there with his daughter and her governess, and in similar rooms wherever his diplomatic assignments took them. Evenings spent reading to each other before the fire had been the best, with Patricia on his lap and Abigail nearby. They had made the most domestic of trios. There was no reason in the world that they could not go on, with the added blessing that he and Abigail would no longer go their separate ways once Patricia was tucked in her bed. And soon there would be other children filling the nursery and playing in the schoolroom.

He crossed his arms and slowly turned full circle around the room, made even more cheerful and bright by the rays of afternoon sunlight streaming in the wide window. *Oh, no, my dear*

Miss Perry. There is no way I'm letting you cheat us out of a richly deserved happily-ever-after.

He had no right to be angry with her—at least very little right. The truth was, the evenings the three of them spent together ended early. More often than not he was out of the house soon after Patricia's bedtime, off to balls, parties, gaming halls, the opera, or some other frivolous entertainment. Always there was an assignation with the mistress of the moment, or a new conquest to be made. He was rarely home before dawn. He understood how Abigail might be wary of him as husband material.

But what about all the times we have spent together? The laughter and conversations shared on shipboard and in coaches and trains, during all our travels? What about all the conversations over quiet meals and chess matches? What about the time we were stranded at the inn in Switzerland during the week-long blizzard and we passed the time learning the local outdoor sports? What about the time in Monaco when the local staff quit and we took over the kitchen and prepared a dinner party for the prince ourselves? What about the time you had that nasty fall when we were in Austria, Miss Perry? Who scrambled down the mountainside and found you? How well he remembered the terror of hunting for her and the joy of finding her, and the horror at the sight of her injuries. *Who nursed you back to health?*

My maid and Dr. von Kaufenberg, she would have answered had she been there. *You were conducting delicate negotiations.*

I stopped in every moment I could spare. Held your hand while you slept. Wiped your tears away when you cried in your sleep, and never mentioned once how seeing you so weak and vulnerable tore at my heart.

He sighed, remembering that he'd put all his fear, worry, and caring aside so that he could answer the first sardonic comment she made when she finally opened her eyes with something equally nonchalant. She had masked pain with wit, and he did his best to let her recover in her own way.

I hunted for you before, and found you. Do you think I won't do it again?

Two doors led off the schoolroom, one to Patricia's bedroom, the other to Abigail's. He had looked in Abigail's room once already, a cursory check to see if she had fled there to be alone. This time he checked Patricia's room, just in case Abigail was hiding in there. Of course, Abigail was not the hiding sort, and was not in his daughter's room. So he went into Abigail's private sanctum, for a thorough look around this time.

Stepping inside gave him the oddest mix of sensations. Though he was impatient to find her, there was also a sense of impropriety, a touch of dark excitement. He felt like a boy breaking rules, a treasure hunter on a quest, and a man about to delve into a lover's most intimate secrets.

Since the room contained so little, his first impression was that it was larger than it actually was. The furniture consisted of a narrow bed with a small night table beside it. An ornate old clothes chest and a washstand with an oval mirror hung above it took up one wall. Abigail's much-used steamer trunk rested on the floor at the foot of the bed. The place was spartan, impersonal, certainly without feminine embellishment. No lace, no flowers, no bric-a-brac, no flower prints or china plates hung on the walls or decorated the mantelpiece. Except for the battered trunk, not a single memento from any of the last four years' travels was visible. This was a place where a woman came to dress and sleep, but not a place where she lived. There was not a hint of vibrant Abigail Perry anywhere in sight. Perhaps she did not see the Kestrel household as her home. It troubled him that the woman who made Patricia's life, and his, so very comfortable lived such an austere existence when she was alone. The walls of the room seemed to close in on him as Martin begin to suspect that bringing Miss Perry to the altar was going to be even more difficult than he'd thought.

Nonsense—he was reading too much into this, making things more complicated than they needed to be. They hadn't been home from Turkey for very long. Who knew when or where the Kestrel household would be off to next? Why would a woman as hardheaded and practical as Abigail turn a room she rarely occupied into some cozy nest?

By now he was quite certain she had left the house. His hope was that she had gone for a long walk to think things over and would return within an hour or two. If she'd had anything more drastic in mind, surely she would have dashed into her room for a few belongings first.

As far as he could tell, no clothes were missing from the wardrobe. Her few good, plain dresses were neatly hung on the rack. Dull things they were, mere lifeless cloth in shades of brown and cream and gray and black. Bonnets were in their boxes; a paisley shawl was folded on a shelf. A neat row of three pairs of shoes shared space on the wardrobe floor with a familiar tapestry carpetbag. He found a drawer containing nightgowns and underthings, and couldn't help but smile at the lack of lace and embroidery on this most feminine of apparel.

Now, this takes staid practicality to ridiculous lengths, Miss Perry. He shoved a high-necked linen nightgown back in the drawer and closed it. And it was ugly, besides. The woman deserved silk and lace next to her skin. He was going to have a red brocade corset made for her, he decided. He wanted to see her in an outlandish, sensual undergarment decorated with black lace and little satin roses. Talking her into wearing it would be a delightful challenge, and seducing her out of it would be more delightful still.

But he had to get her back first.

The washstand held a silver-backed hairbrush, a tortoise comb, and an assortment of hairpins in a china dish. He'd watched her slowly combing out her long sable-brown hair with the brush many times, and did not think she would leave behind an object she seemed so attached to. He stamped on a sentimental impulse to pick up the brush and cradle this intimate reminder of Abigail in his hands; he had no time for sentiment right now.

There was nothing missing, Martin concluded with growing concern as he lifted the lid of her trunk. Not much in there, either, though her reticule was inside, resting on top of a stack of lending library books. Inside the small black handbag he found several months' worth of wages.

If she hadn't taken any money with her, she *had* to be coming back. With that hope in mind, Martin Kestrel left the house to search the nearby streets and small parks. When he came home hours later, she had not returned.

When she still had not returned by nightfall, he went out again. By this time he was frantic. London was a dangerous town, especially for a woman alone. Anything could have happened to her. It was his fault if she was lost, injured, or worse, and he knew it. Though she'd acted rashly by running off, his words and actions had been even more reckless and had driven her off in uncharacteristic panic. He was a man used to having his own way, and he'd made assumptions. He'd been high-handed and full of the arrogant certainty that a mere confession of love would make everything all right, and he'd completely underestimated the woman he thought he knew so well.

He notified the constables of her disappearance long before morning came. The young inspector who turned up on the Kestrel doorstep the next morning was a rude pup named MacQuarrie who ventured impertinent questions about the lady's associates and past and family, to which Martin had no answers. What was worse, MacQuarrie managed to reinforce Abigail's arguments about the perception of impropriety between them, not so much by what he said to Martin, but by looks and significant pauses in the conversation. By the time the man left, with only the vaguest promise to look into the matter, Martin was ready to strike him.

Three days passed with no word from Abigail, nor was there a clue to her whereabouts no matter where Martin and MacQuarrie searched. Fortunately for Martin's sanity, a clue turned up when the post arrived on the third day, in a letter from a lady named Phoebe.

* * *

"Beatrice, I'm quite sure the queen would not be amused if she knew you were able to forge her signature."

Sir Ian Courtney MacLeod looked down the dinner table. His seventeen-year-old-daughter didn't seem in the least affected by the quelling tone in her mother's voice.

"Not just Queen Victoria's signature," the insouciant Beatrice replied. "I've made a study of her handwriting and can duplicate anything she would write."

"But why would you want to?" Her brother Alexander, freshly home from overseas, was holding a fork awkwardly in his left hand, as his right arm was in a sling.

"Perhaps she's planning on committing high treason?" Lucy spoke up.

"Or having Father proclaimed laird of all the MacLeods and lord of Dunvegan Castle," suggested Gabriel, home for his university holiday.

"That might be fun," Beatrice answered. "Would you like to be laird of the clan, Father?"

"I'm laird of quite a clan already," he pointed out, gesturing around the dinner table. Not everyone was home, but the place was packed to the rafters when his roving children and the whole extended family got together. "I prefer staying right here at Skye Court to living in the MacLeods' ancestral seat." He exchanged a glance with his wife. They hadn't considered living anywhere else since they'd brought their growing brood back to his native Isle of Skye off the Scottish coast and moved into the ramshackle old manor house they'd named Skye Court. The place was named after him, in fact, for Ian Courtney MacLeod was known as Court to those closest to him. Those who didn't call him Papa or Uncle, that is. "You know your mother would hate moving," he went on. "Wouldn't you, Hannah?"

"Court, I think the point is—"

"And Lucy would hate to give up her garden after all the work she's put in on it."

"Nightshade and mandrake and hemlock won't grow just anywhere," Alexander put in. "Lucy couldn't possibly leave her poisons behind."

Lucy gave a short, sharp laugh. "Little you know, lad," she told her soldier brother. "As if I'd grow anything so obvious."

Hannah rapped a knife against the rim of a crystal water glass to bring everyone's attention back to the matriarch of the clan. "I think I've had a bit of practice with manipulation—"

"Aye, love, you're a mistress of it."

"Thank you, Court. But if the lot of you think you're going to sidetrack me off the subject of Beatrice having developed yet another skill that could put members of this family in jeopardy, please think again, my darlings."

"Honestly, Mum, what harm could it do?" Gabriel spoke up. "In fact, I was thinking of having Bea ask the queen to write a letter extolling my virtues to my wretched history professor at Muirford."

"After the queen promotes me to regimental commander of the Scots Guards," Alexander spoke up.

"That's just the sort of thing I'm talking about." Hannah turned a stern glance on Gabriel. "And you, heaven help us, are the sober and serious one of the twins. Alec—"

"We were only joking, Mum," Alexander said.

A grown man and a brave young officer who'd seen action and come home wounded yet victorious, he nevertheless quelled beneath his mother's disapproving look like a lad of ten. Court approved this response, for it showed that his son had fine survival skills.

Alexander looked his father's way for aid, but Court only smiled benignly. "I'll go through fire and flood for you, lad," he told Alexander. "But I learned long ago when to stay out of Hannah Gale MacLeod's way."

"It is a wise man who knows his limitations," Hannah said, giving him a warm smile. "Sara, darling," she called upon the family's youngest. "Please explain why Beatrice's latest talent could prove as dangerous as it might be useful."

Sara was fifteen, shy, and even more bookish than Beatrice, if such a thing were possible. Court had already noted that her gaze was directed to her lap, meaning that she was once again violating the household rule about reading during meals. No doubt Hannah had noticed as well, which was why she called Sara out of her reverie now.

Sara didn't even bother to glance up as she said, "Because, as has already been pointed out, forging the queen's handwriting could indeed be used to commit high treason by those who lack scruples. Or Bea's forgery skill could be used by those who serve foreign countries and political policies that run counter to the welfare of the British Empire, should Bea fall into the hands or under the influence of such persons."

"Very good," Hannah acknowledged. "Now put the book away and eat your peas."

"Yes, Mum."

"None of you is to mention this skill of Bea's again," Hannah addressed the people at the table. "Family secrets—"

"—stay in the family," everyone finished with her.

"As if we didn't already know—" Lucy began, but stopped speaking instantly as the dining room door opened.

Mrs. Swift, the housekeeper, came into the room as everyone turned to look, followed closely by a dark-haired young woman in a travel-stained dress. Court rose joyously to greet the newcomer, his arms held wide. "Harriet!" he called happily. "Harriet, you've come home at last!"

She gave a strangled little laugh that was half a sob, and rushed to his embrace. "Harriet," she said on a sigh. "How lovely not to be called Abigail Perry anymore!"

Chapter 5

"**T**hank you for seeing me, Lady Phoebe. It is most kind—"

"Yes, it is," Lady Phoebe Gale cut off her visitor's polite speech.

"I do apologize for the intrusion."

You are not the least bit sorry, she thought. *Nor are you a sorry sight on the eyes. Still, I rather wish I didn't have the pleasure of seeing you like this.*

And seeing him was a pleasure. He was a tall, handsome fellow of the intense-dispositioned, stormy-eyed, raven-haired sort, and she had quite an appreciation of handsome fellows of all kinds. Good looks, of course, were not why she'd allowed this stranger to be showed into her parlor. He looked most out of place in the feminine room, full as it was of delicate furniture, china figurines and many vases of fresh-cut flowers.

At least, Lord Martin Kestrel thought they were strangers. While they had never met, she knew quite a bit about him. In fact, she knew everything about him, except how he had found her and why he was there. So she set aside her irritation at his sudden appearance. She also put aside her concern about another unexpected situation. *Let's see if the two are linked*, she thought, and produced the curious demeanor of a lonely and harmless old lady out of her extensive bag of tricks.

"Excuse my abruptness, my lord. I'm afraid I have very little company these days. Please be seated," She directed him across the feminine room with a flutter of her hand.

Once he'd settled his long frame in one of the tapestry-upholstered chairs tucked into a deep bay window, she rang for tea and took the other seat. He probably did not notice that their positions put the sun to her back on this bright summer day, or perhaps he'd taken the less comfortable seat out of consideration for a fragile old woman. Whatever the cause, she had a better view of him than he did of her, and

Phoebe Gale had spent her life taking even the smallest advantage of her opponents. And there was not a person in the world who could not be judged an enemy, depending on the situation.

She certainly had nothing against the man at the moment, other than the fact that *he* was not the person she'd sent for from the Kestrel household. She studied him under the cover of picking up an embroidery hoop and selecting a skein of green thread from the basket next to her chair.

He was a dark-browed man with a firm, indented chin and eyes like steel. Quite a grand-looking fellow, but tired now and trying to hide it beneath a calm veneer. Not only tired, but worried—she saw that in the lines around his eyes and the tight press of his lips. Lovely lips, they were. Were he to smile, she was certain a pair of dimples would add charm to punctuate the devastating effect. Lucky the woman who got the chance to appreciate the sweet taste of that man's mouth. He was passionate by nature, she could tell simply by the way he held himself under such tightly wound control. *A tiger of a man,* she thought. *A veritable tiger.* She'd had a few tigers in her time, and liked taming them very well, for they could never be completely turned into domesticated tomcats.

"So few ladies do fancywork these days," was her opening gambit as she began to work on the intricate flower design. "And those who practice any sort of domestic art think it rude to work in company. Modern women of the upper classes are no longer supposed to be anything but decorative ornaments in their husbands' homes. I find that a pity, don't you, my lord?"

He was clearly there on business he considered quite urgent, but being a diplomat as well as a gentleman, he held his impatience in check to give a semblance of civility. "Most ladies I know seem content with their lot, Lady Phoebe."

"I think you mistake boredom for contentment. It is an easy error for men to make. Easier than looking beneath the surface, I suppose."

A housemaid brought in the tea. Once the maid was out the door, Phoebe put down her embroidery, passed the man a cup of tea, and said, "Forgive my manners, my lord. Lonely old women do rattle on, given the chance. What can I do to help you?"

Martin Kestrel instantly put down his tea

and leaned forward eagerly. "To be blunt, Lady Phoebe, I'm looking for Abigail Perry."

"Abigail Perry." She gave him a bland smile that covered both annoyance and confusion. She'd sent for the girl, but this man had arrived instead.

"You wrote to her. This is how I found you."

Kestrel took an envelope from his coat pocket and handed it to her. The envelope had been opened.

Phoebe unfolded the piece of paper inside the envelope and glanced at the words she'd written in dark purple ink. "You've read Miss Perry's personal correspondence."

"I'm sorry, Lady Phoebe. I had no choice."

The color of the ink was significant; the words themselves appeared to be merely a friendly note inviting Abigail to meet for an afternoon at a botanical garden, with mentions of favorite flowers and a type of tea Phoebe hoped to find at a specific shop. The code was a simple one; it was the first one Phoebe had taught all her great-nieces and -nephews.

What concerned Phoebe was how her note had ended up in the hands of the man Harriet was assigned to watch and guard.

"Had no choice? How is it that you had no choice but to read Miss Perry's correspondence?"

"It was necessary."

"So you have implied. Where is Miss Perry?"

"I have no idea."

"Really?" she asked quite calmly, while her heart began to race. Surely Rostovich did not have her.

Don't jump to conclusions without proof, you old fool. Stay sharp and deal with facts, not fancy, she chastised herself. *Rostovich is an old enemy, but it is not wise to see him under every rock and in every odd occurrence.*

She was getting old, and the older she got, the more sentimental she became about the members of her own family who were in the game.

"You look uncomfortable, young man," she noted. "Miss Perry must be more than an employee to you." His discomfort seemed to deepen under her sharp gaze. This was an affair of the heart, she decided, but did not show her relief.

"How long have you known Miss Perry?" he

asked. "What is your relationship with her? Would she come to you for help if she were in trouble? If not to you, do you know to whom she would turn?"

"What business do you have prying into Miss Perry's private affairs?"

"I am her employer," he answered.

"I am aware of that, Lord Martin."

He perked up. "She's spoken of me to you? What has she said?"

His eagerness was rather adorable. "Would it please you if I told you she said you are kind, witty, generous, and handsome?"

His stormy eyes suddenly shone with hope, tempered with suspicion. "It would please me," he acknowledged. "But she hasn't said any of those things, has she?"

"She has not."

"Don't test me, my lady, it is cruel."

"Test, not tease—what an interesting way of putting it." The man was clever enough, as well as useful and well thought of by the Crown, or he would not warrant special attention on his foreign assignments.

"You have every right to be suspicious of a stranger coming to inquire about a friend's whereabouts," he told her. "I truly need to know if she's come to you, for I am very concerned for her. She's disappeared," he rushed on, worry overcoming his ingrained civility at last. "She walked away from my home three days ago and has not been seen in the city since."

"Walked away." Phoebe rose to her feet. "Walked away? Why the devil would she do that?" *Rostovich! Dear God, it must have been Rostovich after all! He must have taken her and—*

"It was my fault, I'm afraid, Lady Phoebe."

"You?" Phoebe forced her calm veneer back in place. She truly was getting old to have the façade slip so easily. "Why do you say that, my lord?"

"I asked her to marry me."

Phoebe found herself gaping. "You did what?"

"Proposed. I told her how much I love her, and asked her to become my wife." He ducked his head and looked up at her through thick, dark lashes. "I'm afraid she didn't take it very well. She walked away from my house and has not been seen since."

"She didn't want to marry you?"

"So she said."

"But you don't believe her."

"Let's say that I'm not very good at taking no for an answer."

"You're rather famous for it," she agreed. "That is why the queen sends you to all those odd foreign places as her very special envoy."

"I have been told that I can talk anyone into anything."

"And you see Abigail Perry as your greatest challenge."

He gave her the smile of a man who enjoyed nothing more than a challenge. He rose to his feet as well. "It is very difficult to continue negotiations if one of the parties refuses to show up at the table, Lady Phoebe." He stepped close and took her hands in his.

She was not so old that she was unaffected by this gesture, and his very masculine presence. Pity the woman forced to live with the temptation the man must offer day in and day out, she thought, and barely hid an earthy smile that would have instantly put the lie to her spinster's demeanor. Poor Harriet probably hadn't had a chance. How long had she been in Kestrel's household? Four years, wasn't it? Harriet was a sensible, straitlaced sort, but even angels had been known to fall.

Could Harriet possibly have panicked and run off when faced with too much temptation? Was she so taken by surprise by a sudden declaration that she behaved like a fool? Harriet was no fool. Therefore, her great-niece was most likely in love. The most pragmatic people in the world went all to pieces when Cupid finally got to them. What a pity Kestrel wasn't the sort of person Harriet would think she was supposed to be in love with. As if love cared about what one was supposed to do.

It was a complicated situation, all things considered, and truth tended to be hard on such fragile things as emotions. Of course, Phoebe recalled, it wasn't as if the members of her family were not used to complicated romantic situations. Look at what Court and Hannah had worked through to find love. And who had set in motion the machinations that brought those two together? Why, none other than Europe's premier spymistress, of course.

Lady Phoebe very rarely let herself indulge in sentimentality, but she had a soft spot for her family—when she wasn't using them ruthlessly. She knew it would be wiser for her organization to send Lord Martin Kestrel away, but an urge to matchmake overtook her. Partly because she could use him to run the errand she'd summoned Harriet for, but mostly because she thought the man would look grand next to Harriet in a family portrait.

"It seems you think you are in love with Abigail," Phoebe said, looking him squarely in the eye. "But are you really in love with the woman? Do you really know her? Do you want to make her happy, or do you merely wish to win a debate? She is not a treaty, my lord, or a negotiable piece of property, but a complex and contradictory person. If it is the woman rather than an image of her that you love, perhaps I can be of some help to you."

She gave him some credit when he gave a thoughtful pause rather than answering her instantly. "I appreciate that you do not tell me that marrying Miss Perry is impossible."

"It might be," Phoebe said. "But that is for you and her to decide."

"Please help me find her, then," he said. "So that she and I can continue the discussion she broke off so abruptly. Where is she, Lady Phoebe?"

"I am not completely certain of where she is," she answered, completely honest for once. "But I can hazard a very good guess. She has most likely gone to Scotland."

"Scotland?"

"The Isle of Skye, to be precise, to a family named MacLeod. They have many children," Phoebe added. "Abigail had her training there."

"She was governess to the MacLeod children? I've never heard her mention them."

"She took care of the younger children for years. She is very close to the MacLeods, as am I." Never tell the whole truth when half truths would do; that was Phoebe Gale's philosophy, mixed with a sly sense of humor. "I will be happy to write an introduction to Sir Ian MacLeod for you if you wish to go to Skye to look for her."

He squeezed her hands and gave her a dazzling smile in gratitude. "Thank you, Lady Phoebe. How can I show my appreciation?"

"I do have a favor I'd like to ask, my lord."

"Anything."

"It is a simple task, and one involving the MacLeods. Would you mind acting as a courier for some correspondence I was planning on posting to Sir Ian and Lady MacLeod? It will arrive sooner and safer if carried by hand."

He lightly kissed the backs of her hands before letting them go. "A simple task, indeed," he said. "And one happily performed."

Chapter 6

❝I think, Mum, that I shall change my name."

Hannah had been certain that she'd approached the ruins at the top of the sheep pasture without making a sound, but Harriet, seated with her back turned, was aware of her all the same. Hannah gave her daughter points for her observation skills, and calmly asked, "What name are you thinking of?"

"Several come to mind. What do you think of Caprice?"

Hannah joined her daughter on the ancient, broken wall. Harriet's gaze remained fixed on a distant line of hills while Hannah spoke. "You don't seem the capricious type to me, Harriet."

"But it's such a pretty name."

"And memorable. Anonymity is the watchword for undercover work, remember?"

"I wasn't thinking about a new assignment, I was simply thinking about a change. I wish I was brave and strong and ruthless like you, Mum."

She put a hand on Harriet's shoulder. "Bad dreams again?" Harriet tensed alarmingly under her touch, but shook her head. She knew that her daughter sometimes brooded over what had happened in Austria, but didn't like to talk about it. "I wouldn't want you to change. Not when I've just gotten my own dear Harriet back. What is it, my melancholy one? Don't like being Harriet MacLeod very much right now? Or is it that you don't remember quite how to be yourself at the moment?"

Her daughter had been withdrawn, silent, and sad since returning home three days before. Hannah wasn't sure if she needed to give her child more time to work through whatever was so obviously bothering her, or if she needed to give a loving but bracing lecture on coping with the vicissitudes life threw in one's way. She did know she needed to find out exactly what had transpired to bring Harriet running back home in such a peculiar fashion.

"You must have missed the view," she said when time passed without Harriet answering her last question. "You've been up here every day since you've come home. It is a lovely place, but the wind's cool today," she added as she tucked her shawl tighter around her shoulders.

The foundation of the property's manor house was said to date all the way back to the days when Norsemen had colonized this island off the Scottish coast and named it Skye. The house, rebuilt and expanded many times over the centuries, sat tucked in a small, isolated wooded valley well out of sight of the Portree road. To reach Skye Court you had to first find the narrow track that led up the valley, then ford two streams that rushed down from the Storr along the way. In rainy weather those streams were sometimes dangerously swollen, and the weather was frequently rainy on Skye. One had to *want* to get to Skye Court.

The ruins where they sat were probably those of a medieval defense tower. From up here there was a fine view of the Sound of Raasay, with the Storr Plateau rising at their backs. Between the ruins and the patch of woods that hid the house was a huge green meadow, dotted equally with mossy boulders and a herd of sturdy Highland sheep. A pair of black and white collies raced around the edges of the herd, following the whistles and calls of the shepherd who stood by the drystone fence at the bottom of the hill.

"What about Gabrielle?" Hannah asked after another few minutes of silence passed between them.

Harriet turned a puzzled look on her. "Who's Gabrielle?"

"You could be, if you like, if you ever take a new assignment," Hannah said. "We were discussing your taking a new name."

"So we were," Harriet answered. She rubbed a spot between her eyes. "I have a headache. Don't like Gabrielle," she added, and sighed. "Sounds a bit like Abigail."

Not to Hannah's ear, but she didn't say so. Hannah was well aware that this particular daughter would not admit any sort of weakness to anyone but her. Hannah also knew better than to offer overt comfort or sympathy for Harriet's pain. Pain that was far more than mere headaches, she was sure. The girl had an utterly haunted look that sent worry and anger through Hannah. Whatever had that man done to her? She was certain Harriet's malaise was somehow connected to the toplofty Lord Martin Kestrel.

"What sort of assignment do you have in mind?" Harriet looked her mother in the face at last, and Hannah was disturbed to see the desperation that filled her daughter's eyes. "Something far away?" Harriet asked with a most unseemly eagerness. "I could use a change of pace."

Hannah held up a hand. "Steady on, dear. We have you home at last; let your family enjoy you for a while. Rest and enjoy your holiday away from your flighty ambassador."

"He isn't flighty," Harriet instantly defended the man. Then she shook her head. "Never mind. I don't want to talk about him."

"I see." Meaning, of course, that he was all she wanted to talk about. Interesting. Hannah waited patiently for the story to come out.

Harriet twisted her hands nervously together in her lap and looked out at the distant view of the sea again. "Mum?"

"Yes, love?"

"I have something to confess." Harriet

sighed. "I did not come home just for a month's holiday."

"Ah." Hannah put her hand on Harriet's shoulder. "I suspected as much."

Harriet gave her a half-amused sideways glance. "Was your clue my stumbling home looking like something the cat dragged in?"

"I thought perhaps your luggage had been lost in transit."

"You're a very good liar, Mum. Always the unflappable matriarch welcoming the chicks back to the nest."

"Thank you, love. Pity your brothers Christopher and Michael haven't made their scheduled migrations yet. I've been looking forward to having a full nest for a while this summer. Christopher's finally coming home from America, but we don't expect him for a few days yet. Michael should have been home from university by now, like his twin, but he probably got distracted chasing a bit of skirt—"

"Mother!" Harriet gave the faintest of laughs.

"Well, I'm not an innocent, am I? I know my boys. Aunt Phoebe sent him off on an errand to France after his classes were done, and had some other errand for him after that, I think. A handsome, wicked and charming lad like that loose in the fleshpots of Paris?" She chuckled. "I almost pity the ladies."

"Other people don't have wicked mothers," Harriet answered. "I pity them."

Harriet's brief good humor evaporated like a mist on the moors and Hannah waited through another interval of dismal silence. She watched a hawk circle above the ruins overhead and the collies chasing around the edges of the flock down on the ground. She didn't think Harriet noticed any of the busy world around them, lost as she was in her own personal troubles. Her daughter was too conscientious not to have reported any professional problems the moment she walked in the door three days ago.

Harriet finally emerged from her reverie once more to ask, "What did you think when you first saw me?"

"I thought you'd finally needed to use the trick I taught you about keeping travel money tucked into your shoes, and came flying home for sanctuary. I knew you'd tell me what and why in your own good time."

Harriet chuckled. "No doubt you've been keeping Papa from marching up to me and bluntly demanding what's the matter since I first got home."

How very true. "Your father and I are both concerned. We hate seeing one of our chicks sad."

"I hate being sad," Harriet answered. She made a small, desperate gesture. "I have no right to be sad. And it makes me feel so dull and useless, like someone wrapped me up in soggy wool blankets and left me in a dark closet." She sighed. "And it hurts. Everything hurts." Hannah did not think that Harriet noticed that she'd pressed her hand over her heart while she spoke. Her daughter's gaze wrenched Hannah's heart. "I'm lonely," her daughter said. "In the midst of the place and people I love above all else, I am so lonely. Why is that, Mum?"

This was bad. Very bad indeed. Hannah laid the trouble squarely at the door of Lord Martin Kestrel, certain she had no need for any other suspects. "What did that awful man do to you?" she asked her daughter. "Did he try to seduce you? Did he succeed?" If that dastardly cur had dared lay a hand on her baby chick, she'd flay him alive.

Harriet shook her head. "Oh, no, much worse than that."

"Worse?" Horrid suspicion took hold in Hannah's mind. "What could be worse than being seduced and abandoned by that—"

"He asked me to marry him."

A tear trickled down Harriet's pale cheek. Hannah MacLeod brushed it away, and took her daughter's cold hands in hers. She'd feared something like this would happen.

"You're right," she said. "That is worse."

"There's a man outside."

Mrs. Swift's gruff voice drew Court's attention. He looked up over his reading glasses at the grim-faced housekeeper standing squarely before the library desk. Mrs. Swift was thin as a rail, tough as old leather, and looked even more disapproving than she usually did.

"A stranger," he guessed from her expression. "Did he give a name?"

Mrs. Swift handed over a calling card and stepped back with her thin arms folded tightly across her narrow waist. Disapproval radiated from her like the heat of a furnace blast. Mrs. Swift didn't like strangers. In that, she and Court were in complete agreement.

"What the devil's he doing here?" Court demanded after reading the name and titles of this unexpected visitor.

"Just so," Mrs. Swift said, giving a decisive nod. "I'll tell 'im to shove off, then."

"No," Court told her as she turned toward the library door. "Best find out why he's here. Show him in."

"Hmph," she responded, but marched out to reluctantly do as he bid.

While he waited Court closed the book, put away his glasses, and composed himself to the appearance of a mild-mannered country squire. He folded his hands together on the desktop and called, "Come," when a sharp rap sounded on the door a few moments later. "That will be all, Mrs. Swift," he added when the housekeeper gave every appearance of following Lord Martin Kestrel into the room.

Kestrel stalked in, mud-spattered and disheveled, and looking thoroughly irritated. No doubt the difficult journey from the village and being made to cool his heels by Mrs. Swift had done nothing to soothe the Englishman's mood.

Upon seeing Court, he brushed stray strands of black hair off his forehead and assumed a mild, friendly air as he approached the desk. "Good day, Sir Ian. Thank you for seeing me."

The man did a fine job of controlling his temper, but Court was well aware of Kestrel's strong emotions seething just under the bland mask.

Before Court could offer any greeting, Kestrel took a packet of papers from a case he carried under his arm and held them out, presenting them for inspection like an ambassador offering credentials at a foreign court. When Court did not take the documents immediately, Kestrel placed them on the desk in front of him. The letter on top of the pile was from Phoebe Gale.

As Court picked it up, Kestrel said, "A letter of introduction from a mutual acquaintance, Sir Ian. My reason for imposing on your hospitality might seem a bit odd, and I hope Lady Phoebe's kind words will ease any strain and embarrassment on all sides."

"Perhaps they will," Court said coolly, picking up a very sharp silver letter opener and slitting the top of the envelope. "If you'd let me read the letter."

"Of course, Sir Ian, I—No. We have to talk, man to man." Kestrel leaned forward, placing his palms flat on the desktop, his muscles tense as stone.

Court rose to his feet to look the man in the eye. There was a dangerous edge in the stranger's manner, but Court did not feel the least intimidated. Irritated, yes. The last place Kestrel should be was at Skye Court, and he had every intention of seeing the man on his way as swiftly as possible. "Young man, if you would kindly—"

"I really don't have time for the niceties after coming so far," the world-renowned diplomat snapped. "Where's Abigail? I've come to take her home, and that's all there is to it."

Court kept his expression carefully blank. "Abigail?"

"Miss Abigail Perry. Lady Phoebe told me she would come here."

"And what," Court inquired, mild words masking rising ire, "is Abigail Perry to you?"

"My governess."

"I would not think a man of your years would require a governess."

"My daughter's governess."

"Did you bring your daughter with you?"

"What? No. Of course not."

"Then I don't see why you think you require the services of a governess."

Martin could see that this Sir Ian MacLeod was being deliberately, infuriatingly obtuse and obstructive. He had not come all this way, especially the last several, wretched, bone-wrenching miles, to be thwarted at the last moment so close to his goal. "I have private business with Miss Perry," he said, as calmly as he could manage. "Please read the letter in your hand."

When he was done reading, Sir Ian slowly stroked his chin. He spoke with equal slowness, appearing completely puzzled. "Why would Lady Phoebe send you here?"

The man was a fine actor, Martin concluded as he looked at the man on the other side of the desk, but Martin was certain MacLeod knew why Lady Phoebe had directed Martin to his home. Sir Ian was a big, square-built man, still fit, and with a thick head of hair though he must be somewhere in his fifties. There was a familiar look to the man's eyes Martin found disturbing. They were light eyes, blue-green, the sort of eyes that changed color depending on surroundings and mood. Right now they were the green of an angry ocean, totally at odds with Sir Ian's perplexed expression.

"I am concerned about Miss Perry's welfare," Martin said.

"That is commendable."

"I need to know that she arrived here safely. That she is well. I need to know why—"

Martin bit off the words. He did not know what Abigail had told her former employer, and did not wish to jeopardize her relationship with the MacLeod family. He was so frustrated he wanted to ransack the room or leap across the desk to shake her whereabouts from the other man. When Abigail had first disappeared, he'd almost welcomed pursuing her as a challenge his jaded wits desperately needed, but the hunt had soon stopped being an intellectual exercise. The longer he was away from her, the stronger became the desperate ache to touch her, hold her, keep her. His need for this one elusive woman was frightening in its intensity. He was obsessed, and he didn't care.

And he had had quite enough of being thwarted by all these guardians at the gates. First Lady Phoebe and now this rustic squire stood between him and the woman he wanted.

"See, here, my good man," he said. "All you need to do is send for the woman so I can talk to her."

Sir Ian gave a chuckle that had very little amusement in it. "Well, aren't you the lord of the glen? No, I don't think I—"

Sir Ian's words were cut off as the library door opened. Martin turned hopefully at the swish of skirts, but the woman he saw in the doorway was not Abigail, though for a moment he thought she was. Hope had marred his vision, he supposed, though the woman was of a similar height, build, and coloring to Abigail. This newcomer, attractive though she was, was closer to Sir Ian's age, her dark hair frosted with strands of silver. She wore a plaid wool shawl and there were moisture and grass stains on the hem of her dove-gray skirt.

She looked Martin over with a clear, critical gaze, and said, "You're Kestrel, aren't you?"

"My dear," Sir Ian said quickly, warningly.

She ignored Sir Ian and kept her steady gaze on Martin. "You'll find her up at the ruins," she told him. "Go through the back garden and through the pasture. You can't miss the place."

Martin could have waltzed the woman around the room and kissed her thoroughly. He smiled at her instead, and offered a fervent thank you on his way out.

Court would have followed, but Hannah shut the door and leaned against it to block his way. "What was that about?" he demanded of his wife. "I was about to send the man packing. The last thing Harriet needs is to see him."

Hannah smiled, infuriatingly inscrutable. "The last thing she wants—oh, I quite agree— but I doubt if it's the last thing she needs. And I must say I admire the man's being able to track her down."

"It wasn't cleverness," Court answered, gesturing toward the desk. "Phoebe used him as a messenger for that packet of papers. He has no idea who our daughter really is and I wasn't about to tell him."

"I should hope not. That is between them."

"*That* is a state secret."

"Nonsense." She waved his words away. "More of a family secret, now that Aunt Phoebe's seen fit to send him all the way to

Skye Court. Perhaps you haven't noticed, but Harriet's been pining for that young man." She put a hand against his chest when he tried to get by her to open the door. "Yes, I know, dear," she soothed. "You don't like him—he has a bad reputation with women, abysmal taste in wives, he gambles and keeps bad company, and, oh, yes, he's English. But what you like and what suits Harriet are two different things."

"He doesn't suit Harriet."

"Possibly not, but it isn't up to us. Why don't we have a look at the papers Aunt Phoebe sent? I'm sure they are important."

"They're in code."

"Then we'll send for Beatrice to help us. Crown business comes before family business, remember?"

Court didn't like being handled, manipulated, or distracted by anyone, but he also knew when Hannah would have her way, no matter what. He frowned mightily as he chucked her under the chin. "You'll pay for this, lass."

This growled threat got him no more than a saucy grin, and "Oh, goody."

Wicked woman. He kissed her, then went back to sit at his desk. "Call Beatrice," he said. "I'll wait here and worry about our other daughter."

Chapter 7

E ven from a great distance, the man's
stalking stride was unmistakable. There
was the dark shine of a raven's wing as sunlight touched his windblown hair. The breath
went out of her body at the sight of him, and
she saw bright, brilliant, exploding stars. The
joy was so sharp it hurt, and very nearly drove
her to her knees. Good God, he was there! It
was Martin! He'd come for her! The words
sang in her head and burst from Harriet's
wounded soul. Delight made her dizzy and
giddy, and for an instant she knew she could
fly. She could at least run.

Harriet was halfway down the hill, arms
outstretched with yearning, before the true

horror of the moment washed over her in an ice-cold tidal wave. What sort of fantasy world had she let herself get lost in, to feel such undeserved pleasure at a mere distant glimpse of that wide-shouldered, long-legged form? Martin Kestrel was the last person in the world she wanted to see! It would kill her to see him, to speak to him, knowing she could never—

She could still run. And hide.

Harriet turned around and scampered back to the shelter of the ruins on the hilltop as fast as her heavy skirts would let her.

"Abigail! Wait!"

Martin's shout scattered the sheep. The herdsman called out angrily as Martin sprinted forward through the pasture. The dogs barked and one nipped once at his heels as he ran, but Martin was intent only on reaching his goal now that he'd laid eyes on his elusive prize. He reached the massive ring of stones and broken walls seconds after Abigail ducked into them, saw a flash of scarlet skirt and sable hair amid the weathered stones, and called out again.

"Abigail!"

Harriet flinched away from the name she'd never wanted to hear again. She'd never expected to hear that deep, imperious voice. It sent a thrill through her, surging warmth mixed with cold terror. She did not like being afraid. It did not suit her at all. Nor did she appreciate that the very sight of an unarmed man had sent her into a panic. She was a MacLeod, for God's sake! What would her family think of her cowardly reaction? The teasing would never end if any of them saw her like this. All right, she looked a fright, felt like the worst sort of fool, and was completely and thoroughly confused, but when you were afraid you faced down your fear—and that was that.

Harriet stopped in the center of the ruins, clasped her shaking hands behind her back, and turned to face her foe.

"Martin."

He halted a few feet from her, standing near the base of the broken tower. "You've led me a fine chase, my love," he said as he studied her. "Have you made up your mind yet whether you're happy to see me?"

Not an hour before, her mother had asked her if she loved this man. She had answered that she didn't know. Facing him didn't help her confusion any; seeing him only made her misery worse. Yet seeing him was—

He smiled at her and tears stung behind her

eyes. Her heart hammered so hard she could barely hear herself speak. "I—I—"

Her voice shook as hard as the rest of her. Such a show of weakness would not do at all! Panic was no more an option than giving in to the impulse to throw her arms around the man, now that he stood there so brash and confident before her.

She took a deep breath and tried again. "I do indeed find myself of several minds," she admitted. "However did you find me?"

"Whyever did you run?" he countered.

"I did not run. I walked with great dignity all the way to the train station."

"You could have at least left me a note."

"I should have left my resignation, Lord Martin. I apologize for that lapse, my lord."

He shook a finger at her. "Your disappearance gave me quite a fright, my love. I even called in the constables."

"Oh, dear." Somehow it had not occurred to her that her absence would cause him any distress. She'd been too distressed by his declaration to think. She'd reacted like an animal in pain, and blindly fled to a safe den. It was so unlike her not to think things through. "I should have stayed until things were settled," she told him. "Running away is no method of settling a dilemma at all. How foolish of me."

"Well, Abigail," he said, crossing his arms. His smile softened the words. "At least we're in agreement on the foolishness of your behavior. You need to make it up to me," he added, crossing the space between them in a few steps and taking her into a swift, hard embrace.

His mouth covered hers a moment later, even as she opened it to speak. The kiss was rough and demanding, overpowering with pent-up desire. The moment he touched her, everything ceased for Harriet but primal, singeing heat that burned thought away.

The next thing she was aware of was the shiver of delight going through her as her fingers stroked the hard muscles and soft chest hair revealed by Martin's open shirt. Touching him was so, so—

Then they were on the ground, him flat on his back and her on top of him. She told herself she'd tripped him on purpose, a defensive move to break his hold on her, but she wasn't at all sure why she'd done it, or if she'd done it, and she was still wrapped tightly in Martin's embrace. His lips no longer covered hers, but that lessened her awareness of him not one whit. He was so very . . . hard and large and male. His skin was so warm, and his scent pervasively intoxicating.

"This is not a bit like wrestling with my brothers," she heard herself say, breathless and full of surprised wonder.

They were so close, his chuckle vibrated through both of them. "I should certainly hope not, my love."

There he was, using that word again. As though he had every right to. As if she had a right to be loved by him. She was going to have to correct his mistake, and soon. This was hardly a position in which to begin the conversation.

"Marry me," he said before she could begin. "Marry me today, my darling Abigail."

There he went with that damned name again! The name that damned her. She was up and off him in an instant. He climbed almost as quickly to his feet as she backed swiftly away.

"Good lord, girl, what's the matter? You look like you've seen a ghost. What's wrong? Tell me." Martin held a hand out to her, but she shook her head and dodged away rather than let him touch her. Martin watched the look of haunted revulsion only deepen as she looked at him. His heart sank, and his hopes very nearly went with it. "Is it me?" he asked, voice rough with pain. "Have I ruined myself for you with my philandering? Am I truly too wicked to marry?"

Harriet gasped and barely managed to bite back her instant defense of him. Martin Kestrel had just handed her a weapon she could use to drive him away. The days he'd spent looking for her had clearly put some cracks in his self-assurance. If she had any sense of self-preservation, she would boldly assert that she indeed found his sexual escapades repulsive. Only she didn't have any sense where the man was concerned; she'd had to leave him to realize how much he was a part of her very soul. She was about to hurt him, she had to, but she would not hurt him with a lie. She only prayed that she would not have to wound him with too much truth to make him go away. Martin Kestrel was a tenacious man.

"Wicked? No," she said. "You aren't the one who is wicked. You see, I haven't been completely truthful with you."

"Really?" he said, and smiled as he said it. "I'm shocked. Tell me what awful lie you're trying to put between us."

It annoyed her that he tried not to take the

moment seriously. She lifted her head sharply and looked him in the eye. "My parents were not wed when I was born."

Though she felt no shame about it, it was the truth. As much a truth as the fact that Christopher and Lucy were adopted and Anna was a ward. They were all equally loved and respected in her parents' decidedly irregular household. However, being illegitimate was not looked upon with such leniency out in the wider world. Martin should be shocked and repulsed that a person of such ignoble birth had lived in his house, taught his daughter, dared to lift her head and speak her mind to a man infinitely above her in birth and breeding.

Instead he shrugged. "So you started out life as a bastard."

"Yes."

"How interesting." He rubbed his jaw with his thumb as glanced back down the hill, toward the manor house hidden by its surrounding trees. "That explains it."

"You are supposed to be repudiating and reviling me, Martin." When he didn't respond to this, Harriet let her curiosity get the better of her. "Explains what?"

"Your striking resemblance to both Sir Ian and his lady—?"

"Hannah," she supplied. "You noticed?" Blast! Sometimes the man was far too observant.

"You have his eyes and her coloring and lovely shape. It occurred to me as I made my way among the sheep that Sir Ian's reaction to me was wholly paternal, rather the way I fancy I would respond if some stranger came looking for Patricia. And it appears to me, my love, that your parents are quite thoroughly married."

"Well, yes, *now*, but they weren't when I was born."

"So you have been duly and legally legitimized."

"Yes, but—"

"So there is no scandal. I sympathize with your concern that I might not understand, but fear of facing me with the truth was no cause to run off."

"It was cause enough for me," she asserted. "I am not at all the person you think I am."

"A hint of scandal and mystery always adds to a woman's appeal, my love. Trust me on that." His smile and the glint in his gray eyes took on a sensual edge that sent shivers of excitement through her.

But Harriet dared not let her own weakness lull her into a false belief that they could be together. This was not the time to allow herself to be attracted to the man's rakish charm, or tempted by the carnal pleasure his attitude promised. Yet attraction was something that simply *happened*, something intangible but very real that sang and simmered between them, and always had. She had four years of practice in controlling the longing to touch and be touched, but ever since he'd first kissed her in his London garden she'd become less and less sure of her ability to control her emotions. The passion of a few minutes ago had only strengthened the craving and weakened her will. She had to end this quickly, to sever the connection and cauterize the wounds.

She'd seen an avalanche from a safe distance once. It had come roaring down the mountain, an unstoppable storm of white sweeping all before it, destroying everything in its path. Passion could be like that. The smallest thing could trigger a maelstrom—a turn of the head, an unguarded look, an unintentional touch, a whispered word. Once unleashed passion had its way, what was left broken and devastated after its passing meant nothing to the storm.

But she could not easily make him go away; she couldn't end their association with anything less than the complete truth. She was about to unleash all the devastating passion in Martin Kestrel's fiery nature. Not for love, but for hate—and she was the one who was going to have to try to survive the tempest.

"Speaking of mystery, my love," he said, before she could bring herself to speak. "If you've been legitimized, why do you use the name Perry? Was it your mother's maiden name?"

"Gale," she told him. "My mother was a Gale."

Black, arched brows lowered over his puzzled gray eyes. "But Lady Phoebe is—"

"My great-aunt." She should not admit to anything he did not need to know, but her need for honesty with this man overrode any possible breach of security. "You traced me through her?"

He nodded. "Abigail, I don't—"

"My name is not Abigail," she cut him off, adamant and angry at hearing the hated name from his lips. Angry at herself, and at him for forcing her to this confession. "My name is Harriet MacLeod. And I'm not a bloody governess. I'm a spy!"

Chapter 8

"A spy?" Martin was too stunned to manage more than a whisper.

"A spy," she repeated, her fierce expression daring him to question or refute it.

He didn't understand. He could tell she wasn't joking, but it made no sense. He understood the words *a* and *spy*, but what they had to do with her, or him, the world in general, and what was between them, was not something he could instantly fathom.

"You don't know me," she said, as if in clarification. "You can't love me. I am a stranger."

"Don't be ridiculous," he said, in an attempt to keep the world from spinning out of its orbit. "Of course you're not."

"Not what?" she asked, one hand on her hip and an eyebrow canted sarcastically. "Not who the great Lord Martin Kestrel, in his infinite self-assurance, has decided I am?"

Her voice was different, and not only because the mockery in it grated against his ears. There was a lilt of Highland Scots in it that softened her usual precise enunciation. And her hair was unbound, a thick cascade of wavy dark brown framing the pale, fine-boned oval of her face. And she was wearing a red dress. Abigail never wore red. Her wardrobe was full of brown and black and gray dresses, clothing fit and proper for a governess. A wardrobe she'd abandoned as though it didn't even belong to her.

An identity she'd abandoned?

"Why? I don't understand."

The woman who claimed not to be his Abigail sneered. "You're not supposed to know. Of course you don't understand."

She was mocking him, deliberately trying to make him angry. Why was she still trying to drive him away? Perhaps he had been overzealous in hunting for her, but he wouldn't have persisted if he hadn't been certain, soul-deep certain, that beneath her protests Abigail cared as much for him as he cared for her. *If* she was Abigail . . .

What nonsense. He laughed at himself for half-believing her ridiculous assertion for even half a moment. The sound echoed around the circle of broken walls while Abigail stood with her back to the ruined tower and glared. Her cheeks were pink with emotion and the fresh wind off the sea. Her indignation at his daring to laugh at her gothic tale was plain on her face.

"You are not a spy," he told her, as if saying it would make it so. Why was she so adamantly presenting this rubbish to him?

"I am," she insisted. "Ask my father. Ask the foreign office. No, don't ask them, they'd deny my existence. Father would likely deny it as well."

"Women are not spies. It is not done. You are a nice woman."

"I'm not. And women make very good spies. No one suspects us."

"Besides, why would you spy on me?"

Harriet could see how hard he was fighting not to believe her. A part of her took perverse pleasure in his faith in her, though her pleasure was overridden by the knowledge that faith would soon turn to contempt. And how could she blame him?

"I was not spying on you," she told him. "I was making sure no one spied on you. I also used you as a cover for other covert activities."

Her words wiped the smug assurance off his face. He was beginning to get angry, beginning to unwillingly believe. He took a step toward her, large and menacing, though she doubted he was aware how dangerous he appeared. "What covert activities, pray tell, Miss Perry?"

"MacLeod."

"I don't care what your name is. Tell me what you were doing in my household."

"Serving queen and country."

"You are not a soldier or a diplomat. It is not a woman's place to serve the queen."

She was not used to his assuming she was less capable than he was simply because she wore skirts, and his arrogant superiority lashed her already raw spirit and made her react tartly. "Yet I do serve, and quite competently. Besides, the queen's a woman. If a woman can reign, other women can help her rule."

"Bah." He made a sharp, impatient gesture. "I refuse to believe you led some secret life under my nose."

"Of course you do—because believing it would make you feel like a fool. You will not forgive me for that."

"I will not believe what is patently impossible." He laughed, mockingly. "What did you do, tuck Patricia in bed, then sneak off to shoot anarchists?"

How did he know about that? No, it was only a wild guess. "I am not at liberty to discuss my assignments."

"You're joking." He laughed again, though not very convincingly, while his eyes showed stormy anger. "You are making up this nonsense, aren't you?"

Harriet shook her head. There were several things she would like to tell him about her true activities, but despite the fact that these things involved his life, for the sake of national security Martin Kestrel did not have the privilege of knowing the details. Besides, knowing the facts would only add to his pain, and she would not do that.

She did tell him, "I was inserted into your household staff by Her Majesty's government

109

for the sole purpose of protecting the interests of the British Empire. My undercover work was sanctioned by the minister of a department within the foreign office, and I have successfully carried out missions for that office. I cannot tell you the name of the office or of the minister. I should not tell you as much as I already have, but since your proposal effectively drove me out of cover, and Aunt Phoebe chose to let the cat out of the bag by sending you here, you deserve as much explanation as I can give you." Harriet folded her hands before her and added, "So now you see why I cannot possibly accept your generous proposal of marriage, my lord."

That was cruel and unkind, and she hated herself for saying it, but it was done to drive him away. Though spying was a necessary profession, people outside the espionage brotherhood saw it as a vile necessity and considered those who fed them the information they needed as lowlife scum. She knew very well that Lord Martin Kestrel, lofty ambassador to the courts of the world, shared that common sentiment. He would think a spy who had used him deserved nothing but his contempt. She knew in her aching heart that it would be better for him to spit on her, revile her, and then get on with his life.

She only hoped the truth would not scar him too badly. The first woman he'd married had betrayed him. Now he'd asked her to be his wife, and she'd revealed how she had betrayed him as well. "I never meant to use you," she couldn't keep from saying.

Martin wanted to cover his ears—no, he wanted to cover her mouth with his again, kiss her until there were no words in her, no thoughts in her head, only the driving need that would make her his. There had been passion a few moments ago, a connection greater than the wall of words she tried to erect between them now. There had been no restraint, no need for words. He'd discovered the passion he'd always suspected, roused it, and was half-crazy with desire. There was hunger for him still shining in her eyes. While she talked like a fool, she looked at him with a bold desire he didn't think she was aware of. He could satisfy that passion, remind her that she was a woman, make her revel in being a soft and sensuous woman.

He wanted to have her right now, keep her forever, and completely disregard everything she'd said. Because if it was true . . .

"If you keep babbling like this," he told her, forcing down his temper and his suspicions, "I'll start believing you're mad."

She looked about ready to scream with frustration. "Would my being mad send you away?"

"No. But it might make me lock you up in a safe room where everything has soft edges after the wedding. Especially the bed," he added.

"Trying to make light of the situation won't do any good, Martin. I know it is preposterous. It is also the truth."

It was the sight of unshed tears glimmering in her eyes that disturbed him the most. There was no pity in her gaze, thank God. He might actually have struck her if she showed pity for having duped him.

No. He would not believe it.

"Why lie to me?" he demanded. If he was not going to believe it, he should not keep questioning her. Questions invited her to add more details he'd have to find ways to refute. He wanted to stop the questions, but couldn't. "Why now?"

"I've lied to you for years. I'm not lying to you now."

She had not apologized, he realized. If it was true, and this was a confession, she had yet to say she was sorry. It was that, more than anything else, that Martin found most damning, and convincing.

He was not a kind man. He was not a gentle man. He'd learned to keep his darker emotions leashed most of the time. Now he was very nearly to the point of letting go. He could feel the anger clawing its way past all the barriers he put up, trying to protect his world, his pride, his love for her.

How could he love a woman he'd just met?

Hating her would be easier.

If he took her seriously—

Martin's head pounded with the effort to keep his temper, to keep from shouting. She waited and watched, arms clutched tightly at her waist while the world slowly reeled around the isolated hilltop. Slowly, time measured in the movement of lengthening shadows, her features began to change before his eyes. Or he began to see her through new eyes. The woman he had loved faded, drew away like some pale ghost that had inhabited the form of the stranger she left behind. The woman who called herself Harriet was no less lovely than his prim and proper Abigail—more, really, with her wild flowing hair and full, vulnerable lips. Abigail was always so in control, careful of every word and gesture. How he had admired her poise. He saw now that it had been a thin mask hiding the viper beneath. Before him in Abigail's form was a creature without armor, without stiffness. Without honor, he admitted. Without scruples. A stranger. A traitor. A liar.

One by one these words filled his mind, like drops of poison.

He had been used by the one woman in the world he completely trusted. This was not the first time he'd suffered a woman's betrayal, but it was the worst.

"My daughter," he said at last, voice deathly quiet, but carrying clearly across the windswept ruins. He took a menacing step closer. "Did you ever put my daughter in danger?"

Harriet held tightly onto the impulse to protest that she would never, ever have done anything to harm Patricia. She loved the child as much as if Patricia were her own flesh and blood. For four years she'd been the closest thing to a mother the girl could have. MacLeods did not harm children; just look at the house full of ragamuffins her parents had raised. But she was not facing down the growing wrath of Martin Kestrel to defend her actions.

So, instead of telling him a soothing truth, she forced herself to point out, "I am not the one who took Patricia into situations where she could be put in danger. I did not take your daughter to Italy, Austria, Hungary, Russia, Turkey—"

"I am well aware of the itineraries." He was pale with fury, voice cold, but there was pain as well as anger in his eyes.

"I accompanied Patricia as a member of your household, my lord. If she was ever placed near danger, it was not *my* doing."

"I won't be an absent father!" he shouted. "I won't—"

"Abandon her?" Harriet goaded. "Like her mother did?"

"Keep Sabine out of this. You're no better than she!"

She'd known he would think that way if he ever learned the truth. She knew him too well, and cared too much. She'd stayed too long because she cared. Her mistake hurt them both. But if contempt helped him get over the wound to his pride, she'd accept it gladly. No, not gladly; she was no martyr, but she'd survive somehow.

But, oh, how she wished he'd never kissed her.

"As you say, my lord. I think you should leave now," she said even as he drew closer to her.

She wasn't sure how she'd let herself come to stand with her back to the one wall among all the ruins that was not easy to scramble over. If anger drove him to some drastic action, escaping him would not be easy. She considered calling for help, and realized that in this moment she feared him. How had it come to this?

She refused to back up against the wall, and within a moment they were standing only an inch apart. When he raised his hand it was not to strike her. He ran his thumb across her lips, leaving a trail of warmth that let her know how numb she had become. It left her with a craving, as well. Her lips parted and she almost begged for another touch before she caught herself. She made herself meet his gaze. The fire she saw in his eyes was certainly passionate, but with no softness, tenderness, or fond regard.

"How I could have loved you," he said. Then he turned and walked away.

Harriet did not fall to her knees until she was certain he would not turn around and see her crying.

"You told him the truth, didn't you?" Hannah asked when she met Harriet at the garden gate. She knew the answer from her daughter's defeated expression and red-rimmed eyes.

"Yes," Harriet answered. "I owed it to him."

"The whole truth?"

"No, of course not."

Perhaps Harriet *should* have been honest in all ways with the man who'd come so far to find her. She suspected Harriet was too devoted to duty, letting admirable sentiments get in the way of leading a normal life and finding happiness. And wasn't that bloody stupid? She reminded Hannah of herself at that age.

"One bloody fanatical fool in the family is quite enough, I think," she murmured under her breath as she followed her daughter up the brick path to the house.

The defeated slump of Harriet's shoulders hurt Hannah to the core. What was the girl thinking, that it was her fault? That she wasn't supposed to have fallen in love? When did the heart ever care about what one was supposed to do?

But instead of offering condolences or motherly advice, Hannah waited until they reached the French doors that led into the back parlor before she said, "Your friend didn't come by himself; Phoebe sent him with some documents Beatrice has been translating. No, he didn't know," she added at Harriet's swift, accusing look. "And yes, he's been used again. Don't get all huffy about it." She pushed her daughter inside the house. "We don't have time."

"Why? What—?"

"We have an emergency," Hannah answered. "And we have to come up with a plan."

Chapter 9

He was not drunk. Close, but not quite there yet. Martin stared into the taproom fire and wondered how much more of the fine local whisky it would take to reach the state of numbness he so greatly craved. Whatever it took, he was willing to go the distance. He was no quitter. Not Martin Kestrel.

"Only the biggest fool to have ever lived," he told the dancing flames in the grate. "But never let it be said I give up a project once it's started." Take his latest project for example; following a woman who'd walked out of his life and clearly didn't want to be found, all the way to an island in the Hebrides, so she could utterly, totally, completely crush him and destroy him in the space of the worst hour of his life. "And I've had a few bad hours in my time." He shook his head, drained the glass, and then refilled it from the bottle on the table beside him.

He held up the glass to look at the fire through the rich amber liquid. Flames danced before him, but behind him he thought he glimpsed the movement of a shadow reflected in the glass. Though it made his head spin, Martin leaned forward in the wing-back leather chair and turned to look behind him. Dark outlines of chairs and tables were discernible in the light from the fireplace and from an oil lamp the landlord had left sitting on the bar. Curtains were drawn across the window, letting in not a speck of moonlight. Outside the open taproom door was the inn's entry hall, where a lamp burned low on a shelf by the stairway that led to the guest quarters. It was not a large inn, but the best the coastal village of Portree had to offer.

If the reflection was anything but a drunken fancy, it was likely he'd only gotten an odd glimpse of another patron coming in for the night. Still, he'd heard no door open.

Of course I didn't, he told himself. *I'm drunk and feeling sorry for myself. That sort of thing takes up a man's attention. Not blind drunk yet, though.*

The last thing in the world he wanted was to be capable of logic, or any thought at all. Feelings, feelings were another matter. He refused to acknowledge heartache, but he was willing to nurse fury, humiliation, resentment, indignation, betrayal, and hatred until he could forge them into a hard armor that he could place around his heart to protect him forever.

Martin finished his whisky and poured another. After he finished that he stood, picked up the bottle that was still a third full, and made his way up the staircase to his room. He did not stagger; he'd had far too much practice at debauchery. He was a gentleman, a nobleman, a member of the ruling class. He'd also had plenty of practice at being one thing and showing something else. In a way, he and Abig— Harriet the Harridan were alike. No, no, not a bit! He was an honorable man. *I do not prevaricate—I am a diplomat.*

He pushed open the door to his room. *She, on the other hand is—*

Here.

Martin did not know why he closed the door and put himself squarely in front of it as he said, "What the devil are you doing in my bedroom?"

"Martin, we need to talk."

He lifted his head proudly and looked down his long, straight nose at her. The room was a bit fuzzy around the edges, but he could see her clearly. "That is Lord Martin to you, madam. Unless you have come to apologize—"

"I haven't."

"Then we have nothing to discuss." He should tell her to get out. He should open the door and toss her out bodily if she refused to go. She did not deserve any better treatment. But he couldn't take his gaze from her, even though he had *not* missed her in the few hours since they'd parted.

She came nearer and peered at him closely, then gave a decisive nod. "Right. You're drunk."

"My state is no affair of yours." He knew he sounded clear and lucid, and looked sober as a judge. Abi—Harriet knew him too well. Damn her.

"Affairs of state are both of our affair."

He puzzled this out for a moment, but all he could manage to respond with was, "What?"

She was still lovely, viper though he knew

122

her to be. Why was that? He knew her to be false, evil, cruel. Why did she have to be so, so . . . round in all the right places? The swelling of her breasts beneath the riding jacket and simple white shirtwaist she wore riveted his gaze. And her scent . . . So very . . . Was that lilacs? Being near her was like breathing in spring. Her dark hair shone in the lamplight and the hint of pink in her cheeks was so very lively, and how sweet it would be to run his thumbs over those bright spots and cup her jaw in his palm while he turned her face up for just one kiss. One long, delicious, forbidden taste of—

"Martin!"

At her sharp tone the bottle dropped from his numb fingers. He swore and she snatched it by the neck before it crashed to the floor. "Making a fool of me again, I see," he said coldly.

"Always cleaning up, more like."

"Get out." He spoke coldly, and none too quietly.

"Shh," she said. "Old man MacLeod's not that deaf. The point of having a secret meeting is that no one notices."

"Secret? What MacLeod?" It took him a moment to recall the name of the inn's owner. "Is everyone on this sheep-infested island named MacLeod?"

"If they're not named MacDonald, aye, mostly, but we're not all close clan relations. And cattle are the chief export of Skye, my lord. Every Englishman who likes his beef knows that."

"I'm not a child for you to be giving lessons to."

"You asked a question. But you're right, I've resigned the position of governess—"

"Been dismissed."

"As you wish, Martin. It's a different position I've come to discuss with you altogether."

He smirked, looking her over boldly from head to toe, then gestured toward the bed. "I can think of several positions to start with."

She put the bottle down on the washstand while he wished his wits were clearer. He'd worked hard to become drunk because of her, but needed his senses sharp in her presence. It was not just his thoughts she affected; oh, no. His body was not under such tight-leashed control, either. She was not a governess anymore, not a pure and shining example of modest womanhood up on a pedestal to be wooed and won. She was on the ground now, had shown herself to be a woman of the world. That made her available, an object of lust, rightful prey for a man's baser instincts. How lovely it would be to take his revenge by living out all his fantasies with that lovely, lush body of hers.

"It's not safe to be alone with me," he warned.

Harriet carried a gun and several knives about her person, but she did not mention to Martin that she was also dangerous to be alone with. She knew what he meant, and he was absolutely right. His hair was tousled, he was coatless, his vest was unbuttoned, and the collar of his white shirt was undone, revealing his strong throat and curls of dark chest hair. His cheeks and square jaw were outlined by a day's growth of blue-black beard. There was a languidness to his movements, a loose sensuality about his mouth, and a hungry glint had replaced the usual cool assessment in his eyes. Whisky and the day's turmoil had wiped away much of his inhibitions. He looked thoroughly disreputable and dangerous, and to a woman of her background this rascal's guise was far more appealing than the carefully groomed, controlled charm of Martin Kestrel the diplomat.

She could easily have moved into those lithe, muscular arms, succumbed to the urge to touch and be touched. She was quite aware that they were alone together in a bedroom, and was not unaffected by his reference to sexual positions. She had a vivid imagination, and wasn't made of stone. She drew on her years of practice to hide the flesh-and-blood woman's earthy cravings behind her usual mask of self-possession.

Martin was a person of masks as much as she was, he simply didn't acknowledge it. Perhaps everyone was. She didn't bring it up for philosophical debate. Of course, she was here to discuss roleplaying with him. Not in a context that had anything to do with soul searching, but in a far more practical way. She really wished there was another way to do this.

"I should tell you why I'm here," she said.

"You said we needed to talk. We've talked. Now get out." His words were laced with grim anger, but he didn't move away from the door.

She did not show how his words pricked small wounds in her soul. She folded her gloved hands in front of her and restrained the sigh that threatened to escape her lips. "I need your help," she told him.

"Why don't you say you need me?" His lips

formed a smirk, but the expression in his eyes was darker and more intense. "I know it would be a lie, of course, but I'd like to hear it."

"I did not expect this conversation to be easy, Martin."

"My lord."

She nodded. "As you wish, my lord."

His smirk turned into a very wicked smile. "I'd love to hear you say that as well, to everything I want."

For some reason, she had not expected sexual innuendo from him. At least not until after she posed her proposition to him, and then what she expected was bitter, caustic teasing that she'd told herself she could live with.

"You are going to give me a very hard time aren't you, my lord?"

His answering laugh was low and sinister. "Very hard indeed."

Her cheeks burned bright red, and redder still when a quick glance below his belt buckle confirmed that the man was not joking. "Martin, are you drunker than you look?"

"Probably."

Harriet supposed she should have waited until tomorrow morning to ask him for help, instead of rushing off right after her mother suggested the plan. What had she been thinking? The man needed, deserved, time to calm down, to regain rationality and equilibrium—just as she did. She wasn't at the top of her form either, or she wouldn't have rashly slipped into his room for a midnight tête-à-tête.

But tomorrow he would take the ferry back to the mainland, and from there who knew where he'd head? To his parents, to be with Patricia? She couldn't confront him there. To his London home? Back to the house party he'd left on the Isle of Wight? To the continent? She could trace him, of course, but that would waste precious time.

The window of opportunity was right now. She didn't want to think that her hieing after him so rapidly was the result of not being able to bear never seeing him again. No, her heart could not be so foolish and impulsive. This was business. She had to concentrate, and make Martin do the same.

"Martin. My lord," she amended at his crooked eyebrow. "I have a favor to ask of you."

"Ah." He smiled, and he reminded Harriet of a large, black, stalking cat, a panther to be exact. "You need me."

"Yes."

He threw back his head and laughed.

"I could kick you," Harriet vented her exasperation.

"And scratch and bite and claw, I hope. From flat on your back."

"Martin!"

He put his finger over his lips. "Shh. Remember old man MacLeod."

Harriet fumed in silence for a few moments. She had to admit that she'd left herself open for every jab he'd delivered. The man had the right to give her a certain amount of grief; she accepted that. What was disturbing was how his suggestions dovetailed so succinctly with what she needed to discuss. "I've come to grovel for a favor. Will you please let me get on with it?"

"Or off with it," he suggested. He waved toward the whisky bottle on the washstand. "Pour me a drink."

No *please*, she noted, and sighed. He probably expected her to tell him he'd had enough. Well, she wasn't there to nursemaid him, or play the disapproving governess. "Very well." She turned.

"Take off your gloves first."

She glanced over her shoulder and caught

the glint of wicked amusement in his eyes. "Very well," she said, mild as you please.

Slowly, with a certain amount of insinuation, she peeled the thin kidskin riding gloves off her fingers. He watched her hands with a riveted attention that she found disturbing. One by one she let the discarded gloves drop to the floor, the action taking on a sensuality she hadn't consciously intended. Then she poured a measure of amber liquid into a glass. He snatched at her hand when she brought the drink to him, but she danced back, only letting him have the glass. He drank the potent single malt whisky in a gulp.

"Another." He held out the glass. "And take off your coat."

All too aware of the tension radiating from the man, Harriet undid the coat and slipped out of it with a minimum of fuss, draping it neatly over the back of a chair before bringing him the whisky. "There's only so far I'm willing to go, you know, before we have our talk."

His gaze held a disturbing mixture of contempt and hunger. One hurt her, the other she found unwillingly fascinating. He said, "I notice you did not say you wouldn't go further."

"Let's talk."

He drank. "Undo your hair."

She would go this far, and no further. Some long-suppressed corner of her mind whispered, *Why not?* She hated having her hair pinned up, anyway.

Martin moved to the bed. He stretched out on his side on top of the blue bedspread, leaning back on the piled-up pillows, his glass held casually in one hand. He smiled his dangerous, tempting, black-cat smile as he watched her take down her hair, as pleased with himself as some Oriental potentate having his every wish fulfilled by his favorite concubine. What *had* he been up to during those private meetings with the Turkish sultan?

"I won't dance for you now, effendi," she said after she shook out her long hair around her shoulders. "Don't bother to ask."

"I don't have my water pipe with me, anyway."

Harriet took a seat in the room's one chair, across the room from the bed. She tried not to notice that he'd undone several more buttons of his shirt. She also ignored the impulse to settle on the bed beside him and help him slip the garment the rest of the way off. She hadn't allowed herself to think of Martin Kestrel as a

131

male for the last four years, at least not in any context concerning her own mating urges. She'd tried not to *have* mating urges. But now her carefully ordered thinking was topsy-turvy, her life was a complete disaster, and all those repressed urges threatened to bubble out of control. It was only going to get worse, if things worked out as she needed them to.

Remember that he has good reason to hate you, she reminded herself. *For he's not likely to let you forget.* This job was not going to be easy or fun. *Do what you have to,* she ordered herself sternly. *Then go home and get back to licking your wounds. They'll only be worse when you're done.*

"I should like to see you naked," he said, proving her point.

"We can't always have what we want when we want it," she snapped back before she could stop herself.

"I've waited four years." He drained his last glass of whisky and let the glass drop to the floor. He crooked a finger. "If a woman comes to a man's room she only has one thing on her mind."

"Tidying up, most likely," Harriet answered. "Scrubbing the floors, airing the linens."

"That wasn't what I meant and you know it."

"But some bait doesn't bear rising to, does it, Martin—my lord?" Harriet forced her thoughts back to her objective, and kept her gaze away from the hard muscles of Martin's chest. "May I leave off groveling for a while and discuss business?"

"We were discussing business. I've always paid you for your services."

The contempt in his voice brought her angry gaze to his. "I never took any of your money, my lord. Not a penny, or a pound, and I gave Patricia the finest education a girl is likely to receive in this unenlightened age. Furthermore—" Harriet bit her tongue. Justifications were not necessary; she had served her country.

"Furthermore, what?"

"Nothing." She'd risen to her feet during her tirade. Harriet shook her head, shifting the thick tendrils of hair framing her face. How the man could make her lose control so easily after all these years, she did not understand. Perhaps it had something to do with bare chests and beds, but she liked to think that she was not so easily susceptible to his flagrantly displayed charms. It had been a bad day; she was tired and rattled. That was all.

She stiffened her spine, took her seat once

more, straightened her skirts, and asked, "Where was I?"

Mention of his daughter seemed to have taken some of the lecherous pleasure at taunting her out of him. "You were about to attempt to talk me into something." He glared at her through narrowed eyes. "You're going to try to make me believe I should help you with some sort of undercover assignment, is my guess."

"For a man who has just met me, you know me too bloody well."

"Don't swear. It isn't ladylike." He smirked. "Oh, right. You're not a lady."

She hated that they so easily descended into bickering. If Patricia had behaved this way, Harriet would have put her down for a nap. She supposed that after such a trying day she and Martin both needed rest, but she was so keyed up she didn't know how that was possible. Perhaps she should ask to join him in a drink—which would, of course, be no more ladylike than swearing. Men got to have all the fun; women who joined them got called very ugly names.

"Very well," he finally agreed. "What do you want?"

"To go to a party."

Martin sat up so fast his head swam, and only an act of sheer will kept him from hurtling face first onto the braided rug on the floor. It took a moment for his eyes to come back into focus, and when they did he saw Harriet MacLeod gazing at him with a look of mild concern, and her usual calm demeanor.

"A party?" he demanded of this odd mixture of complete stranger and longtime acquaintance. "What are you talking about? What sort of party?"

"Let me explain."

Her hands were clenched so tightly together in her lap that her knuckles were white. Nerves? He saw the strain around her lips and eyes. She was a consummate actress, the little traitor, but he doubted these signs of strain were part of an act. He took great pleasure in seeing her perturbed.

"This should be quite an explanation," he observed. "You hate having to come to me for help, don't you? Of course." He rubbed his jaw. "You wouldn't be willing to put yourself in my debt."

"Even drunk, you're too bloody perceptive."

"I'll take that as a compliment, and stop swearing. Tell me."

135

She took a deep breath, and seemed totally unaware of the delightful way her breasts shifted beneath the starched material of her white blouse. Martin imagined them uncovered while she talked.

"It is a complicated story, and I cannot tell you all of it. To those uninvolved in the game, the details always sound quite preposterous anyway."

He understood what she meant by the game, of course. In his own diplomatic capacity he was very much a player in the rivalry between the British Empire and czarist Russia. Russia schemed to expand its borders, England countered with schemes to preserve the current balance of world power. The Great Game, as some romantic in the foreign office had dubbed the power struggle decades ago, was played on many levels, some official, many covert. Martin fought the war with words, negotiating delicate treaties between the Empire and governments that were courted with equal fervor by the Russians. His was the clean, honest way: a game played by fair rules.

His lip curled back in disgust at the game she played. "Spies." He might as well have spit as said the word. "I'm getting used to your preposterous tales, Miss MacLeod. Do go on."

"The short version of the story is that a courier carrying vital information needs to be met at a certain time and place. The person who was supposed to meet that courier has been delayed. The meeting is to take place at a very private house party on a secluded estate. When I heard the location, I recalled that you had turned down an invitation to that specific party to accept the Hazlemoors' invitation instead. You could still go to that party—and take me with you." She smiled. "You see, when one ignores all the secretive trappings, it is really a very simple plan. I need a way in, you have an invitation. I meet the courier, I leave, no one is any the wiser."

Somehow he was certain it could not be as simple as she said. He must have received four or five invitations for the same time that he chose to spend in the Hazlemoors' wholesome company.

He smiled bitterly. If he hadn't gone to Freddie Hazlemoor's and been bombarded by eligible maidens, his thoughts would not have turned to marriage. Then he would not have proposed to his governess and he would not now be sitting in a room in Scotland with the treacherous woman who'd torn his life and soul to shreds.

He crossed his arms. "Good God, how I wish I'd gone off to Sir Anthony Strake's for a fortnight of good old-fashioned debauchery."

"You still can," Harriet said. "But you have to take me with you."

Martin stood even more quickly than he'd sat up, and it was even more of a mistake. This time when the room spun, it kept right on spinning. He could barely manage to croak out, "Take *you* to that den of iniquity!"

The last thing he heard was Harriet very calmly saying, "I could go as your mistress."

Chapter 10

Martin woke with an aching head and to the sound of rain blowing hard and heavy against the windowpane. He also woke with two thoughts. One was never to touch the local whisky again. The second was that it had been quite a dream. An image of Harriet with her hair down and her clothing in disarray swam through his head. To combat the headache he let his imagination take the notion further, baring her shoulders and calling up an image of ripe, round breasts. He had not let himself think of her as a woman for so very long, but now every thought of her was of carnal revenge. She was traitorous, false—how right it would be to make her pay for her crimes against him in his bed. He groaned at the notion, half in pain, half in regret for letting the opportunity to use her as she deserved slip away so easily the night before.

"That was a dream," he reminded himself. The sound of his own voice, though it was only a whisper, sent a fresh jolt of pain through him. Getting up and dressed was not something he particularly wanted to do, but the sooner he was away from the Isle of Skye and temptation named Harriet, the better. It was all he could do to shave and change out of the clothes he'd slept in before stumbling downstairs, where he was immediately confronted by the landlord.

"G'day, m'lord," the old man said before Martin could utter a word. "Yon carriage is waiting to take you to Mallaig." He gestured toward the door, and had it open a moment later.

Wind drove in a heavy spray of cold rain that hit Martin squarely in the face. Martin didn't remember requesting a carriage, but the idea of riding a horse through this weather, with a pounding head besides, did not seem a promising way of spending the day. He wiped cold water off his aching brow and said,

"Fine." He quickly settled his bill and went out through the downpour to the waiting carriage.

He'd taken his seat and closed the door behind him before he realized there was someone else occupying the dim interior. He should have noticed sooner, he supposed, as it was not a big conveyance, and the large bonnet and wide skirts of the woman seated opposite him took up a certain amount of space. A hatbox and carpetbag took up the rest of the woman's seat.

"I beg your pardon," he said, swiftly taking off his hat. "I had no idea this is a public coach."

"It's not." Harriet leaned forward, her lovely, smiling face framed by the curving arc of her bonnet brim. "Did you cut yourself shaving, Martin?" she inquired, all mild solicitation.

"You! What are you doing in my carriage?"

"It's not your carriage, it's my family's carriage."

Her words effectively stopped him from telling her to get out, and the carriage began moving before he could step out himself. "Harriet," he complained as he was jolted back into his seat.

"Miserable day, isn't it?" she asked, glancing out the window, then turning a pleasant look on him as though this was another start to one of their many journeys rather than an abduction by a woman who had betrayed all his trust and belief in her. "You could jump out if you like," she added. "But Gabriel's driving rather faster than conditions warrant, you might have noticed. You'd probably survive, but why spend weeks mending broken bones on a relatively remote Scottish island, when you can be enjoying the decadent pleasures of—say, Sir Anthony Strake's house party?"

So it hadn't been a dream. Martin rubbed his aching forehead and glanced out the window as the carriage rattled at a fast clip down a narrow road. There was sea on one side and hills on the other. "Perhaps I'll push you out," he suggested.

"That would not be a gentlemanly thing to do. And despite what you think of me, you would never harm a woman."

"More's the pity." He gave her a dark look from under lowered brows. "Why are you plaguing me, woman? Didn't I tell you that I never want to see you again?"

Harriet looked thoughtful for a few moments before answering, "No, I don't recall your actually using those exact words."

"Don't mince shades of meanings with me, woman. I am the diplomat here," he reminded her.

"You are a true and dutiful servant of the queen, my lord," Harriet said. "And your service to the queen is needed at this very moment." She managed to keep the smile on her face even though he sent her a look guaranteed to peel the skin off lesser beings than His Mighty Lordship Martin Kestrel.

He held up a hand. "I am not taking you to Strake's party. It is not in the cards, my dear. Not on the agenda."

"I'm glad you remember the conversation."

"Most of it," he admitted. "I hoped it was a dream. A nightmare," he added.

Harriet remembered too well his watching her as she paid him for the conversation with bit by bit of shed clothing. The memory of his heated gaze burned into her skin and memories and had kept her from getting any sleep at all the night before. Perhaps it had been fear of nightmares of her own that kept her from sleep, or fear that her dreams would have continued the erotic aspects of the visit far beyond her control.

The road was rough and the weather foul. The coach bounced along at breakneck speed, throwing up gouts of mud and water as the driver sped toward the ferry dock at the southern tip of the island. Harriet wanted to shout up to her younger brother to slow down before he killed them, but that would be a show of nerves. She refused to look anywhere but at Martin Kestrel, or to concentrate on anything but the task at hand. "It's a pity you fell asleep before we settled this last night."

He lifted an elegant eyebrow sarcastically. "What? You aren't going to tell me that I agreed to some mad scheme while I was drunk?"

She might have shaken her head, but nerves and the lurching of the carriage already had her quite queasy enough. Yet he looked worse than she felt. It was all she could do to keep from offering to soothe his aching brow, despite the fierce look he turned on her.

"I never have treated you like a fool, my lord, despite what you think. I won't start now."

"You're happy to treat me as a pawn."

"Not happy," she said. "Never happy. And I'm not asking you to be a pawn, but to be a shield. Not a passive role, but an active one. At least I *am* asking you this time. You are the one in control of the situation, my lord."

His attention focused with a sudden, frightening intensity that left her gasping for air. Something dark stirred in his eyes; his lips curved in a smile that was as cruel as it was compelling. "Really?"

His voice held a silky purr, one with steel behind it, and Harriet's heart began to race at the sight of the dissolute stranger suddenly seated across from her. Soon they would be at the ferry dock at Mallaig. She needed him to agree to help her before he could walk onto the boat and disappear from her life forever.

"I need your help, Martin," she pleaded. "I would rather you do so to serve your country— there are lives of innocent British citizens at stake if the information falls into the wrong hands—but if you would rather help me for the sake of revenge, so be it." He continued to glare at her. She could see that thunderstorm temper of his building behind the bitter look, and did not have time for pride. "Please help me. Name your price, and I will pay it."

There was a demon seated on Martin Kestrel's shoulder, whispering, *Go on, man, do it. You know what she's offering. Take it. Take her!* Exquisite images of satiating every lustful fantasy danced in his head, and stroked a fever through his blood. *Use her. Think of those long legs wrapped around you, of those ripe breasts in you hands.*

She'd betrayed him. She'd made a fool of him. He wanted revenge. Most important, he still desperately wanted her. He had four years of secretly wanting her and trying *not* to want her to make up for. She was under his skin and in his blood. How could he go on with his life until he had her out of his system? The idea of having power over her was more intoxicating than last night's whisky.

Martin leaned back. It was not a large carriage, so there was not much room on the upholstered bench beside him. He patted the narrow space and said, "Come sit beside me and ask me nicely."

"And change the balance of the coach with Gabriel driving like a fiend?" she answered. "I think not."

She glanced quickly to her left, out the small

window that showed a view of the sea. His eyes had adjusted to the faint light enough to recognize that she was frightened of the drive through the storm. He remembered driving a coach through the night on an icy mountain road with a stoic young woman who showed not a hint of nerves. But Harriet . . . Harriet was not so well armored.

He patted the seat again. "Come here."

"Do you want to tip us over?"

"Do you want my help?"

Harriet said a very unsuitable word, bunched her skirts out of her way, and moved out of her seat just as the carriage came to a sharp curve in the road. She gasped and swayed toward the door. Martin caught her around the waist and dragged her down beside him. He put his arm around her, pulled her as close as possible in the tight space, and said, "Isn't this nice?"

After a significant hesitation, Harriet answered, "Yes, my lord."

He liked her like this, warm and pliant in the crook of his arm. Martin put a finger under her chin and tilted her face up to his. "Now," he said, lips close to hers. "What is it you want to be to me?"

Harriet opened her lips to speak, but his mouth covered hers before she could make a sound. After a while she did make a sound, a small, helpless one that sent a sharp pang of desire through him. He very much wanted to go further but made himself lift his head and look her in the eyes. They were still in the negotiating stage, after all. It was going to be ever so much more a victory if she capitulated to his terms of her own free will.

"Sorry for the interruption," he said. "I believe you were about to answer my question."

"You look as smug as the cat who caught the canary," she replied.

He gave a faint, one-shoulder shrug. "Your technique needs work, my dear, but with practice I'm sure you'll learn to make kissing a more pleasurable experience for me. You've ever been a quick study." She looked outraged. He smiled. "What was that question?"

She stiffened, her green eyes flashed with fury, but she kept to the point and asked, "Will you take me to Sir Anthony Strake's house party?"

"As?" he coaxed.

"I would be there under the pretense that I

am your mistress. I would be acting the role of—"

"Acting?" He shook his head. "I don't see why there should be any acting involved."

"Martin . . ."

"Do you need my help?"

"Do you think I'd be debasing myself this way if the need wasn't desperate?"

"Debasing." He smiled slowly. He stroked her cheek. "What a lovely word."

Her fingers closed around his wrist, but she did not try to push his hand away from her face. She said, "I see you're going to be unreasonable."

"I've had enough games from you," he answered. "First a false governess, now you want to play at being a lover. It will not do."

Her grip grew tighter around his wrist. "Why not?"

"Because, my dear harlot, someone needs to make an honest woman of you."

"The name is Harriet, not—"

"I know what I meant." He stroked his fingers down her throat and flattened his palm over her heart. "Honesty is a relative thing; you've taught me that. If you want to go to

Strake's as my mistress, you have to *be* my mistress."

She went very still, and very pale. Green fire blazed in her eyes when they met his. "You want my virtue in exchange for your cooperation?"

"I want your body. I'm sure you gave up your virtue years ago." He was not sure of that at all; she did not kiss like a woman skilled in the art of love. Then again, perhaps her lovers had not been interested in skill. He required it in his.

Anger and indignation crackled from Harriet as Martin waited for her reply. The rattle and sway of the coach began to lessen. Martin caught a glimpse of scattered houses along the roadside out of the corner of his eye, but he kept his attention focused on his beautiful adversary. Bright spots of color had appeared on her pale cheeks. Embarrassment? Fury that he would not be swayed into letting her have her own way, by talk of loyalty and duty to the Empire, was more likely.

Finally Harriet said, "This is the point where I should slap your face and call you a cad."

"If we were following a standard scenario, I suppose that would be the appropriate response to such a vile suggestion," he agreed.

"The only reason I would slap a man's face would be to challenge him to a duel, my lord. Of course, if I were to challenge you, you would choose foils or sabres—and you'd end up winning anyway, because you're much better with edged weapons than I'll ever be."

"I don't see how I can lose this match with you at all," he told her. His head still pounded, and the wound from her betrayal was still too open and fresh for him to be anything but cruel. "You see," he went on, with a very cold smile, "if you say no, then we part company, and good riddance to you. If you say yes, then I'll take my pleasure with your pretty body for a few days, and then say good riddance to you. I have nothing to lose."

"Martin, how long do you plan to act like a bastard over this?"

"How long do you have, my dear?"

"As long as it takes to get what I need."

"I take it your answer is yes, then?"

She looked away as the carriage came to a stop. "We're here," she said. "I'll think about it," she added, and slipped from his grasp and out of the coach before he had a chance to stop her.

Chapter 11

"Harriet, what is going on with you and that man?"

Harriet stood facing the water, her back to the village and to the man who was the main source of her troubles. The rain lashed down hard enough to obscure the view of the mainland across the strait, hard enough to disguise any tears she might shed.

She was glad Gabriel spoke before he had touched her, or she might have lashed out violently at the person behind her. She had never been so on edge before, so ready to do something wild and reckless and out of control. The simple explanation was that Martin Kestrel had finally driven her mad. She'd always suspected he would someday. Four years in the man's charismatic company had taken far more out of her than she'd realized. She'd always thought she'd kept her objectivity intact, but knew now she'd been lying to herself.

She was so angry at Martin she wanted to kill him.

The gall of the man! The arrogant, superior impudence of that rutting stallion to dare suggest she—

"Harriet?"

She whirled to face her brother. "What?" Gabriel took a quick step back. "This is all your blasted twin's fault," she complained.

"Things generally are," he agreed, though she could tell he didn't know what she meant, but was anxious to soothe her. "But what's Michael have to do with you and Lord Martin?"

Everything!

She managed, just barely, not to shout this at Gabriel. It wasn't his fault Michael was young and reckless. It wasn't his fault that Martin Kestrel was an ass. She might possibly lay some of the blame for Martin's behavior at her own door, but that only increased her anger. At herself and at him and at the rainy, gray world in general.

And speaking of reckless—"Did you have to drive like that?"

"You said you were in a hurry."

She reached up and chucked him under the chin. "You're not as mild-mannered a scholar as you like to pretend." That was the problem with her family; none of them was mild-mannered at all, even the ones who desperately tried to be.

He grinned. "Does that mean you're letting me come with you?"

"You're going as far as the train station in Fort William and no farther."

He glanced back at the carriage. "I don't think you should be alone with that man. He has a dissolute look to him."

"And what would you know about being dissolute, my lad?"

His eyes twinkled as he answered, "I do go to school with Michael, lass."

It occurred to Harriet that she might have missed out on vital information she was going to need in dealing with Martin's demand, by being denied a university education.

"You're shaking, Harriet. Come along, we're getting soaked out here."

Gabriel put his arm around her shoulder

and led Harriet inside the small building where passengers waited by the ferry dock. There were bare wooden benches where one could perch uncomfortably, and a stove in the center of the small room gave out a bit of welcome heat.

Harriet nodded a greeting to the woman seated stiff and straight on the bench. She was working on a piece of sewing, a trunk and other traveling bags piled beside her. Harriet received a disapproving nod in return. Harriet smiled, having had years to learn to interpret the myriad nuances to be found in Mrs. Swift's disapproval. She was glad to see that her traveling companion had found her own way from Skye Court to the village of Mallaig.

Though Harriet let her brother lead her to a spot near the stove, she didn't tell him that cold had nothing to do with the way her treacherous body was quaking. She dared not tell Gabriel the price Martin demanded for his help. She could imagine several scenarios that could come out of dropping that bit of knowledge in a MacLeod man's ear. They ranged from one to a dozen of her male relatives making Martin Kestrel pay for his salacious effrontery in any number of gruesome, painful ways.

While thoughts of retribution were pleasant, defending her honor at this point would cause a delay they could ill afford. Women had to be the sensible ones.

Harriet stripped off her gloves and held her hands out toward the warmth that radiated up from the stove. "Ah," she said. "How long until the ferry arrives?"

"Momentarily," Gabriel answered. He glanced toward the door. Harriet heard it open, but the shiver that was a mixture of fear, anticipation, and something far more primal told her that Martin Kestrel had walked into the room. She did not turn to face him, but listened as Gabriel went on very softly, "You need someone you can count on." He shot a quick glare at Martin.

Harriet glanced once more at the stern woman minding the trunks. "I'll have Mrs. Swift."

"She's an old woman. And Kestrel doesn't look particularly promising," Gabriel said. "He's not family."

She smiled slightly at Gabriel's assessment of the woman who had been many things at many times, most recently the housekeeper at Skye Court. Of Martin she said, "He looks better when his valet takes him in hand. Besides, all he has to do is get me where I need to be. I'll do the rest."

"Let *me* go, disguised as Michael."

"That possibility has been discussed and discarded already. If Michael is in trouble—which we do not know to be true but have to assume, then there is possibly a trap waiting at Strake House." Harriet traced a finger down her brother's nose. "If someone holds Michael prisoner and is waiting to intercept the courier, having a man who looks exactly like Michael walk in the door would certainly put a spanner in the works. We'd lose the courier, and more importantly, the chance to find Michael."

"But Michael might not be in trouble."

She knew he said it because he wanted it to be true. "Very likely not," she reassured him. "I'll probably meet him at Strake's, and all will be well." She hoped the rascal had been way-laid or delayed for some inconsequential reason and was even now taking up his assignment. But the way the documents had reached Aunt Phoebe was worrisome. So was the cryptic message scrawled on the bottom of one of the sheets of paper. They didn't know if anything was actually wrong, but they didn't

dare take chances. Lives were at stake. Someone had to get into the exclusive house party
and find out what was going on.

Alexander had volunteered for the mission,
but he didn't have the temperament for playing a gambling, whoring noble. Besides, he was
still nursing his injured arm and shoulder. Father had outright said, "No!" when Harriet
pointed out that she had a way in. He had declared that they'd wait for Christopher and
give the job to him. But Mother had seen the
sense of sending Harriet, and had made all the
necessary arrangements.

And because they had to assume that
Michael MacLeod's life was in danger, Harriet
would accede to the payment Kestrel demanded for his help. She would not be a whore
for her country; not even patriotism would
make her sell herself into a man's bed. But she
would do whatever was required to save her
brother's life.

*And young Michael MacLeod had damned well
better be in deep, life-threatening, tortured trouble,*
she told herself. *Or I'll kill him myself.*

With that thought, she turned and angrily
marched up to where Martin Kestrel leaned
with his arms crossed, fuming by the door. His

gaze burned into her with every step she took. "Very well," she said when she reached him.

His arm snaked around her waist, drawing her so close that she was intimately aware of his hard body pressing against hers. "Very well, what?" he asked.

"Let me go," she whispered urgently, dizzy with the awareness of Martin's maleness, and of the outrage that would burst out of Gabriel if this embrace went on any longer. She put her hands on Martin's shoulders, and pushed. "I'll do whatever you want once we're away from Skye, but release me before my brother makes a scene. Besides, my da's an elder of the kirk," she added when Martin released her after a moment's hesitation. "If the scandal of your touching me like that got out, you'd have a wife rather than a temporary mistress before you got off the island, my lord. We wouldn't want that, would we?" she added with a grim smile.

Martin was frightened—so frightened that the meaning of her words did not sink in for a moment. Because in the last few minutes he had made the awful discovery that once having Harriet in his arms, he did not want to let her go. He'd even been jealous when he walked in there and found her talking to her brother. A man she *said* was her brother. How could he be sure anything she told him was true?

He told her in no uncertain terms, "I'll make sure you live up to the bargain. Try to play me false and you will regret it."

"The ferry's in," she said in answer. "Let's get started, shall we?"

"You want me to thump him? Your mum said I could if he got out of hand," Mrs. Swift said.

Martin stood behind them, lounging in the open bedroom doorway.

The journey had been a long and uncomfortable one; from Skye to Fort William by carriage, by train from there to Glasgow, and another train from Glasgow across the border into the north of England. They'd finally ended up at this inn in the Northumbrian village closest to Sir Anthony Strake's country estate. Tomorrow they would proceed to Strake House. Harriet was all in favor of riding on through the night to their final destination, but there was no available transportation. Martin had dispatched telegraphs from Glasgow, one to his friend Strake announcing his arrival. He'd told Harriet the soonest they could expect a carriage to be sent was the next morning. Besides, Martin had insisted on waiting for the arrival of his valet and his wardrobe. He was correct about the importance of appearances; they couldn't walk into a house party full of the wealthy and the titled looking like a pair of refugees from the windswept Hebrides. One needed style, elegance, and fashion to mingle among the elite if one did not want to raise brows, incite gossip, and call attention to oneself.

Harriet's cover was to be a pretty ornament dangling adoringly on Lord Martin Kestrel's arm. Being an ornament took a great deal of work, and she was nowhere near prepared to assume the role yet. Despite all the hours spent working on the project while they traveled, she and Mrs. Swift still had so much to do.

"He's still there," Mrs. Swift said. She lifted a white brocade dress from the trunk and looked critically at the bodice. "Hmm," she said. "Shall I slam the door on him?"

Harriet sighed. She had been trying to ignore Martin's presence as they sorted through her clothing. "You deal with the dress," she finally told Mrs. Swift. "I'll deal with the—with

Lord Martin." She turned to the man in the doorway and said, "What?"

He held out a hand. "Come have dinner with me. I have a private room for the two of us," he added with a bitter look at Mrs. Swift. He had been quite disgruntled at having the other woman as a chaperone the whole way here. Mrs. Swift had been impervious to his glare, and Harriet had been amused and uncomfortable with his dark, hungry looks by turns. Conversation had been at a minimum, contact nonexistent, and Harriet had been dreading this confrontation since their arrival at the inn. Still, she faced him with aplomb and stiff courtesy.

"Thank you, my lord, but as you can see, I am rather busy at the moment."

"Doing what?"

"Making myself unpresentable to polite society. One does not become a doxy overnight, you know."

He chuckled. "My dear, I believe that is exactly how it is done."

"Nevertheless—"

"Dinner," he said, coming forward and taking her by the arm. "Now."

He drew her forward, and Harriet went

along without further protest. Though his imperious behavior had a great deal to do with her capitulation, the lure of a hot meal had an influence over her as well. "A meat pie would be nice," she said. "And a cup of tea. I'd kill for a good, strong cup of tea."

"Your tastes are plebeian, my dear," he told her. He led her down a flight of stairs and into a small, private dining room. For a country inn the room was quite elegantly appointed, paneled in dark wood, the walls hung with portraits of dogs, horses, and hunting scenes. Silverware, crystal goblets, and china in a blue and red floral design were set out on an embroidered linen tablecloth. A crystal bowl holding fragrant red and white roses adorned the center of the table. A sideboard held silver chafing dishes and several bottles of wine to go with the meal. Candlelight gleamed golden over it all.

"All that's missing is the Gypsy violinist," she said as she looked around.

"You, woman, have no appreciation for the finer things." He gestured her gallantly toward the table.

It was not that she was unfamiliar with the finer things in life, or even with sharing a private meal with Martin Kestrel while on the road, but context was so important, wasn't it? Somehow she doubted this evening's repast would be followed by a companionable game of chess, or a discussion of a book they'd both read. *Well, at least he's willing to feed me,* she thought as she sat in the chair he held out for her.

Perhaps I should simply order her to my bed, Martin thought as he went to the sideboard. He felt her gaze on him, as real as a caressing touch along his back and shoulders. Odd that he should be so sensitized to her awareness of him. Or perhaps he only imagined he held her attention. She might be making a mental shopping list behind her appraising stare. He'd thought an intimate meal, some excellent wine, and the two of them alone before retiring for the night would have a soothing effect on the situation, ease the awkwardness of the circumstances for her. She was probably thinking that he was serving her now so that he could service her later, which was the sort of rude, cynical thing he'd be thinking in her situation. And they had always thought a great deal alike.

No, we haven't, Martin sternly reminded himself. He had never known what went on behind that lovely, liar's face, but only thought he

SUSAN SIZEMORE

had. He didn't know now, wasn't going to ask, and her thoughts on any subject did not matter. The point was not to care what went on behind her serene expression, not to want her opinions or crave a smile or a glance of approval. Her face was for kissing, tasting, touching. What mattered was soft skin and supple, skilled lips.

"You are a bad habit," he told her. He turned, empty-handed, and took a seat. He waved toward the row of silver serving dishes and said, "You have permission to serve me my dinner."

She snorted, a most unladylike sound that drew an unwilling smile from him. "Oh, please." Harriet tossed her napkin on the table, and got up and brought him back a heaping plate of food and a glass of wine. "Shall I cut your meat for you, too?" she inquired, hovering at his shoulder.

"No," he said, "but I could use having my neck rubbed."

When her hands settled at the sides of his throat he thought she might choke him. She divined his thought, for she leaned down and whispered, her warm breath brushing his ear, "Oh, no, my hands alone aren't strong enough

166

for that." She slowly traced a forefinger around his throat, just under his collar. Her touch left a trail of fire even as she said, "Now . . . if I had a cord of some sort . . ."

Never mind her actual words, the sultry tone was enough to drive any hunger for food from his mind. He pushed the chair away from the table, snagged her around the waist, and drew her down on his lap so quickly it left her gasping in surprise. He liked that he could surprise her, having had more than his share of surprises from her lately. He laughed as she kissed him, knowing that she didn't mean to, but they both let it happen. The taste of her mouth was honey sweet, insistent, and he was eager to oblige. And then her hand was in his hair, caressed his cheek, and her weight pressed against his loins arousingly. He groaned, and his hand came up to cup her breast, his thumb questing to find a hint of nipple beneath all the layers of clothing and corseting between him and the heavenly touch of naked flesh.

Harriet knew she should not be doing this, it had just *happened*. She was tired, overwrought, and so very fearful of being out of control. She told herself she was kissing him because it showed both of them that he did not have all the power. But she also kissed him because, though he had kissed her several times, she had never kissed anyone before, and didn't see why she should wait until mighty Lord Martin ordered her to put her lips to his to serve his vengeful pleasure. And he would. She had no doubt that he would demand a great deal that he considered his rightful due before this liaison ended. But now she was taking as well as giving, and it was a heady sensation to close her eyes as her tongue delved delicately into the heat of his mouth. She immersed her senses in blind tactile awareness of the texture of his lips, the scent of his skin, the smoothness of a freshly shaved cheek beneath her fingers. It was wrong, it was morally repugnant, but it was very, very pleasurable.

The impulse died in a jolt of panic when she became aware that his hand sought her breast. She was off his lap and halfway across the room within moments. She did not run for the door—oh, no, she was not that much of a coward. Instead she approached the chafing dishes, trying hard not to betray any quivering of her limbs, and pretended to choose between beef and lamb. When she was certain that her hands were not shaking, she filled a plate and went back to her place opposite Martin.

He watched her the whole time. When she finally looked at him, he said, "You're blushing."

"It's warm in here," she answered.

"Very," he agreed, and passed her his glass of wine.

She took a sip and passed the crystal goblet back to him. She couldn't help but notice that he put the glass to his lips in the exact spot where she had. For some reason, the gesture sent an intense erotic shiver through her, as though her lips felt the brush of his even across the distance. His gaze did not leave hers the entire time. Something was going to get out of hand very soon, Harriet thought. The only question was, which of them would make the fatal move?

She almost laughed at her melodramatic choice of words. *Fatal* meant dead. She understood fatalities all too well. Preventing real, irrevocable, gone-forever-and-you-can't-get-them-back deaths was why she'd made a deal with the devil seated opposite her. What was at stake in her dealings with Martin were things important only to her. What were lost innocence, squashed pride, abandoned principles, and a broken heart worth, in comparison with the greater good? *Quite a lot from where I'm sitting,* she complained silently.

Of course, if she hadn't spent the last four years making a fool of him, from his point of view, the man might not be so truculent now. One had to look at these things from all sides.

"Why?"

"Why what, my dear?"

Harriet blinked, bringing her attention to bear on Martin in the flesh. "Am I?" she asked. "Your *dear*?"

"No."

"I didn't think so."

He shrugged. "It's a general term I use for all my mistresses." He took another sip of wine. "It's useful when I can't recall their names when I wake up beside them."

"I can see how that could be useful," Harriet answered, and deliberately set about slicing and eating several forkfuls of roast beef. She didn't taste a thing. She did not let herself contemplate his string of mistresses, of which she was about to become another. How would he compare her to all those skilled, beautiful

women he called *dear*? She beat down a spark
of satisfaction that at least he would remember
her, because he counted bedding her as a conquest of a hated enemy.

All the time, she was aware of him sitting
back and looking at her with an almost feral
watchfulness. She *felt* his gaze, like a caress on
her skin, and deeper inside.

"When I wake up beside them naked," he
added.

She put her fork and knife neatly on either
side of her plate. Her senses reeled as her mind
filled with images of beds and naked flesh—
touching . . . She had to swallow, but her voice
was steady when she spoke. "Personally, I
think that if two people are going to wake up
naked together, they should at least exchange
proper introductions beforehand." She also
thought they should have the blessings of the
kirk in the bonds of holy wedlock, but this
didn't seem the proper time to bring it up.

"Speaking of introductions," he said. "What
do I call you besides *my dear*?"

For a few moments Harriet had no idea what
he was talking about. When he noticed her
staring at him in confusion he added, "You do

have a disguise picked out for this assignment, don't you? A false identity?"

A knot of misery curdled in Harriet's stomach, and an ache began in her temples. She'd just sloughed off one false identity and loathed the notion of assuming a false image again so soon. "Blast it all! I can barely remember who I am, and now I have to do it all over again."

Martin wasn't at all sure what to make of Harriet's words. He had some sort of vague assumption that playacting must be second nature to the woman, that she assumed and shed personas as easily as a snake sloughed off its skin—and that she was just as treacherous. Instead, she sounded tired and petulant and seemed almost confused by the masquerade that lay before her.

"You haven't thought this through very carefully, have you?" he asked, genuinely curious, and rather abashed. "This isn't some carefully thought-out, long-range—"

"Of course not!" she snapped at him. She threw her napkin on the table. "This is an impromptu, thrown-together mess. When one has an emergency one has to improvise."

"I see," he said, rubbing his jaw. "How shall I introduce you when we reach Strake House?"

he asked. "Where did we meet? How long have you been my mistress? Do you have a profession other than courtesan? Are you on the stage? A milliner? An opera singer? Do you dance at the ballet? Are you English? French? Are you Harriet MacLeod of the Isle of Skye come to see how the daring and degenerate live?" He tilted his head to one side and studied her intently in the gold glow of the candlelit room. "*Are* you Harriet MacLeod?"

Harriet rested her elbows on the table and regarded him with her chin propped on her folded hands. "I am in fact Harriet MacLeod," she asserted. "Just not tomorrow, or the day or two after. And you are a clever one, my lord, bringing up details I should already have thought of. Getting here took up all my attention, so now we have to plan how to get the disguise right."

"We?"

"You brought it up. And it is your cover, as well."

"I have a legitimate reason for being at Strake's. You are simply using me—as you have used me all along."

"You have made the bargain and agreed to a price, my lord," she countered, stung by the sudden darkness in his tone. "So you are a participant in the exercise, not a pawn. In fact, you are the one in control of this situation. You know it, relish it, and have no plans of letting me forget it."

He did not know why it bothered him that she threw the truth in his face. "And you aren't going to let me forget it, either."

"Precisely, my lord."

"Speaking of not forgetting things. . . ." He rose imperiously to his feet. "We're finished here." He came around the table, drew her to her feet, and turned her toward the door with his arm hooked around her waist. "It is time, my dear," Martin Kestrel told his new mistress as a rush of ravenous anticipation went through him, "for us to go to bed."

Chapter 12

∽⟡⟡∽

He couldn't wait until they reached the bedroom. It was dark at the top of the stairs, and there was no one around. That one kiss, one brief whisper touch had only whetted his appetite. He pressed her back against the wall, using his size and strength to overwhelm. He gave her no chance to bolt like some scared fawn this time. Her lips were soft against his when he touched them, her mouth accepting, but her body was stiff, unyielding, when he wanted her to melt against him as she had earlier. He wanted to *feel* her, and for her to be as aware of his hardness as he was of her opulent curves.

"Will you at least try to work up some enthusiasm for the role?" he whispered, after taking a moment to nuzzle her ear. "Touch me," he urged, feeling as though he were acting like the director of some lunatic, lurid stage production. His fingers sought and found the buttons of the high-necked bodice of her traveling dress. His impulse was to rip the clothes from her body right there in the hall. But he'd undressed many a woman in his time, the flat buttons were easy to undo even in the dark, and his fingers were quick and clever. Harriet stayed very still, he could not even feel her breathing, as one by one he undid them until he felt satiny warm skin beneath his palm. "Touch me," he ordered again, and ground his hips against her, the action bringing a small shocked sound from her lips.

Harriet was not unaware of male anatomy. Papa and Uncle Andrew had taught her myriad ways to damage it. More to the point, Aunt Phoebe had once spent an entire revealing day going through a very detailed picture book with her. Besides, she'd grown up on a working farm and had many brothers. Harriet knew about men and mating, but she had never known a man sexually. Never known this personal touch. She could only assume there must be some instinct at work for female to respond to male, because moving her hand between their bodies to find the hard bulge beneath his trousers was the most natural thing in the world.

He groaned as she touched him, and his mouth pressed down on her throat. Buttons popped as his hand dipped suddenly beneath her corset and chemise, his fingertips skimming a hardening nipple. Harriet turned her head and her back arched, compelled by a sensation at once languid and urgent. Her breasts felt heavy, sensitized as his fingers stroked and stroked over the hardened nub. His mouth trailed down from the base of her throat until he buried his face in the cleft between her breasts. She felt him breathe in the scent of her, and shuddered as his tongue slowly traced the inside curves of her bosom.

She supposed she should protest being groped like a whore in some back alley, but the pleasure was so shockingly intense that the analogy didn't occur to her at first. When it did, the humiliation that rushed through her was barely enough to temper the coiling heat of growing arousal.

She tangled her hand in Martin's hair and

tugged, but ended up having to pull hard to get his attention. His eyes flamed with anger when he finally lifted his head from between her nearly exposed breasts. She pushed against his shoulder, but he didn't move. So she slipped her hand beneath the waistband of his trousers and whispered, "You have two choices. I scream and wake the house. Or I squeeze very hard . . . right here . . . and you do the screaming."

Moving very carefully, Martin disengaged himself and moved away from her. The anger in his eyes was deadly. "You made a bargain," he reminded her. Soft as his voice was, she felt it like flame brushed across her skin.

Quivering inside, and with emotions all a jumble, Harriet managed to give a curt nod, and led him to the bedroom at the end of the hall. She felt him following behind like a stalking panther. The lamps were lit inside, but she noticed immediately that Mrs. Swift had vacated the premises for her own sleeping quarters. A pity, for Harriet felt drastically in need of a chaperone right now. Well, she'd dealt with this man before; she could do so again. Of course, in all the years before, she had not felt his touch and responded to it with primal, animal weakness.

She made sure the door was closed before she said, "I'm well aware of our arrangement. Please don't mention it in public again." She pointed toward the hallway. "From this point on, anywhere besides a room in which we are completely alone is public."

He stalked forward, face like a thundercloud, his fists clenched at his sides. "Are you dictating to me?" He reached her and put heavy hands on her shoulders. "Do you dare dictate to me? Do you dare imply that I can't keep your petty, dirty secrets?"

This was threatening to get seriously out of hand. His temper was already hot and she was close to boiling over herself. Maybe she'd held herself under too much control in the last years, for a look, a word, a touch from him set her off in so many ways that she couldn't hope to contain them. She had not known how furious the man and the whole situation was going to make her when the thing started. This was too personal, too much a travesty of what she'd always wanted.

Always? Since the night they'd first met?

Oh, God. Oh, yes. The realization hit her by surprise, bringing the sting of tears behind her eyes, but Harriet put it and her simmering anger aside to deal with the seething man whose grip on her shoulders was painfully tight.

"You are bruising me," she said. "If that is what you wish to do, so be it. I will be at your disposal, my lord. I had not heard that you were cruel to the women you fornicate with, but I hardly have detailed information about your bedroom habits."

"You soon will." Though his lip curled in a very ugly sneer, she felt his grip loosen noticeably, but he did not take his hands off her. "You weren't acting particularly 'disposable' out in the hall."

"I apologize. I should not have touched you like that. There."

Her repentance took him by surprise, wiping the ugly sneer slowly from his handsome features. He almost smiled. "It wasn't the touching I minded, it was the threat."

"I am tired. My nerves are not as steady as they appear—and what if someone saw us like that?" She hated the hint of hysteria that crept into her voice with her last words.

He actually blushed, and his gaze slid from hers. He cleared his throat, but he didn't stop holding her. "That was a bit impulsive of me," he admitted. "And a bit crude. I promise you, my dear—" His hands left her shoulders and he began unfastening her buttons again.

Harriet stilled the impulse to push his hands away from her clothing. She also fought down the urge to panic and run. "Promise me what?" she demanded.

"That my behavior for the rest of the night will not be so crude."

Martin heard Harriet's murmured, "Oh, dear," and managed, just barely, not to smile. Her words, coupled with her earlier behavior, told him all he needed to know. He didn't want to believe it, but in moments of high stress Harriet reacted far more as the starchy governess than the worldly sophisticate. He really did not want to believe her an innocent in the ways of love, but despite what he wanted to believe, of one thing he was sure. She was more than nervous, more than angry, and more than manipulative. She was also a virgin. It was really quite infuriating.

The truth was, he wasn't quite sure what to do with a virgin.

Other than attracting unicorns, he wasn't sure what virgins were good for. He was a man of the world, in search of carnal pleasure and elegant sensual diversion. He had never bedded a virgin. Even his wife had been less than pure on their wedding night. Oh, Sabine had done a fine job of distracting him from the knowledge, and he'd been innocent enough in the ways of women to be easily distracted. But later, looking back on his honeymoon with the insatiable Sabine through the eyes of an experienced womanizer, he knew that his wife had not been as pure as the driven snow.

He was fairly certain that Harriet was. A worldly virgin, a sophisticated virgin, a hardheaded, calculating, sensible, serious, and yes, even patriotic virgin. Bloody hell.

If one was setting out on the path of righteousness within the bonds of holy wedlock, having a virgin bride was a good way to start out. What man wanted a virgin mistress? Some men did, of course; they liked the idea of training a girl to their tastes. They also likened taking a girl's maidenhead to collecting some sort of trophy. Martin found this sort of man disgusting.

He'd said several crude things to Harriet on

the subject of her virtue in the last few days, and he had meant every word as he said it. He'd wanted desperately to believe the worst of her, because she'd hurt and humiliated him beyond bearing. He couldn't forget what she'd done. He didn't forgive her. He wasn't going to step back now and forgive her the debt she'd agreed to, because she was willing to pay more than he'd bargained for. He'd wanted to take her as both punishment and reward and to work out some of the burning sense of betrayal he thought would drive him mad.

And because he wanted her. Desperately. He'd wanted her for four damned years, but he'd kept a vow that turned out to be as false as her identity. He had held off telling her how much he cared, until he couldn't take it any more. He'd offered the woman he loved honorable marriage. Then he'd demanded a very dishonorable arrangement with the strumpet who'd trampled on his very soul. And now . . . and now . . .

"Martin? Martin?" Harriet waved a hand in front of his face. "Martin, what are you staring at?"

"Your bosom."

"No, you're not. My bosom is not located

somewhere beyond the top of my head. You've been staring at the wall for at least a minute."

"Have I? Sorry." He lowered his gaze to the expanse of soft, round cleavage peeking up over Harriet's corset. He did not recall having finished unfastening her clothing, but the bodice of her blue wool traveling dress was lying on the floor, and the chemise she wore beneath it was pulled down around her waist. She stood before him, still in her heavy skirts and petticoats, but bare-armed, her upper body clad only in the plain white corset. Her dark hair swept across bare white shoulders. Not Venus rising from the waves, perhaps, but the effect was stunning all the same.

A woman with breasts like that should display them in black lace and red satin. Now that they had his attention, his hands reached. He couldn't help himself.

She closed her eyes and arched into his touch, her tongue moistening her slightly parted lips. Maybe he was mistaken. Maybe she was truly the finest actress of the century, a rival for Bernhardt. He hoped so, because, virgin or vixen, he was going to make love to her tonight.

Martin fondled her breasts for only a few

moments. He wanted more, but he stepped back and turned away instead, smiling when she asked, "What are you doing?" The answer was obvious. The tremor in her voice touched a deep chord of sympathy inside him, though he told himself sympathy was wasted on the treacherous Miss MacLeod. He did not turn around until he was completely undressed.

"Oh, my," Harriet said. Her eyes grew very wide, and a hand came up to cover her mouth. "How very—interesting."

Her gaze did not immediately go to his groin and his growing erection. Though instinct warred with the decision, he stood very still and let her look her fill for a few intense moments. He was not sure if it was a chance draft of air that sang against his skin and prickled the hair on his arms and chest, or if it was the intensity of her regard that stirred his skin with sudden sparks of heat.

"Magnificent, actually," she added after her gaze skimmed his shoulders and chest and all the way down to his bare toes curled in the rug, and slowly back up the length of his legs and muscular thighs.

His breath caught on a hard wave of desire, but he still managed to chuckle at her words, and hardened further, his penis straining upward. "Seen enough?" he asked. "I'm not a statue at a museum, you know."

Her cheeks and throat were bright pink, her breasts rose and fell with the increased rate of her breathing, and her wide eyes glittered. He relished the effect the sight of him had on her.

"I know," she answered. "You're not wearing a fig leaf."

"You won't be wearing so much as a fig yourself in a few moments, my dear."

"Hmm," she said, and gestured. "Would you mind turning around?"

A knot of suspicion clenched in his gut as he said, "Promise me you won't try to run from the room or throw yourself out the window if I do."

She didn't even glance toward door or window. She couldn't seem to take her eyes from him. "Don't be ridiculous. I want to see your backside."

He was very aware of her taking a step closer to him, though he didn't think she was. Banter, he saw, was the best form of seduction to use with his dear untried Harriet. Though his throbbing member warned him to hurry up and let it be about its business, he said,

"Woman, you're making me feel like a horse at market."

"A mighty, rampant stallion you are indeed, my lord."

Martin refrained from commenting and turned slowly, so that he was facing away from her. After a few seconds of aching silence, he felt the warm brush of material against the back of his leg. Sensation raced from the point of contact all the way up his spine. He turned his head to find Harriet standing very close behind him. The combination of curiosity mixed with trepidation on her face made her look young, vulnerable, and so very desirable.

"May I touch you?"

The question was asked in a soft, shy voice, and Martin managed a tight nod. He wanted her to touch him, had demanded it not half an hour before. He fought to remain passive and let it happen.

He did not look like a marble statue. Harriet had decided that with her first look at him. Nor did he feel like one. His muscles were not cool beneath her touch. He was not perfect in the way of a Greek god, yet this tall, long-limbed man was just right, from the width of his shoulders down the long vee of his back into a narrow waist and firm, flat buttocks.

At first all she could manage was to lay her palms flat on his shoulder blades and absorb the heat of his skin. When she flexed her fingers and made her way slowly down the length of his back to the base of his spine, he wiggled under the gentle touch.

"My lord," she said, "you're ticklish."

"If you tell anyone, I'll deny it," he answered through gritted teeth.

"My lips are sealed." It wasn't as if she was going to publicly proclaim the details of their liaison from the rooftops. Curiosity overcame the stab of resentment and she continued her examination. She brushed her cheek against his shoulder and further down his back, ventured to cup his rear in her hands, and ran her thumbs in small circles over his narrow hips. He was a well-made man, beautifully muscled. "And here I always attributed your fine form to your tailor's skill."

"Hmph," he muttered. "Cheeky wench."

"I'm not the one standing here naked."

"But you are the one petting the naked man."

She cleared her throat. "Yes, well . . . you said it was all right."

"Feel free to continue."

She ventured further down, through and around, making tactile contact with parts of him she wasn't quite up to looking at just yet. Picture books weren't much help when the man was real and right in front of you. When she touched some places he gasped; others, he moaned.

"Have you . . . had . . . enough yet?" he asked.

A stab of fear went through her, mixed with an equally devastating wave of longing. She felt as if she were about to plunge into some deep, bottomless pit, and the secrets down in the darkness beckoned, promising unknown delights. Demons calling her to jump. Her fall was right in front of her, and her demon was named Martin.

"Harriet," he urged her for an answer.

"Well—" she equivocated. "That does depend on what happens next, doesn't it?"

"This," he said, and turned around and scooped her up in his arms.

189

Chapter 13

"**M**artin!" she cried, more shocked than afraid. Then he deposited her in the center of the bed, and she was afraid. She would have bolted, but he knelt on her skirts and held her down with one hand on her stomach. "I—I—" She could make no other coherent sound come out.

"Don't be frightened," he soothed.

"Easy for you to say," she snarled back. "You're not, not—"

"A virgin?" He looked at her with an altogether encouraging smile. She considered spitting at him as he stroked hair off her cheeks, and caressed her breasts. "Don't worry, my dear, we'll have that fixed in no time."

In her panic Harriet's accent had reverted to a rich Highland lilt, but when she swore at him a moment later, she might as well have been a Cockney guttersnipe. He tapped her on the cheek. "Where did you learn those words?"

"Mrs. Swift was my nanny."

That led to other questions he wanted to ask, but this was not the time or place. He had Harriet in his bed, where he'd always wanted her—or at least a woman who resembled her in the physical ways that mattered—and here he planned to stay with her until morning.

He was naked; now it was her turn. Fortunately, he'd had a bit of experience along those lines. Despite wanting to get her naked as quickly as possible, Martin first took off her shoes, and rolled the sensible stockings down her long, shapely legs. Then he started with her skirt and petticoats. He didn't ask for any help and Harriet didn't offer any, though she did oblige him when he requested that she lift her hips so he could slide the heavy layers of wool and linen off her. He cradled her round bottom in his hands for a few moments after he did so, appreciating the weight and shape of her before he proceeded to finish undoing her corset. Martin kissed and stroked each centimeter of flesh as it came to light. And such lovely, rich, creamy flesh it was.

Sometimes her fingers traced across a spot after he had moved on to another, as though making sure the place he'd stimulated truly existed. How very unaware she'd been of her own body and all the pleasures it contained.

Harriet's hands drifted to his shoulders after her chemise and corset landed on the floor, and she said in a breathy voice, "You could always find employment as a ladies' maid."

He looked up from kissing a spot just beneath her left breast and said, "I'll keep that in mind should I ever need to assume an undercover identity."

"You'd look fetching in a maid's uniform," she agreed, and tugged on his hair. "But only if you grew a mustache first."

"What an odd duck you are," he said, and eased her back onto the pile of pillows at the head of the bed. *And what an odd duck I am,* he thought, delighted to be luxuriating in this slow seduction punctuated by silly conversation. His rage and the urge for rapine were past, and this was far more fun. Revenge could wait until tomorrow.

Harriet didn't protest when she felt him undoing her drawers; she was far too curious to find out what happened next. This was not at all what she'd thought *it* would be like. She'd thought he'd be harsh, rough, quick. But no, he was torturing her by taking his time. And what a fascinating brand of torture it was—both sweet and sharp, and there was a deep, dark mystery to it somehow. Where he touched her she tingled, the sensation stirring both pleasure and a yearning that almost burned under her skin. Could the man have magic in his fingers? In his lips?

After he bared her breasts he kissed each of them for a long time, then drew her nipples into his mouth to tease them with his tongue and his teeth, and it was—nice. More than nice, it was a melting, aching, yearning feeling that caused her to arch her back and fling her head from side to side on the pillows and want to ask him to never stop. Until he moved on to drawing down her drawers and kissing around her navel, and that was nice too.

"What are you doing?" she asked, languor lacing with panic when he spread her legs wide and moved further down her body. His only answer was a deep laugh that she felt more than heard against the soft skin of her inner thighs. "And here I thought I would lie back and think of England," she murmured, and he laughed again. Only this time, he laughed as his tongue touched a swollen, throbbing spot at the juncture of her legs. She jerked and arched her back from a pleasure so devastating that her body turned momentarily to fire.

The sound she made was not quite a scream, because a purr of indescribable pleasure issued from deep in the back of her throat.

Martin glanced up the length of her body. "Shall I do that again?"

Harriet's hands were twisted in the bed linens and she was panting. "No—yes—I—if you wouldn't mind."

Martin lowered his head and put his whole attention to tasting, teasing, and arousing her. She'd always known he had a wicked tongue, but she's never suspected that he could do *this* with it. Heat flowed through her from the places he touched. Her head swam as she was flung into a dizzy delirium. She ground her hips against his mouth and banged her heels against the mattress as desire shot through her, each jolt stronger than the next. She'd never suspected she could lose control so easily, so completely, and she couldn't mind. She could only want more.

And he gave her more, until she quite simply exploded. It was the most frighteningly wonderful, intense experience she had ever known. It was like climbing a mountain to reach the sun and bursting into flame the moment she reached the highest peak.

"How do you feel?" Martin asked, when her shuddering stilled and the panting breath that burned in her lungs slowed a little.

He lay next to her so that her breasts pressed against his wide chest and his hard penis rested against her belly. His fingers drifted between her thighs and began a slow, gentle stroking. Slowly, delicately, he moved first one finger, then another inside her. She wriggled against this touch, but he persisted, giving her no choice but to accept his questing intrusion.

She had thought the shattering climax had wrung everything out of her, but her body began to quicken again at this gentle invasion. She made small, needy sounds, and without realizing it, her fingers closed around the base of Martin's penis and began to match the rhythm of his fingers inside her.

"How do you feel?" Martin asked again, voice tight with strain. "Shall I tell you how you feel? Your body is singing. You've never felt more alive, but you still haven't had enough. Nowhere near enough." He spoke slowly and his fingers moved slowly, punctuating each and every word.

Harriet strained upward, meeting each of his movements as his fingers curled and flexed and probed. Her body did want more, more stimulation, more release, more of Martin. All of Martin.

He responded to the hungry sound that came from somewhere deep in her soul, shifting to put himself between her wide-splayed legs. Within a moment she felt the hard thickness of him pressing, separating soft warm flesh, pushing inward, filling her slowly. She felt him shaking with the effort to hold back, to control the instinct to ram his length all the way home within her surrounding flesh. The sensation of her body being joined to his was strange for only a moment, but it was not an unwelcome strangeness. A burning craving grew to discover what taking the whole, hot length of his penis into her would be like. It was inevitable, natural, needful . . . Her hips

197

lifted of their own accord, her senses straining for more.

He slowed further, and a whimper escaped her throat. "Mar-tin . . ." she said, breath catching on his name.

He grew completely still, and she whimpered again.

"Am I hurting you?"

His concern raced to her heart, but she couldn't bear it anymore. She lifted her head and demanded, "Would you *please* get on with fornicating!"

"Harriet!"

And his control broke with the word. And his concentration broke, and his hips bucked, desire overcoming control. Laughter broke over them both like a refreshing wave that eased the pain as he breached the thin barrier, burying himself as deep in her as he possibly could go.

There was a certain amount of discomfort, but her body was primed enough by the pleasure that came before to accept the necessity. She closed her eyes and held on tight, gripping the straining muscles of his back. The heady sensation of being stretched and filled, the heated friction sent waves and waves of fire through her, and her senses soon took her beyond the ability to think, to do anything but ride the swelling of the waves. Soon the building torrent overwhelmed her to the point where she knew she was going to drown, and she didn't mind at all.

"Good God," Martin murmured as he collapsed, exhausted and sated, on top of Harriet's soft form. He lay still, getting his breath back, getting his bearings back. Perhaps he slept for a while, but eventually he stirred. Harriet slowly opened heavy-lidded eyes as he lifted his head from the pillow of her breasts.

He kissed her. When he was done she ran her tongue over her lips and asked, "Is that me I tasted?"

He traced the outline of her lips. "Couldn't be anyone else at this point."

She breathed a deep sigh. "I think my bones have melted; I feel all floaty and creamy. Is that supposed to happen?"

He couldn't help but smile, and take a certain amount of pride in his work. "If it was good. You'll be sore in the morning, though."

"I expect so." She sighed again, and slowly

combed her fingers through his hair. "I'm not quite sure what happened. I thought I was supposed to be the one who served your every whim and desire."

"I promise to be a demanding lover tomorrow night. Let us consider tonight as a dress rehearsal for your playing my mistress."

"Tomorrow," she said, and sighed again. They snuggled closely together with her head over his heart and his arms around her without discussion or thought. The last thing Martin heard before deep sleep claimed him was, "Tomorrow."

Chapter 14

The next thing Martin heard was the door banging open and a woman's gruff voice announcing loudly, "Your man's here."

Martin blinked through sleep-drugged eyes. He stared without comprehension at the thin, angry woman who glared right back at him until Harriet sat up with the bedcoverings bunched around her and said, "Thank you, Mrs. Swift."

Martin blinked, and recognized the harridan as Harriet's maid. Then it occurred to him that her announcement probably meant that his valet had arrived with the luggage. Glad as he was for this news, he glared back at the woman and demanded, "Why didn't you knock?"

Mrs. Swift ignored him. "I brought you bath-water," she said to Harriet. Sniffing disapprovingly, she added, "I can see you need it."

Martin watched in confused awe when Harriet slipped meekly out of bed without meeting the woman's gaze or issuing a rebuke at the servant's presumption, and quickly stepped behind the screen that shielded a hip bath from the rest of the room. Mrs. Swift cast one more venomous glare his way and followed her mistress, carrying a steaming pail of water in each hand. Once the women were out of sight, Martin got up, stretched his own strained muscles, and dressed in yesterday's clothing. He would give Harriet some privacy by finding Cadwell, and then bespeak a separate room so he could properly bathe and clean up himself. He was roaringly hungry, and quite pleased with himself, and a wave of amusement overtook him when he recalled Harriet mentioning that the formidable Mrs. Swift had once been her nanny. No wonder the clever, commanding Miss MacLeod had slunk off to obey her maid's bidding. Lord knew, Harriet deserved every comeuppance the world could throw her way.

Martin heard whispers from behind the screen, and tiptoed forward to eavesdrop with a gleeful sense of anticipation on hearing Harriet receive a thorough dressing-down.

What he heard was the maid saying, "I left a knife for you under the pillows."

"I know, Mrs. Swift. I found it."

"You could have used it."

"I don't renege on my bargains."

"If your da finds out about this he'll have the toff's balls on biscuits."

"I suppose he would—but Papa isn't going to find out, is he?"

"I don't know why your ma let you—"

"We don't have time to discuss it now. Hand me the sponge, please."

Martin almost clutched his genitals protectively. A pang of guilt went through him as he gave a quick glance back at the rumpled bed. A knife under the pillows? Good lord, was there really a weapon? Then he reminded himself that Harriet had agreed to the price; he had forced nothing on her. She had held to the bargain—he snorted—and been honorably dishonored. What a strange world this was, full of lady spies, mysterious couriers, and well-armed chambermaids. Not his world, not an admirable one, but certainly an interesting view of reality to visit for a while.

He also realized in disgust that he was spying on the spy. This would not do at all.

"Harriet, I am picking up bad habits from you," he called over the screen.

"And what's she picking up from you?" Mrs. Swift called back.

He did not deign to reply, and went off in search of his well-mannered, discreet valet.

By the time he returned Harriet was in the process of getting dressed, and was not that far along in her toilette. Martin closed the door and leaned against it, arms and long legs crossed, a smile curling his lips. His attention focused immediately on the confection of creamy lace and pink satin roses and ribbons that tightly cinched Harriet's trim waist and forced her bosom up at a most provocative, inviting angle. It was a piece of underclothing made to send a man mad imagining the erotic possibilities.

Though he delighted in the sight of this erotic confection, he stared at Harriet suspiciously and asked, "Where did you get that?"

"I borrowed it from my mother."

"Your father is a lucky man."

Harriet blushed a fetching shade of pink, all

over as far as Martin could tell. She ran a hand down the length of the sexy lace corset, cleared her throat, and said, "My lord, there are some things I'd rather not think about."

Martin considered what it would be like to think of his own parents as sexually active humans, and rubbed a hand along his jaw. "Yes, I see what you mean."

Harriet turned her back on him and continued dressing. Martin took a seat in a deep chair near the fireplace where a fire had been made up to drive away the morning damp. He stretched out his legs, glanced out the window at the pewter-gray sky beyond the branches of a dripping tree, and said, "Do you know what I miss on a day like today?"

"Italy," Harriet replied automatically as her head emerged from the white brocade skirt that had just been pulled over her head.

"You know me too well." He chuckled.

Then the sound died in his throat. Damn the woman! She *did* know him, and was still playing him. Despite the intimacy they'd shared last night, she was still a stranger to him. He had to keep up his guard, remember that they were using each other. His sole reason for allowing the charade was for the sex. His body tightened as images of the ways he intended to take her flashed through his mind. He doubted there'd be time enough in the next few days to indulge every fantasy, but he'd make every moment he had her in his bed count. He promised himself she wouldn't forget him when they were through. In fact, he couldn't help but smugly indulge in the knowledge that he had had her first. He did not admire men who boasted of deflowering, but she knew and he knew, and that was more than enough. He momentarily considered asking Harriet if her nether regions were aching this morning, but Mrs. Swift's formidable presence kept him quiet. *No wonder Harriet turned out as she did, with that harpy for a nanny. I almost feel sorry for her.*

Martin hardened his heart against tender feelings and looked over his prize with a connoisseur's eye. She stood with her back to him while Mrs. Swift finished fastening the bodice of her dress. He was used to seeing Harriet's sable hair fastened simply behind her head; now it was arranged in a more elaborate upswept style, and the view of the back of her long neck pleased him immensely. He would leave a great many kisses and caresses on her throat before he was done. "Turn around," he commanded. He frowned when she did as he told her without any demur. He almost wished she'd argued, until he got a good look at the plunging neckline of her bodice and could do nothing but stare.

Harriet didn't understand why Martin's lips hardened in a thin line, or the flash of anger in his eyes. She brushed a hand over her skirt and asked, "Don't you like it? Isn't it suitable? It was my coming-out dress."

"You're still coming out of it."

Harriet looked down at her chest. "Mrs. Swift altered the bodice a bit."

He was on his feet, tense with outrage. "I won't have you going out dressed like—"

"Your mistress," she interjected.

He forced a smile. "Yes. Of course. I see. And so will everyone else." She could tell it was forced because when he really smiled, his dimples went very deep, and they barely showed at all now. He got up and slowly circled around her, making an inspection with his hands held behind his back. "I will enjoy showing you off."

Rather like prime horseflesh, Harriet thought, and tried very hard not to resent what was the whole point of the exercise. She hoped she qualified as being worth showing off, but she certainly didn't want to be the loveliest, most seductive courtesan at Sir Anthony's affair. She didn't want to draw attention to herself. Still, for a confusing moment she felt an aching jealousy that she would not compare well to the other women, and Martin's fancy would light on some beautiful young thing that he would go off with and—

All right, she had recently advised him to take a new mistress, but she hadn't *meant* it.

She was not sure what she meant about anything at the moment—certainly not about what she felt when she looked at Martin Kestrel. She wished she had some time to sort everything out. Perhaps she would have liked to wake up in his arms and hold on to an illusion of love for at least a little while. She had probably not slept so well or felt so safe in her life as she had lying beside Martin last night. Mrs. Swift's arrival had given her no time to bring any illusions into the waking world. Perhaps she should be grateful, and maybe she would be later. Right now the best she could hope to do was play the role to the hilt. If that meant clinging to his arm and boldly showing her bosom to the world while he smiled like a dog fancier with a new pet, so be it.

She lifted her head proudly. "I am ready, my lord, if you would care to leave now."

"The carriage has arrived from Strake House," he acknowledged. "But I am not quite ready to leave yet."

A jolt of near panic went through Harriet. She had to get this over with *now*! For the sake of the nation! For her brother! And, dear God, yes, for herself! "But I—"

He held up a hand to still her protest, but it was to Mrs. Swift he spoke. "Lady Phoebe sent along a trunk of clothing for your mistress with my man. Go see to it. I want a word alone with you," he told Harriet. Mrs. Swift turned a withering look on Lord Martin and a cautionary one on Harriet, but leave she did, grumbling.

When she was gone, Martin rose from his chair and gestured for Harriet to come toward him. Harriet stepped forward, half wanting him to take her in his arms and kiss her as he had the night before. The rest of her impulses were so jangled and confused she had trouble catching on to them. Wary and high-strung, she asked, "What do you want?"

"You," he answered succinctly, his gaze running over her with a hunger she recognized and couldn't help but respond to. Her blood sang and sparked, but she stopped a foot from him and kept perfectly still. He cupped her jaw in his big warm hand and then ran his fingers down her throat and across her collarbones, leaving pure fire in his wake. "Pity I don't have time to toss you on your back right now," he added. Outrage flared in her, but he continued. "We are both anxious to arrive at Strake House, each for our own reasons."

His thumb continued a slow, circular path tracing her exposed throat and bosom. His touch made it very clear to her that he was anticipating their activities at Strake's house party. Her outrage died and she could barely keep from closing her eyes, throwing her head back, and moaning. She took a step back from him before her legs turned completely to butter. It annoyed her that his slightest touch could dominate her so—but four years of simmering lust for him, and she was at its mercy. She could only hope the fever would run its course in the next few days.

"Do you dislike my touch so? Never mind," he went on before giving her time to answer.

"There are things I want to know, questions I want answered, and I don't want any chance of being overheard." He gestured her toward one of the chairs by the fireplace.

Rather stiff and sore from last night's exertions, she was glad to settle into the well-upholstered seat while he went to lean against the white-tiled mantel.

"I'm not interested in discussing your assignment at the moment," he began. "There was something I should have asked when I—when you—Damn it, Harriet," he complained, "you've gotten me tongue-tied, and you know how I hate that!"

He looked as if he were about to smash one of the china figurines on the mantel in his frustration. That, or march forward and lay hands roughly on her as he had the night before. She hated that she caused him such pained agitation. She hated even worse that he felt such a strong need to delve into their tangled, shadowed past. She sighed. "You are right, I owe you whatever explanation I am free to give you, and Strake House would not be the place to hold this discussion."

"I am frequently right," he declared.

"Yes, Martin."

He pointed a finger sternly at her. "Patronize me and I'll beat you."

She meekly lowered her gaze. "Yes, my lord."

"Unless, of course, you like that sort of thing. Then I'll refuse to beat you."

She shot indignantly to her feet. "Martin!"

"Ha! You accused me of liking it last night. I see you don't take any kindlier to accusations of that sort of perversion than I do."

Harriet settled into the chair once more. "Touché, Martin." She glanced at the mantel clock, then out of the window. The rain had stopped, and it looked like the clouds were finally clearing. Except in Martin's stormy gray eyes, she saw, when she made herself meet his gaze again. She had not wanted to hurt him; never planned on it. She had almost given up her life for him, and wounded her soul in the process. He should never have known. It was all her fault, for she had stayed too long at his side, filling a role someone else could have easily taken over. But Patricia had needed her and he needed her—and she had let herself need them. "What a fool I've been," she said, with a heartfelt sigh.

Martin did not dispute this claim. "But I was

the one taken for a fool. Why?" He came to kneel in front of her chair, his expression wild with pain. *"Why?"*

"It's—" Harriet had difficulty finding the words. She touched her temples, which had begun to ache.

"You can't tell me?" he questioned. "You won't? Which is it?"

"Both," she said. "Neither." She shook her head. "You deserve the truth, Martin."

"Is it me?" He looked and sounded so devastated that she reached for his hands. "Is it my loyalty to my country that's in question? Is that why you were set to watch me?"

"No!" She was so shocked at the question that she shouted the answer. "Of course not. Your loyalty has never been in question, only your taste in women I mean—"

He was up and away from her in an instant. Harriet stared at her empty hands, then looked to where he'd retreated. The anger and pain that radiated from him filled the room.

Harriet twisted her hands in her lap. "I put that badly—but there's no way to put it in a good light. It was Sabine."

"What does Sabine have to do with you?" he demanded. "You never even met her."

"That is true, but—"

"Wait a moment. *Sabine* was a spy?"

She saw him go white, and hurried to quash the awful thought she knew had come into his head. "As it turned out, she wasn't. Your Italian countess married you because she was enamored of you. Your marriage was a reckless act of passion, not a political maneuver. But there were suspicions . . ." She watched him begin to prowl the room. "And the Russian lover she ran off with *did* initially seduce her to get information about the very delicate diplomatic assignments you undertook."

"I never discussed such things with my wife. She had no interest in my . . . life outside the bedroom," he said, his voice laced with bitter fury.

"My whole assignment started out under false assumptions," she admitted. "Some information about treaty negotiations you had access to fell into the wrong hands. Your father was demanding that the foreign office do something to protect you."

"I do not work for the foreign office."

"But you are frequently asked to intercede in delicate situations by the foreign office. That makes your safety the government's concern.

Therefore, it was decided to shield you—from the dangers of your assignments, from your wife. Maintaining the fiction that your work is unofficial has been useful in dealing with anti-British sentiment."

"Odd," he said. "I never thought of it as a fiction. I try to be a neutral voice trying to bring all parties together—rather than the instrument of British imperial policy, handing down uncompromising pronouncements."

"You are an idealist, Martin. Please never change."

He sneered at her. "Thanks to you, I'm not quite the idealist I was a week ago."

"Yes, I know." She sighed and rubbed her temples again. *Nor am I quite so pure myself,* she thought, but kept her own shattered ideals to herself. "My initial assignment was to keep an eye on Sabine while I tried to find out who on your staff was passing information to Britain's adversaries. By the time I arrived, Sabine had already run off. I was briefed about the scandal when I arrived at the embassy, and decided to go ahead with the assignment. Patricia *did* need someone to look after her in all that uproar, and it was necessary to determine if Sabine really was the source of the leak. It

215

turned out she wasn't, by the way. It was your brother's mistress."

"The one he fought the duel over?"

"Yes. Sabine's lover bribed your brother's lover when he couldn't get Sabine to help him. Of course, he also became besotted with your wife and deserted his assignment to run off with her. Very unprofessional."

Which is the pot calling the kettle black, she thought. Sabine and her lover had paid with their lives for this desertion, though not before the pair had tried to cause Martin trouble he need never know about.

"I stayed on," she finished, "because no one notices a governess, even in the household of a man who travels to the centers of world intrigue. There were messages for me to deliver, intelligence to gather. I was really a very small cog in the espionage wheel. Mostly, I cared for your daughter as a proper governess should."

And watched your back. Her principal assignment had been to direct the small group of operatives assigned to protect the unofficial ambassador whose skills were so very valuable to England.

Martin glanced toward the bed. "A proper governess indeed."

"Well, that was a different assignment. One adapts to circumstances." Harriet rose to her feet.

Nothing showed in Martin's face, his earlier agitation well hidden. "One does adapt indeed, my dear . . . mistress." He came to her side and held out his arm. "And I believe it is time for us to go."

Chapter 15

"**P**erhaps I shall call you Caress," Martin said, running the back of his hand across Harriet's cheek. "Or Fancy," he said. "I think I'll introduce you as Fancy the flower vendor. What do you think of that?"

They sat close together on the narrow carriage seat. He had his arm around her shoulders, holding her against his long, hard body. She was very aware of him and told herself that was all to the good, that it helped her adapt to her part. Yet the awareness made her head reel and prodded her imagination into places she'd never let herself dream of before.

She and Martin had been occupying the drive to Strake House with light conversation, for which Harriet was grateful. She was too keyed up for any more serious discussion about past, present, or future at the moment. Martin seemed to sense her nervousness or perhaps he was reacting to his own discomfort, rather than trying to alleviate hers.

In reply to his latest flight of imagination, she said, "I think Fancy sounds rather cheap and common."

"Well—"

"Picking up that sort of woman wouldn't do your reputation any good, Martin. While I suppose I could manage a Cockney accent, think about what your friends would say about you if you consorted openly with a Covent Garden flower girl."

"You are annoyingly sensible much of the time, my dear."

"But the rest of the time I'm a blasted fool. A fool for you," she added, smiling dreamily as she dropped her head onto his shoulder.

"Fluttering your eyelashes when you did that was a bit much," he advised her on her performance. "What *shall* I call you?" he asked, seriously this time. "We've turned into the drive and will be at the house soon."

She wondered if he could hear her heart banging nervously inside her chest.

"I have it," he said before she could answer him. "I've always liked the name Cora. Let's say your name is Cora Bell. You're the daughter of servants on one of my family's estates. I interviewed you when you came to London looking for work, liked what I saw, and offered you your current position in my bed."

"How very medieval of you, Martin."

"Yes, but it's an easy explanation of why you've not been seen at the opera or on the stage or the other sorts of places men like Strake acquire their fancy women. It is a good cover story."

Indeed it was. Harriet lifted her head to look Martin in the eye. "Please don't take this as an insult, but I think you could be very good at this."

A flicker of disapproval crossed his eyes, but he said, "Thank you, Cora. That's the nicest thing you've ever said to me."

"Oh, no, it is you I have to thank, my lord," she answered, assuming the awed eagerness of a country girl lucky enough to have caught the attention of a wealthy, handsome nobleman.

Martin nodded and patted her lightly on the thigh. "I am eager to discover all the ways you intend to express that thanks. Ah," he said with a smug, deeply dimpled smile as the carriage rolled to a halt. "We're here."

"It's not the painted jezebels I mind," Mrs. Swift announced. She stood behind Harriet, fastening her into the freshly ironed ice-blue gown "Cora" was wearing down to dinner. "Girl has to do the best she can, however she can, in this world. Oh, no, it's them so-called ladies, married women showing off their toff lovers like they didn't know it was a sin. You should hear their maids twittering and gossiping belowstairs."

Harriet turned her gaze from the dressing room mirror where she'd been pinning up her hair, and smiled at the grizzled older woman. "You know I would very much like to hear any gossip you might find relevant."

Mrs. Swift gave a curt nod. "Have a report for you later tonight. Nice frock, this," she added, smoothing a silver-beaded panel at the back of the skirt.

"Aunt Phoebe's a godsend to send along proper attire," Harriet said. She glanced in the

222

mirror at the gracefully plunging décolletage of the off-the-shoulder bodice. "Mother must have wired her. I wonder where she found clothes like this in such a hurry?"

"Pulled 'em out of her own closet," was Mrs. Swift's opinion. "Old girl still has spunk."

"I suppose one could call it that."

Harriet turned back to the mirror and picked up a necklace. She had to admit the finery made her feel better. Mrs. Swift was a fine seamstress, but her efforts paled in comparison to the examples of the dressmaker's art Harriet had encountered in the few hours she'd been in Strake House. Perhaps it was true among the demimonde that the more time you spent on your back, the more money you got to spend on what you wore on your back. Or perhaps they worked on some sort of barter system. She would have to ask Martin when they had a moment alone.

Lord Martin had been greeted effusively by his host. Sir Anthony was delighted Martin had changed his mind and had made much of him during the day, ensuring that Sir Anthony's association with so important a member of the nobility was made known to everyone gathered in the house. Martin put on an air of bonhomie and had a word for every man, a smile for every woman. There was a picnic luncheon in one of the huge estate's many gardens, a polo game, and billiards and cards in a gaming room the size of a palace ballroom. The men took part in these activities, while the women looked on admiringly until it was time to go upstairs and change for dinner. It was all dreadfully boring. Harriet had spent the day being the self-effacing ornament, taking in everything while blending into the crowd. So far, no one she'd encountered fit the particulars of the courier she was there to meet. The man she was to meet would be wearing a gold lily stickpin. She'd have to keep looking and putting up with an atmosphere she found distasteful and unnerving.

Martin does not belong here, she thought. *He's a responsible man, a good father. He has nothing in common with this decadent lot.* It had been wrong of her to use his slight acquaintance with Sir Anthony Strake and drag him into this den of iniquity. *Where he seems to be having a perfectly lovely time,* she reminded herself. How long would this operation take? How many nights would she find herself in Lord Martin's bed, paying for his help? And why did her body tingle and tighten with excitement at the prospect of more nights with Martin? She had no choice but to make love to him; she wasn't supposed to like it.

"Hope we can leave tomorrow," Mrs. Swift said.

"Yes." The word was drawn out of Harriet slowly, with more reluctance than there should have been. "There are quite a few people here, more than I expected, somehow. I'm not sure if that's going to make the task easier or more difficult." She received a grunt in response. "They're an odd lot, I think," Harriet went on. "I get the impression that Sir Anthony didn't arrange this party only for the pleasure of entertaining his friends. There's a certain cold-eyed professionalism among some of the men at the card tables."

"He's probably pimping," Mrs. Swift contributed. "Not all the gentlemen brought a lady friend with 'em, I heard. And there's plenty of strapping young lads about, for the ladies of quality that came on their own."

Harriet shook her head in disgust. "What an unsavory fellow."

"Give a house too many bedrooms and you're asking for trouble," was Mrs. Swift's opinion of country house architecture.

And to think her brother Michael had been supposed to show up at this party, where apparently he fit in easily with the rest of the guest list. She was going to have to read that young man a strong lecture when she saw him. Still, she saw how a large number of people gathered to commit acts of moral and ethical ambiguity would make an excellent rendezvous point for clandestine meetings. Now all she had to do was make contact with the lily-wearing courier and discover if there were others at Strake House with an interest in acquiring the same information she was there to collect. If Michael had been compromised . . .

She didn't want to think that Michael might be hurt, or worse.

Fortunately, the door that separated her dressing room from the bedroom of the guest suite opened before she let her thoughts run off in wild, frightened speculation. Martin stood in the doorway, dressed in formal black and white. She saw his reflection in the mirror, then turned to look at him in the flesh. He stared at her. She was not sure whether his expression indicated disapproval or awe.

"Well?" she asked.

"You're wearing paint on your face."

Harriet put her hand up to her face, careful not to touch the dusting of rice powder Mrs. Swift had applied to her cheeks. "I must say it felt rather odd at first, but I don't notice it now. Do you like it?"

Martin did not like it. He did not like it at all. He almost told her so, and that, furthermore, nice women did not paint their faces like trollops or aged dames who pretended to still be in the first bloom of youth. But pointing this out would show a concern for her reputation and for her as a person that it was ridiculous for him to feel. He put on his best neutral diplomat's expression and said smoothly, "It does lend a certain allure and glamour, Cora, my dear."

"Cora needs all the allure and glamour she can get."

"She'll do." He had to work very hard to keep the words from coming out as an angry growl.

He had never seen her look more lovely,

more alluring. That he now had to take her downstairs and show her off before the hungry eyes and dirty minds of the other men sent waves of possessive fury through him. He knew the men would see her in that magnificent dress and think of nothing but what she would look like out of it. He felt that way himself—but that was all right for him! Why had he agreed to bring her here?

Because she wanted him to, he made himself recall. And he'd agreed out of a longing for revenge, restitution, the hope of humiliating and using her the way she'd humiliated and used him. It had made a certain amount of immature, twisted sense at the time. *It still makes sense,* his lower self argued. *She is lovely, she is yours. Show her off and bask in the others' envy when you're the one who takes her upstairs to bed. Let them imagine the things you're doing behind closed doors.* His imagination took flight at the possibilities.

What pleasure he was going to get from punishing her for her deception—but that would have to wait for later.

"You're smiling like a cat with all the cream," she said.

"And feeling like it," he answered, holding out his hand. "Come." When she came to him he brushed his lips across one bare shoulder and then the other, and left a lingering kiss at the base of her neck. "Such lovely, soft skin," he murmured, letting his hands roam where his lips had touched. She arched back against him, and he heard her breath catch. "Cream indeed," he murmured against her skin.

A shiver of pure desire shot through Harriet, memories of the night before and thoughts of the night to come running riot through her thoughts. She wanted to turn around, tear off the man's shirt, and pull him down with her onto the floor! Did he think she was made of stone? That she could be touched by him and not react? She managed to get the impulse under control and said, "My lord, you are attempting to excite my base emotions."

His hands skimmed over her, not quite touching anywhere but leaving a trail of heat, nonetheless. "Is it working?"

"Yes."

"Wrinkle that gown and you'll be the one who irons it," Mrs. Swift contributed.

Harriet blushed while Martin gave the

woman a poisonous look. "Are you referring to me, madam?"

Mrs. Swift's fists rested on her narrow hips, and she looked them both over disapprovingly. "You mess up my handiwork and you pay for it."

Martin knew the termagant who'd left a knife at Harriet's disposal the night before was referring more than to the dress. He was not used to being thwarted by anyone, and certainly not a servant, so he chose to ignore her.

"Let us go down to dinner, my dear," he said, taking Harriet's arm and leading her from the dressing room. "I don't like that woman," he whispered as he and Harriet entered the white and gold bedroom. The bed beneath a draped canopy was huge, the carpet so thick they moved in utter silence. He would be far happier to stay there than go down to dinner, but not with Mrs. Swift still in the area. "She's part bulldog and part viper."

"She's a dear," Harriet whispered, and received a skeptically canted eyebrow in answer. She laughed. "Really."

Martin refrained from further comment as they made their way down to the main floor of Strake House. Harriet's attention left him to focus on the others in the reception hall when they reached the bottom of the sweeping grand staircase. It was a subtle thing, but he noticed the moment she stopped being herself and assumed the persona of his lady friend. He shouldn't have minded, since "Cora" put her arm through his and moved closer as they came to a halt before their host. But he missed Harriet—who was proving to be not unlike Abigail, only far more interesting.

Harriet did not know why Martin stiffened suddenly and his mood shifted to barely concealed annoyance. She could not afford to ask him what was wrong or show concern in any way. So instead she smiled at Sir Anthony, and giggled with delight when he bent to kiss her hand. She was not wearing evening gloves, and found the touch of anyone's lips but Martin's unpleasant, though she certainly gave no sign of this.

She also didn't balk when Sir Anthony put a finger under her chin and looked her over with knowledgeable eyes. She boldly stared into his. They were a pale, watery blue, cold and shrewd. He was of medium height, lean and fit-looking, with thinning fair hair and a thick-lipped mouth. The silver brocade vest and the

231

velvet collar of his evening coat were not in the best of taste. He did not compare favorably at all to Martin's understated elegance.

"She's lovely, my lord," Sir Anthony said to Martin. "An absolute stunner."

The words galled, and she half expected him to ask how much Martin wanted for her. "How kind of you, Sir Anthony," she murmured.

"Several new guests have arrived today," their host continued to Martin. "Come and meet them," he urged, steering Martin toward the center of the reception room.

Under the guise of flirting, Harriet took the opportunity to study the people they passed. She received smiles and nods from several men, and a hot-eyed assessment from a pot-bellied fellow that left her wanting to run up-stairs and take a hot, soapy bath. She accepted a glass of champagne off a servant's tray and took a long drink, instead. While she did not see the courier, she did establish that she was not opposed to striking up acquaintances with gentlemen other than the one she was there with.

The room was hot from the blazing crystal chandeliers and the press of bodies in the crowded room. Conversation was too loud.

The mingled scents of heavy perfumes hung in the air and the champagne did not settle well in her empty stomach. Harriet longed to ask Martin to take her away from this awful place.

Then Martin turned his head and smiled reassuringly at her. It was only the briefest glance; she wasn't sure he knew he did it, and she had no idea how he'd sensed her mood, but her heart melted when he looked at her. Her soul lifted out of the morass of tangled fears and recriminations that had been tearing her up for days, and took flight. She felt as if she were rushing toward heaven, and it was in his arms . . .

She caught on to the joy and pushed it firmly down. There was no permanent solace to be found in Martin Kestrel's arms, and it was her own damned fault. Her spirits sank once more, but her nerves were now steady as steel, and her mind on her mission.

"Here we are," Sir Anthony announced as they reached a couple standing near the wide entrance to the dining room. "Lady El—"

"Lady Ellen?"

"Lord Martin?"

Harriet looked from Martin to the young woman who'd spoken his name. That they knew each other was obvious. That each was surprised to see the other there was equally obvious. Lady Ellen, a vivid woman with auburn hair, dressed in emerald-green and emerald jewelry, was pale, round-eyed, and speechless, though her mouth hung open.

Martin recovered his aplomb immediately, and kissed the lady's hand. "I see you left the Hazlemoor party early as well, my dear," he said. "Wise choice on both our parts, don't you think?"

Lady Ellen responded warmly to Martin's charm. "Yes," she said. "Yes, indeed. It is *so* good to see you again, Martin. No need for formality here at Anthony's, is there?"

"No formality necessary at all," Sir Anthony chimed in. "So you two know each other?"

"Mutual friends introduced us recently," Martin explained.

"Dreadfully dull people," Lady Ellen added. "I fled their games of charades and theatricals as soon as decently possible. A day after you, Martin. If I'd known you knew Anthony we could have come here together."

Harriet wasn't sure how this Lady Ellen person managed it, but the next thing she knew, Lady Ellen was the one clinging to Martin's arm while Sir Anthony beamed on the pair, and she was relegated to the back of this happy little group. Conversation went on without her.

Fine, Harriet thought after a moment of impotent fury. *All right, then. I'll just have a look around, why don't I?* Not that she would be missed, it seemed.

She did not get far before the butler announced that dinner was served. The next thing Harriet knew, she was being escorted into the dining room on the arm of a man who was not Martin. Cora Bell ended up having dinner seated between two men she didn't know, while she caught glimpses of Martin down the long length of the table chatting merrily away with his vivacious little friend Lady Ellen.

I'm going to kill him, Harriet thought, her fish fork gripped in a way it was not meant to be used. *That's it; I'm simply going to kill him.*

Chapter 16

"**W**here did you get off to?"

"Where did *I* get off to? I'm not the one who—"

"You could have had the decency, the propriety, to go into dinner with me, my dear."

"Really? I don't recall your coming to look for me, my lord."

"That is hardly my place. You are here with me."

"I thought you were with Lady Ellen. Your good friend Lady Ellen." She sniffed.

"I hardly know the woman."

"Would that be in the social or biblical sense that you know that red-haired hussy?"

"What business is it of yours how I know her?"

Harriet clamped her mouth shut on what she'd been about to say next. She did not believe she was having such a fit of jealousy, knew she had no right to, but she *was* jealous, and it felt rather good to snarl at the man for leaving her in the lurch.

Except that he hadn't. She took a deep breath and tried hard to clear her head. He'd left her alone to do her job. She should be grateful. Instead she was furious, and a phlegmatic, dour Scotswoman she was not. She did not lose her temper or her self-possession often, but when she did . . . well, she wasn't going to anymore.

And why was he forgetting that he'd left her alone to do her job? The man was acting like an ignored lover.

And so was she.

She whirled away from the large, glaring man confronting her on the terrace. She pressed her lips together and began counting slowly. Martin stood behind her, so close that the heat of his body warmed her skin. Behind them, across the wide terrace with its huge pots of night-blooming flowers and topiary bushes, were the French doors of the crowded ballroom, thrown open to the mild summer night. Light, laughter, and the strains of a waltz came from inside.

A few moments before, she had been circulating through the ballroom, chatting, flirting, avoiding groping hands, and looking for her contact. Then Martin had come striding up, large and menacing, his gray eyes as dark as a thunderhead, and dragged her out there to demand explanations from her. She'd come gladly, prepared to demand explanations of her own.

Totally foolish behavior for two intelligent, civilized, sophisticated adults who were not really in love.

Harriet forced herself to focus on the view before her, which was magnificent. Below the terrace, a reflecting pool threw back moonlight and lantern light. Wide paths lined with marble statues and topiary beasts stretched out along its sides. A fountain rose out of the far end of the pool, and beyond that paths led off to mazes and knot gardens and distant grottoes surrounded by the shadows of tall trees. The night was filled with the scents of herbs and roses. Couples strolled along the paths and lounged on the benches set in the gardens. Laughter and faint light shone through the trees from a distant corner of the grounds.

"This place is so beautiful," she said with a sigh. Martin stepped closer and put his arms around her waist. "But the people aren't very nice." She couldn't help but close her eyes and savor the sensation of being enfolded by his large, forceful presence.

"A very unsavory lot indeed," he agreed. His muscles were no longer hard and tense with anger when he pulled her against him, but she was no less aware of the strength and power of the man. When he chuckled, she felt it all the way through her. He leaned forward and whispered in her ear, "My dear, why do you think I turned down Sir Anthony's invitation to begin with?"

"Well, I didn't think they were your sort. You've always been so much more—"

"Discriminating in my lovers? Discreet in my affairs?"

"Nicer." He chuckled again, and somehow managed to pull her even closer. "You're crushing my bustle."

"I won't tell Mrs. Swift if you won't."

"A wise man, as well as a nice one."

"You know very well I am not nice." His hands smoothed over her waist and across her breasts. The faint touch set her senses humming. "You're trying to flatter me into taking you for a long walk in the garden," he informed her.

She leaned her head back against his chest. She was quite comfortable right there. "Am I?"

"Yes. It's a very romantic garden."

"I can see that from here."

"But you can't experience life at a distance, my dear. Or moonlit gardens."

He was annoyingly correct that she spent most of her time observing rather than living life. It went with the profession, but she was not feeling very professional at the moment. She wanted to go down into the dark garden with Martin and do what the other couples there were doing. Perhaps lie on a bed of roses, and—

"I wonder what's going on in that small wood over there?" she asked, pointing toward the lights in the distance.

Martin slipped his arms from around her and took her hand. White teeth gleamed in the moonlight as he smiled at her. "Let's find out."

She descended the marble steps to the gardens as quickly and eagerly as a curious child. Maybe it was the moonlight. Maybe it was the company. Maybe it was the clasp of his fingers, so sure and strong entwined with hers. Whatever it was, Harriet felt light as thistledown, and as floaty. Because it was dark, and the gardens of Strake House came as close to being a fairyland as Harriet had ever seen, she let herself believe this closeness she and Martin shared was real—at least out there in the rose-scented moonlight.

Past the rearing bronzes of the fountain, beyond the darkly beckoning entrance to the boxwood maze, they stopped to kiss in the shadow of a white marble statue. Their lips clung, their hands clung, and their bodies strained to be so close together that Harriet felt for an instant of rushing passion that they'd become one. It was so intense that her soul begged for her to somehow make it real, make it never end, to love Martin forever and never lose him. But that could never be . . .

Martin didn't know why Harriet cried out and whirled away from him to the other side of the statue, leaving his arms empty and his senses in turmoil. He shook his head and tried to clear his mind before he followed after her.

At first he thought she'd run off, then he saw that she'd stepped back into the shadows and was looking up at the marble creature on the plinth.

He couldn't help but smile when he followed her gaze. "I'm afraid most men's private parts can't compare with mythological proportions such as that."

"And a good thing," she answered. "What would one use it for, a coat rack?"

"Shall we find out?" he asked, and stripped off his jacket. Harriet put her hand over her mouth and laughed when he hung the coat up on the protruding part of the marble faun.

"Where does one find something like that? Did the Hellfire Club hold a jumble sale?" she asked.

A nice girl would not know about the last century's most infamous gentlemen's club, and Harriet would not be trying to divert him like this unless something was disturbing her. Hadn't she liked being kissed? She'd certainly seemed to be enjoying it as much as he was, before she broke away. Perhaps she'd been enjoying it too much. Or perhaps she was regretting having given herself to him. He didn't know, and wasn't sure he wanted to ask. Perhaps nothing was wrong at all, and her mind was more on business than on lovemaking. That was too bad, because she'd had hours to look for her blasted courier. Now it was time for her to concentrate on fulfilling her part of the bargain. To concentrate on pleasing him.

But none of the tangled logic twisted up with lust changed the fact that he instinctively knew she was upset, and just as instinctively longed to comfort her. Then again, there was no reason a man could not comfort a woman in a lusty, amorous fashion, was there?

"Why don't we go back to the house?" he suggested.

Harriet backed away from him and turned once more toward the lights in the distance. "Soon," she answered. She pointed. "See the white limestone path shining in the moonlight?"

"It's impossible to miss in the moonlight," he answered.

"Can you hear the music coming from the woods?"

He could indeed hear the faint strains of melody played on pipes and a stringed instrument. There was a wildness to the sounds he disliked. He glanced suspiciously at the now-covered rampant faun. He suspected they might not want to join the entertainment taking place in the woods. "Perhaps," he began, but Harriet hurried off up the shining path before he could finish. *A babe into the haunted woods*, he thought with a sigh, and snatched down his coat and followed protectively after her.

Harriet did not know what she was running from or to, for she wasn't thinking clearly. And she hated it, hated it with a passion almost as great as her passion for Martin Kestrel. She liked order. She liked being in control. She liked being a calm, calculating chess master and not the witless pawn of desperate events and her own emotions.

"This is no way to run a rescue," she murmured to herself as she made her way toward music and firelight and a crowd of people, to insulate her from her reactions to Martin.

"What did you say, my dear?" Martin asked, closer behind her than she thought. She almost gave in to the impulse to pick up her skirts and run like she had the devil on her heels. "It was only one kiss, my love," he added when she said nothing. His hand landed on her shoulder, though he didn't try to hold her back. "Are you afraid you liked it too much?"

Stop being right all the time! she thought, but held her tongue on the words. "Just around here," she said as they reached a point where the path curved around a huge ancient oak tree.

When she first stepped around the tree, her gaze was drawn immediately to a giant bonfire that blazed in the center of the clearing. It was so bright she had to blink a few times to adjust her eyes, and even when she did she could not fathom for a few moments what she was seeing. When the scene did come into focus, she was assaulted with detail that overwhelmed comprehension.

Naked bodies with masked faces writhed in the firelight, dancing not to the music of the blindfolded musicians, but to a more primal rhythm. Fornicating bodies were everywhere. She saw not only couples, but also combinations of three and four people forming frantic patterns of flesh twined with flesh. There were heaving bodies on the ground, draped over boulders, backed up against trees, kneeling before the fire. Groups broke and reformed in quick, mindless succession. Flushed skin, mouths sucking breasts and penises, grasping hands everywhere, pumping organs, jiggling breasts, and buttocks filled her sight.

"Oh, God," she gasped, her stomach twisting in revulsion. "Oh, God!"

She whirled, and ran straight into Martin. "Don't fret," he said. "Let's—*oof*!"

Harriet shoved hysterically into him, pushing him off the path. She needed to run, and woe betide anyone or thing that got in her way.

Martin spun around as his shoulder hit a tree. Harriet was already far down the path, racing headlong the way they'd come. He cursed and continued swearing as he ran after her. He cursed the disgusting exhibition in the clearing. He cursed ever having allowed her to see such a sick spectacle. He cursed himself roundly for a fool who thought that just because she could joke about a lewd statue, that she would not be deeply affected by the sight of a full-out orgy when she came upon it. He truly had not suspected any gathering in the clearing would be for such vile purposes. There were couples sharing dalliances all around the shadowed gardens; how could he have known the worst of it was being performed around a cheery fire to the accompaniment of music?

He didn't catch up with her until she reached their bedroom, and even then she slammed the door and the key was turning in the lock when he set his shoulder to the wood and forced his way inside. Once in the room, Martin slammed and locked the door himself.

He heard Harriet sobbing before he saw her, and moved quickly to where she was kneeling on the far side of the bed. Her face was pressed into the blue satin bedcover, and her sable-brown hair had fallen down around her bare shoulders, which shook with her weeping. She was the most utterly forlorn thing he had ever seen. When Martin knelt beside her he was almost afraid to touch her at first, though he leaned closer when she sobbed out a word against the thick hanging bedcover.

"What, my love?" he asked gently. "What did you say?"

She did not turn her head, but her voice was stronger when she spoke again. "Vile." She pounded a fist against the side of the bed. "Disgusting. Ugly. Degenerate. Vile. I didn't know." She struck the mattress again and again. "I've seen pictures . . . and the statues . . . and last night was . . . but this, this . . ." She bunched up cloth in her fists. "I didn't know!"

He kept his voice as soft and gentle as he could manage. "Know what, my sweet?"

"Aunt Phoebe never said it was so . . . so . . . awful! I can't do that." She turned her head and he saw the wild terror that filled her eyes. "I won't do that!" she declared. "Not even for you! Not even for—"

Martin took her face in his hands, and wouldn't let her go when she tried to shake him off. "You never get hysterical." He spoke quietly, firmly, and he refused to let her look away from him. "You would hate to let anything disturb you so much that you ran from it. Because if you ran from something, you would think it necessary to face it down until you were no longer disturbed by it. But some things do not bear facing. Some things are not worth facing. So you are not hysterical, nor are you disturbed by that distasteful, silly display of flailing body parts out in the garden. People who behave like that are beneath your notice. You do not suffer fools, and those are the worst sort of fools—desperately unhappy, empty people who know nothing about love."

She blinked, tears clinging to her long, thick lashes. His words seemed to have calmed her somewhat. She sniffled. "They know about sex."

He shook his head. "That was not sex, my sweet."

"It looked like—"

He kissed a tear from her cheek, and she stiffened at even this slight brush of his lips on her skin. "It looked like what it was; anonymous and deluded and dirty. Forgive me for letting you witness such a thing." She looked confused and vulnerable, but she was getting back some of the control she so valued.

"Forgive you?" She sounded so very bitter. "Did you know?"

"I had a suspicion, but—"

Suddenly a ripple of shock went through her and she pulled away. She was on her feet when she demanded, "Did you expect me to join in that disgusting display of—"

"How dare you?" he demanded in return, on his feet as well now. "I wanted you as a mistress, not as a whore!"

"Is there a difference?"

He had not thought so, a day or two ago, when he'd made this monstrous bargain with someone he thought was a woman of the world. And she'd lived up to the bargain, even when it turned out she was—once again—not the person she seemed to be at all. She must hate him for this. Perhaps she had always hated him; how was he to know?

He could point out that she was the one who had asked to come there, that she was the one who had proposed posing as his mistress. Of course, then she could throw back in his face that he was the one who insisted she actually *become* his mistress. She had agreed to pay a high price, but perhaps she now feared it might be too high a price to bear.

"It is not me you are angry with," he said. "It is yourself. It is not the fools at the orgy that repulsed you, but your own conscience acting up that sent you running."

"Stop being reasonable with me," she demanded. "Stop it right now. You only want your own way; we both know that."

He was shocked. "What are you talking about?"

She pointed toward the bed. "You know."

"Ah," he said, and showed deep dimples when he smiled. "I see. You're afraid you'll like it too much when I make love to you again. My dearest, you can never like making love with me too much."

Harriet knew full well the man could talk the birds out of the trees and have them eating out of his hand. She'd heard him spin sugar webs of reason and logic around some of the shrewdest and most clear-headed men in Europe and get his way every time. She was furious to have his skills turned on her.

"I could never enjoy making love to anyone after seeing the ugly truth of what lust is," she told him. "Don't try to make me think I can."

She saw the gleam of challenge come into his eyes and knew immediately that she had said the wrong thing.

"All right," he answered, stalking closer. "I won't make you think anything." His arms surrounded her the instant she tried to turn away. He pulled her closer, pressing her body close to his. Just before his mouth covered hers, he finished confidently, "You won't have to think. I'll do the thinking for you, and you will *know*."

Chapter 17

◦─◦◯◯◦─◦

She had no idea what he meant, but she wasn't ready for this, she didn't want this!

She expected his kiss to be rough, for his mouth to be hard on hers, for his hands to be harsh and demanding. She flinched, then prepared to fight when his hands and lips touched hers.

His lips brushed across hers like a whisper, a promise, a suggestion, a temptation, and then were gone. "Close your eyes," he commanded softly. "And don't think of anything else but me kissing you."

She responded to the sensual promise in his voice even as she fought it, and her eyes slowly closed.

Martin whispered, "Your lips are warm honey on mine, sweet, ripe. I can taste your smile, drink in your laughter with my mouth to yours. You taste of urgency, hunger, completion, and paradise. Our souls touch when our lips touch. There is lightning when our mouths come together, giving and taking, a promise of much, much more, without any need for words."

He kissed her then, not on the lips he praised so extravagantly, but on the tip of her nose, on the tip of her chin, and on her cheeks and temples and forehead. Somehow her awakened imagination transferred each teasing little kiss to the lips sensitized by his words.

"Let your skin remember my touch," he whispered in her ear, and kissed her earlobe, drawing it briefly between his lips. "Remember last night."

She felt the warmth of his hand at her throat, skimming over her face, across her bosom, but only the heat touched her, stirred her, left her tingling. This touch that was not a touch swirled slowly over her for a long time, almost frightening at first, almost soothing, conjuring the images of the night before. Remembering was so vivid it was as though it were happening all over again. She felt herself growing warm and pliant while his voice continued weaving a spell over her. Heat rose in her and her bones melted from remembered heat until she doubted she could have stood without the strength of his arm around her waist.

"Your skin is smoother than the satin that covers it, alive and wanting. Remember wanting. Want me."

He filled her inner vision, filled her senses. Memories flooded through her, mixed with something more urgent than memory.

"Yearn," he said, defining the stirring for her.

"Oh, do shut up and kiss me," she heard herself say, realizing how close their lips were to each other.

"Why don't you kiss me?" he suggested.

A few minutes ago she'd never wanted to kiss anyone again. She'd never wanted to look upon or perform the act of sex again. But all the blasted diplomat had had to do was *talk* to her and she was on the verge of changing her mind on the subject of carnal relation yet again. She was not a changeable sort of person.

"Passion is a powerful incentive," he said, reading her mind in her hesitation. "Real passion will not be denied. Real passion survives."

Did this real passion survive ugliness such as they'd witnessed tonight? It must, as she could no longer keep herself from running her hands through his black hair and drawing his head to hers until their lips met and clung, and something as wild and bright as sunlight burst through her.

While he kissed her he lifted her off her feet and carried her to the bed. When he put her on the bed, he held her down with one hand flat on her stomach while he tossed aside pillows with the other.

"Ah," he said, and held up one of Mrs. Swift's knives. He was grinning as he knelt beside her. "At least we won't have to worry about ironing out all the wrinkles."

She was not frightened of the man holding her down and brandishing a knife for an instant. She probably could have managed a way to disarm him, but protested instead, "This is my aunt's dress! You can't cut it off me!"

"I'm in a hurry," he explained.

"The thing has buttons!"

"And I have a knife. I'll be gentle," he added, still grinning. "At least with the knife."

Harriet was so flabbergasted she stayed perfectly still while he sliced very, very carefully, but with surprising speed, through first one and then the other narrow sleeves of the off-the-shoulder gown. Satin tore and silver beads scattered and soon her bodice and the undergarments beneath were a piece of history, and in several pieces. When the top half of her body was bare and open to his view, he leaned over her and looked his fill. He watched her bare breasts with intense scrutiny as her nipples tightened, and lifted a brow sardonically at her when they did.

"The air in the room is cool," she offered in explanation.

"I know how to warm them." He dipped his head to suckle and tease each breast in turn.

Her hands roamed over his back and shoulders, drawing a moan of frustration from her when she encountered cloth instead of skin. "My turn," she muttered, and reached for the hilt of the knife he'd dropped onto the bed.

"Now, Harriet—!" he exclaimed when he lifted his head and saw what she held.

His momentary alarm made her laugh. The fact that he knew about the secreted knife meant he'd overheard yesterday's conversation with Mrs. Swift, and that he assumed she knew how to use a weapon. She did, but he was the last person in the world she'd ever wanted to hurt, especially after this sweet seduction.

Giving herself to Martin was wrong, but making love to Martin did not feel wrong, and what did it matter right now if he did not love her? He wanted her as much as she wanted him, and passion would have to do, with Martin Kestrel in her bed looking at her with a twinkle in his eye, one hand on her breast and the other undoing the buttons of his shirt.

And, oh yes, about the knife . . .

"I'll be gentle," she said.

"I'd rather you'd hurry."

"All right."

"But *carefully*."

"Of course."

Within a short while and with his enthusiastic assistance, Martin's tailoring was as shredded as her dress. They kissed and touched, and giggled like naughty children while fine wool and linen mingled like May Day ribbons with the beaded blue satin of her gown.

"Now we have to face Cadwell as well as Mrs. Swift," Martin pointed out as they finished undressing each other.

Harriet was so breathless from laughter and arousal that she could barely form words to answer. "We're too old to be sent to bed without our supper."

"Spoken like a governess." His voice was husky with need despite the humor. He swatted her gently on the rump. "Besides, we're in bed already."

"So we are," she agreed and rolled on top of him, reveling in the contact of his hard muscles against her softer, smaller frame. From this angle, his erection pressed hard against her bare belly. His hands cupped her buttocks and darted between her thighs, extracting a sharp jolt of pleasure. She gasped and slid up his body. She took the time to kiss around his navel and run her palms through the dark hair covering his chest. He lay on his back and bunched his fists in the bedclothes, letting her caress and arouse him.

"What are you doing?" he asked when, at last, she positioned herself with her knees on either side of his hips.

"I was scared tonight. I've always been told to confront what frightens me," she said, grasping his shaft. She stroked him until he moaned, and then maneuvered their positions to the exact point where their bodies were meant to join. His hips bucked, but she eluded his thrust until she was ready. "If you fall off a horse, for example, you should get right back on." She managed to get the words out, though she was about to lose all control. She eased herself down until the tip of his penis was planted a little way inside her. Her breath caught on a gasp as his heat and hardness filled her. "A—stallion—in this case," she finished, and thrust her hips down, taking him swiftly and completely into her body.

From that point on she lost all coherence. Words and thoughts fled before the rising, endless tide of sensation. She closed her eyes and lost herself in the glorious flood. At some point their positions shifted so she was on her back and Martin was over her, in her, and then the great shuddering spasms of pleasure began and she was aware of nothing until the exhausted, sated man collapsed on top of her. She gradually became aware of his lips lazily nuzzling her throat and of her fingers slowly combing through his thick, sweat-damp hair.

"You see," he mumbled against her throat. "It isn't always bad."

No. And it wasn't always for always, either. She'd have to resign herself to holding on to the memories and learn to live without him.

Four years and two nights. There were plenty
of memories to last her there, the bitter and the
sweet. Especially the memories created in the
last two nights, things her body as well as her
mind would remember always. She supposed
she could look to Aunt Phoebe's example and
manage to live the rest of her life as both a spinster and a fallen woman. The point was not to
feel sorry for yourself, and she could learn to
do that in time.

Her thoughts drifted, but her deeply satisfied body melted into the deep featherbed. She
could not have moved if she tried. She had
Martin's warmth and weight to share, and took
infinite comfort in the way they fit so neatly together. She wept a little as she fell asleep, joy
and sadness mixed together.

Martin dozed, but came awake enough to
pull a blanket over them before settling spoon
fashion beside Harriet again. Half-awake, he
kissed her shoulder and smiled against her
loose hair, and tried to remember that he hated
and loathed her for a liar, a betrayer, and a spy.
She was a stranger in his bed, he reminded
himself, a conspirator and a skilled actress
who'd deceived him for years. He should take
pleasure from using her, not from comforting

her, not from simply lying beside her through the night, not for acting like a man gentling a virgin bride, when he should be toying with a sexual plaything. It was not right and fair that he kept following the impulse to treat her like a cherished lover, rather than a temporary mistress. Not fair at all.

He must put his foot down, be stern, cruel, extract the revenge he was owed with exquisite humiliation. Only then could honor be satisfied. It was not enough to have her for a lover. He must treat her to the same dose of mortification she'd fed him.

"Tomorrow," he murmured, putting an arm closer around her and sighing with contentment. "I'll take my revenge tomorrow."

Chapter 18

"**H**urry up, woman."

Harriet glared at Martin's broad, black-clad back from across the bedroom, and answered, "Yes, my lord."

"Your tone leaves a great deal to be desired, my dear."

"I was only trying to be polite, my lord."

"I would prefer it if you were expeditious. How long does it take for a woman to put on clothes meant to be taken off? Quite a while, apparently."

"Yes, my lord." She was wearing scarlet this morning, and feeling quite the scarlet woman under the lash of his tongue. She bit hers and finished pinning up her hair. *He* was the one who had chased Mrs. Swift out, leaving Harriet to finish her toilette on her own.

He whirled to face her, dark brows lowered over stormy gray eyes. "Don't mock me."

She did not recall having done so, but kept her eyes lowered and her tone mild as milk. "No, my lord."

He opened the door and gestured her forward. "You'll do as you are. I want my breakfast and some company besides that of women."

He was acting thoroughly irritated and insufferable this morning. He'd woken up that way, and it had only gotten worse as they'd bathed and dressed. She could not do or say a thing to please him, and he'd even managed to astonish Mrs. Swift with a high-handed word or two.

Harriet might say that he was not the man she had gone to bed with, except she was used to all of Martin Kestrel's moods, the dark and the light, the expansive and the snappish, the playful and the punitive. He was definitely in the dark this morning. She'd learned long ago that when he was like this, the best way to deal with him was to remain meek and mild and accommodating, until the right moment to stick a pin in his pomposity presented itself.

Out in the wide hallway, he took her hand and hurried her downstairs and into the dining room. The room was crowded with late-rising, bleary-eyed revelers taking their turns at a long buffet table set up along one wall. Servants moved about, keeping the chafing dishes filled, removing used plates and serving drinks. Wine, ale, and brandy were already being poured out. Harriet hoped that she could acquire a cup of strong tea.

She studiously kept herself from wondering which of the ordinary-looking men and women sharing a perfectly normal breakfast had taken part in last night's masked debauchery. Her own personal debauchery, and the wicked speculation on whether there would be time for any more of it, was much on her mind as she followed Martin to the breakfast board. Time was short—the dates set for the rendezvous with the courier ended today. If she did not make contact today, that meant the courier had been waylaid by the opposition and some other way of retrieving the information must be found. And what of Michael? Worry ate at her, though she still didn't know if there was anything wrong with her wayward younger brother. Her instincts told her there was, but how could she trust any instinct or impulse when her head and heart were in such an uproar over Martin?

He still had her hand clasped in his. The pressure he exerted was not gentle, but she was rather glad of this sign of his claim on her. A week ago she would have been furious at this feminine reaction to belonging to a male, but when it came to this male, she discovered she didn't mind a bit. Next week she would mask the heartbreak of never seeing Martin again with starchy pride, but for now she accepted that she wanted to belong to him, and for now she did.

Gazing at the man's marvelously broad shoulders and strong profile was a lovely way to spend the morning, but there was a roomful of other people there that she needed to turn her attention to, she reminded herself sternly. Martin finally loosed her hand long enough for them to fill plates. Harriet cast her gaze around the room once more, but her inspection was interrupted by the approach of their cheerfully smiling host.

"Lord Martin," the man said, sounding as if Martin Kestrel were his best friend and private property. "Come join me on the terrace for breakfast, my lord. The garden is lovely today."

Harriet tried to catch Martin's eye, to indicate that she'd rather circulate among the crowd in the room, but he didn't even glance her way. He gave Strake a thin smile and said, "Gladly. Come along, Cora."

Cora Bell had no choice but to follow her lord and master outdoors into the warm sunlight, to a group of tables that overlooked the pool below the terrace. It was indeed a beautiful day, though in the daylight she could see that the bronze figures of the fountain at the other end of the pool were naked gods and goddesses disporting themselves in a most unseemly fashion. After encountering the rampant faun statue the night before, Harriet was quite unshockable by any of Sir Anthony Strake's tasteless bric-a-brac.

Fortunately for her hunt for the courier, there were several people at the outdoor tables that she had not encountered before. There was also Lady Ellen. Harriet's jaw clenched at the sight of the woman, and at the way she rose to her feet with a welcoming smile and gesture for Martin to take the empty seat beside her, without taking any notice of Harriet at all.

That was all right; Harriet did not want to be noticed. It was just that she didn't want Martin being noticed by any other woman, and she certainly didn't want Martin noticing in return. Harriet was left standing back from the table holding her plate, as there was no other empty seat available. She gritted her teeth, swallowed her anger and pride, and reminded herself that she was not there to dance attendance on Martin Kestrel. That didn't stop the pain of being so casually brushed aside, nor did it ease the jealousy she had no right to feel. All she could do was hope her feelings did not show.

But she had no luck there, as a man who'd come up beside her announced cheerfully in an American accent, "If that fool doesn't want you, sweetheart, I know I do."

Harriet turned to face the speaker, and as she did, her plate was snatched out of her hands and a quick kiss was pressed on her cheek. "Thief!" she announced, wide-eyed at the sight of the man now holding her breakfast.

"Of hearts and breakfasts," he announced irrepressibly. His dark eyes were full of the devil, as was his smile. "There's an empty table over here." He took her elbow and guided her away from Martin's table. "Where we can share my breakfast in private."

"Your breakfast?" Harriet laughed despite her indignation, and went with this handsome man with the American accent. She didn't even look to see if Martin noticed before she walked away.

Martin deliberately turned his back on his mistress while Lady Ellen chatted on about the day, the pleasure of his company, the joys of a relaxed country house party, and God knew what else. Though she put her hand over his and squeezed it suggestively, he had only a vague awareness of her. His mind was completely on Harriet. He didn't want it to be, and he didn't let it show, but there it was.

He was acting like an ass, and knew it. Harriet had made a fool of him, and he was in danger of forgetting how much she'd wronged him. For example, he'd woken up that morning with her sleeping peacefully in his arms, and he'd spent the time he wasn't distracted by her warm, pliant body cradled against his justifying her outrageous behavior as only doing her job. A woman wasn't supposed to have a job, and certainly not the sort Harriet performed with such aplomb. It was unseemly, distasteful, ridiculous—and he certainly could not countenance the woman's living a secret life within his own household.

Such behavior deserved contempt and punishment, and that, by God, he resolved before she awoke and smiled at him, was just what she was going to receive at his hands! It was what he'd intended all along by bringing her to Strake House. He'd simply lost the point of the exercise because the familiar habits of their false friendship were hard to break. What he'd felt for the woman he'd wanted to marry had died on that hillside on Skye. What was left, all that needed to be left, was lust. Now that he'd had her, the fever for her would burn out and he could move on.

Only, as he lay beside her, their naked bodies so close that it was hard to know where he ended and she began, what he'd felt had gone beyond lust straight to utter contentment. There had been lust, too, of course. He couldn't think now why he hadn't taken her, first thing that morning. In fact, he couldn't think of one good reason that he shouldn't take her back upstairs right now and start the morning out the way he should have, by riding her good and hard until some of the fever was burned out of his system.

Anticipation drove him to his feet. "Excuse me," he managed to say to Lady Ellen. He turned, for some reason expecting Harriet to be standing meekly behind him. Of course, she was not there. He frowned and very nearly bellowed out her name in angry frustration.

Lady Ellen said, "Your pretty friend is over there." Martin noticed her malicious smile when she pointed toward a table on the other side of the terrace.

He followed her gesture, and immediately saw Harriet seated close beside a slender man with thick, reddish-brown hair. The pair were sharing a plate, and some joke, for they were both smiling. Then Harriet's smile turned into laughter and the stranger flicked a stray wisp of hair away from her face, brushing her cheek in the process. Martin's world suddenly turned to angry red. He was across the width of the terrace and standing menacingly over Harriet's chair within a few heartbeats.

"What the—" he began furiously.

"Fox," the strange man cut him off, and rose smoothly to his feet. "My name's Fox," he added when Martin ignored the long-fingered hand the man held out to him. "My friends call me Kit." He was as tall as Martin, with a lean, wiry build, and strong, handsome features. "I know we haven't been properly introduced, Lord Martin, is it?" the man called Fox went on in a thick, outlandish accent. "But Miss Cora here's told me about all I need to know about you."

Cora? Who the devil was Cora? Was there a note of underlying menace in the man's tone? Martin didn't know or care. He was prepared to call the man out to a duel for behaving so familiarly with Harriet. Then Martin recalled that Harriet *was* Cora, it was the name he'd bestowed on her himself. But he intensely disliked hearing it from anyone else's lips. She was *his* Cora, just as she'd been *his* Abigail. *His* Harriet? Yes, damn it, *his*!

The question and vehement answer drew him up sharply, and drove a bit of sanity back into his head. He was being jealous of a phantom woman. He didn't know who she really was. Which didn't stop him from wanting to fight over possession of her.

Harriet sat and watched the bristling meeting with ironic amusement. The two men looked for all the world like a pair of dogs preparing to fight over a bone. A tasty one, she hoped, with a bit of meat on it. Her amusement lasted only moments, and she rose to her feet to defuse the confrontation before everyone else on the terrace took note of it. Harriet was certain that the other guests were the sort that eagerly scented out rancor and jealousy and egged it on for amusement's sake. Lady Ellen was already avidly watching Lord Martin's every move. The last thing she intended was to draw any attention to herself; she remembered her job, even if other people did not.

"Gentlemen," she said quietly. "There are sharks in the water. They are drawn to the scent of blood. Try not to act like fools on my account."

That said, she walked away, going down the terrace steps. She did not pause to see which of the men was following her until she reached the pool and clearly saw his reflection looming behind her. She sighed when strong, skilled hands began massaging shoulders she had not realized were tight with tension.

"I know this sounds ridiculous, Martin, considering where we are and what we've been doing," she said while her muscles began to relax and her blood started to simmer under his touch. "But we are not here to create a scandal."

"Then you should stay away from rogues like Mr. Fox."

She was not going to fight about whom either of them had shared their breakfast with, though the temptation to bring up his dalliance with Lady Ellen was hot on her tongue. There was no more time to allow feelings to interfere with duty.

"If I stayed away from rogues today," she whispered to him, "I would not be able to get my job done."

"Bah," he muttered, the sound bitter and contemptuous. His hands dropped away from her shoulders, and he stepped back as she turned to face him.

It took all of her willpower not to let that small, irritating sound lead her into another argument where they could talk for hours and never get a thing settled. Sometimes it seemed to her that they shared one mind and hardly needed words at all. Other times she felt as if they used words from the same language but didn't understand each other at all.

Instead of allowing herself the infinitely

more stimulating option of an argument with Martin Kestrel, she said, "I'm told that Sir Anthony has arranged fencing matches for this afternoon. No doubt this is in honor of your reputation."

"Yes," Martin growled. "He was enthusing over the prospect of wagering on his dear friend's prowess with a sword last night."

"And I'm sure there was some mention made of your knowing how to fence, as well," she couldn't help but add, her gaze dropping to the bulge in Martin's trousers before she met his eyes again. Martin grinned, and the hurt anger in his eyes was replaced by a wicked twinkle.

"Naughty wench."

"I try, my lord." She put her arm through his "I shall enjoy watching you fence, my lord."

"You'll prefer my swordplay," he answered, letting her lead him toward the house. "But I'll let you mingle for a while. As long as you stay away from that Fox fellow," he warned.

Chapter 19

~~~♦♦~~~

Martin did not like to lose. He didn't suppose any man did, but some accepted defeat more easily than others. Not Martin Kestrel. Though fencing was a hobby, it was a serious one. Had the world's wars still been fought by sword-wielding knights on horseback, he might have made his career as a soldier. As it was, he spent his life trying to avoid wars by wielding words, and saved his talent with the sword for bloodless competition with foil, epee, and saber. Though Martin had studied the conventions of the sport with Italian masters, his early and best training had come from his half-Spanish godfather, who claimed to have been among the last of the Barbary pirates in his youth. Wherever the Duke of Pyneham had learned his skill, he'd passed quite a few useful tricks on to Martin, who never failed to use them to his advantage.

And he learned quickly that fencing with Sir Anthony's friends required every dirty trick he'd ever learned. There was a great deal of wagering among the spectators in the long window-lined gallery used for the exercise, and at first none of the betting was on Lord Martin Kestrel. Martin welcomed the challenge and set about ruthlessly defeating every challenger who came against him.

I wish he wasn't taking so many risks, Harriet thought as she stood among a group of tittering women.

The ladies clapped and cooed at every touch of the tips of the long fencing foils against the padded white garments that protected the competitors' torsos, while the watching men clapped and commented knowingly whether they were aficionados or not. Harriet doubted most of the spectators knew the names of the feints and parries, or what constituted points in the combat of clashing swords. What the women did recognize was that the fencing match was a fine, athletic way for a man to show off his body.

Martin's broad shoulders, muscular thighs, arms, and long legs looked especially elegant and graceful as he moved purposefully up and down the length of the hallway. His black hair and fair coloring were certainly set off handsomely by the white fencing gear. All the women commented on it. Harriet received quite a few envious looks, and actually found herself smiling smugly back a few times.

Honestly, don't be an idiot. He isn't mine to preen over.

But he certainly looked good as he worked up a sweat, his expression showing sharp concentration and fierce determination. The man looked like a medieval warrior. Lady Ellen even commented that she wished she'd offered Martin a handkerchief to wear as her token. Harriet repressed the urge to give the other woman a blistering look.

Harriet would have been happier if the men wore protective masks instead of fighting with their heads bare. The thin fencing foils they wielded were blunted at the tip, but the tip could still prove dangerous if thrust into an eye or vulnerable throat. She was in the habit of being protective of Martin Kestrel even when the danger was minimal. Watching the man's back was an ingrained habit after four years.

Well, that assignment was over. He was a big boy who was voluntarily showing off his prowess and could take care of himself. She even tried to tell herself that Lady Ellen was welcome to him. Then she sidled out of the crowd of women and spotted a group of men who did not seem particularly interested in the fencing. This group stood by one of the tall windows in a warm shaft of sunlight. The windows were flanked by flowering plants in huge blue and white porcelain pots, obscuring her view of the members of this group.

It was such a simple assignment, but proving terribly frustrating to carry out. Where was the man wearing a gold lily stickpin in his cravat or lapel? The courier was a man who knew a man who passed secret information from a Russian double agent in Vienna on through this anonymous chain of spies until the information reached the hands of the British secret service. Her brother Michael was supposed to be the person who represented the British. It was supposed to have been a simple operation that a young man on holiday from university could easily handle.

It was possible that Michael had been tortured into revealing that the courier was to be at this party. It was possible that the courier had heard some rumor that Michael was missing and was being cautious. It was possible that there was a Russian agent at the party hunting for the courier as well. Many things were possible. Harriet felt time nipping at her heels and wanted something, *anything* to happen. Only she had to find the man with the blasted stickpin first!

When she stepped around the potted plant, Harriet was pleased to note that there were at least two men in the group that she had not met before. She smiled and moved closer, but before she could so much as utter a word or even flutter an eyelash, a hand snagged her arm and she was spun around.

"We meet again," Kit said. He looked her up and down, dark eyes glittering and a smile dancing on his wide mouth. "You do clean up pretty," he told her.

"Would that be considered a compliment in America?"

"No, Miss Cora," he answered. "In New Orleans we compliment women in French." He steered her away from her objective and toward a door at the other end of the gallery. While she wanted to scream in frustration and had a childish urge to kick him, he leaned his head close to hers and said, "When we're alone I'll speak to you in French, *chère*."

"I'd rather you didn't," she told him.

His smile was irrepressible. The way to the door took them past where the men were fencing. "What other language would you like? I'm fluent in several. Fluent in many things," he added.

"Flirting and teasing being high on the list."

"Would I flirt with you, Miss Cora?"

The fencing foil that was suddenly pressed against Kit's throat interrupted whatever answer she would have made.

It seemed to take forever to look up and up the length of the slender line of metal until Harriet finally met the raging fury in Martin Kestrel's gray eyes. There was a moment of exquisite silence, but his gaze flicked contemptuously over her for only a second before he concentrated his attention on the man he held at sword's point.

"Oh, dear," Harriet murmured, and then became aware of the staring crowd gathering around them. "You are causing a scene, my lord," she warned. The worst of it was, she didn't understand why he was doing it.

"Take your hand off her." Martin spoke quietly, but his low voice was full of threat.

Kit's response was a raised eyebrow and the slightest of shrugs. "Pull a real weapon on me and I might consider it," was his cool answer.

"Gladly," Martin said, and tossed down the foil. "Name your weapon."

"*Martin.*" A duel. She didn't believe it. Was he mad? Had he really challenged another man to a duel? "This is the sort of behavior I expect from your brother," she told Martin. She glared at Kit. "And you—"

"Well?" Martin urged Kit. He ignored her.

Kit's smiling attention was completely on Martin. "What are we fightin' over, sir? The hand of the lady?"

Harriet pulled away from Kit. "My hand is not up for barter."

Martin gave a mirthless laugh. His eyes were wild. "It is not her hand either of us is interested in."

Kit showed a hint of anger for the first time. "Really?" He sneered at Martin. "Seems to me that a man who's willing to lose a woman in a fight doesn't deserve to have her in the first place."

"I do not believe I am hearing this." Harriet pulled away from Kit. "You're acting like a pair of idiots."

She looked around at the avid spectators, but there was no use calling for help or sanity from this crowd. The eagerness with which the confrontation was being watched was sickening. Sharks indeed, scenting real blood as well as gossip this time. There was an eager gasp when the man who'd come from America reached into an interior coat pocket.

What he brought out was a deck of cards. He fanned them in one hand and his smile was as sharp as a knife when he said, "My weapon of choice, sir."

"Fine," Martin said, nostrils flared with contempt.

"Martin," Harriet warned. He didn't listen. "Kit!"

Kit only smiled at her. "You're going to be going home with me, little lady."

"I am not."

"You haven't won her yet," Martin informed his opponent.

"Yes, I have," Kit answered. "You, Lord Martin, are a dilettante. Among my many accomplishments, *I* include Mississippi riverboat gambler." He glanced at Sir Anthony, who was standing nearby. "If you'll show the way to your gaming room, sir, we can get this duel started."

. There was some laughter, and quite a bit of comment. Bets on the outcome were already being laid. Harriet decided it was best simply to walk away and let the antagonists get whatever was poisoning them out of their systems. She had a man with a lily to find.

But as if being gambled over wasn't humiliating enough, Martin grabbed her by the arm and dragged her off to the gaming room. She protested the whole way, which only drew more attention and comments from the crowd. Shame burned through her, and growing anger. Worst of all was the pain that Martin could think so little of her that he was willing to give her up to the turn of a card. Kit was right about one thing; any man who treated a woman—treated *her*—with such contempt wasn't worthy of being loved.

"Whatever happens, no matter what punishment you think I deserve," she whispered as they stepped through the card room door, "know that you and I are through."

Martin pretended he didn't hear her. Whatever his initial motive was, he knew that he'd taken it too far and that there was no going back. The insane thing was, he almost didn't know how it had started. He remembered that he'd already been annoyed at a bungling opponent's blatant attempts to cheat, and he was already angry with himself for his behavior toward Harriet that morning, and angry for being angry because she deserved any treatment he cared to give her. Into all this confusion and fury, what did he see out of the corner of his eye but Harriet casually strolling off arm in arm with her new American friend, as though Martin didn't matter at all. And she was smiling at the scoundrel. *Smiling!*

That was when the red rage descended on him like a curtain blocking out all sanity, and the next thing he knew he'd challenged Kit Fox to a duel. For some reason, it had all seemed perfectly reasonable at the time. Which made him not only a fool, but the worst sort of dastardly villain. It would serve him right if the American gambler won this card game, for

Martin couldn't back out now. To refuse to fight with the chosen weapon meant he would default the match. Harriet would go to Fox anyway. She could protest all she liked, but Sir Anthony would gleefully ensure that to the victor went the spoils, even if Martin had to be restrained to do it. Sir Anthony would never let anything besmirch the "honor" of his house by letting a man renege on a bet.

Of course, he thought with grim humor, with the spoils went Mrs. Swift. Not that that was any real consolation. Win or lose the game, he realized when he glanced sideways at her hard, unyielding anger, he had lost her before ever really finding her.

"Damn," he muttered, but no one, least of all Harriet, paid him any mind. Everyone was caught up in the entertainment. Actually, Lady Ellen did smile at him when he looked around. Perhaps she thought he'd seek consolation in her arms once he'd lost his mistress to the gambler. "Damn," he said again, even more fervently.

In the wood-paneled gaming room, he paused to strip off the fencing rig and wipe the sweat off his face. Then he sat down in his shirtsleeves opposite Kit Fox. Sir Anthony took a third chair, and Fox passed his deck of cards to their host, to act as dealer.

"I'd prefer a fresh deck," Martin said, his request an open implication that Fox's deck was marked.

Fox didn't complain that he was being called a card cheat, but nodded his agreement. "Straight draw poker," he said when a servant brought the new deck. "You know the game?" Martin nodded. "Good. I wouldn't want to tax Your Lordship's skills with anything more lively."

"Shut up and play," Martin replied.

A stack of chips was placed before him and Fox. Though there was no ante or stakes in this game, the chips were necessary for smooth play. Sir Anthony shuffled and cut the cards, then dealt the players five cards each.

Martin schooled his emotions, his muscles, and his features, and settled down to play. He might not have played on a Mississippi riverboat but he was no less a professional gambler than Mr. Fox. What was the diplomacy he practiced at the highest-level negotiating tables of the world, if not gambling for the most important stakes imaginable? What was winning a hand of cards next to preventing a war? A calm confidence came over him the moment the play began. When all five cards were in his hand, he began to smile.

The room was silent, people barely breathing, all eyes centered on the gaming table. To Martin they became no more than statues, unimportant pieces of furniture. Even knowing that the seething Harriet stood directly behind him had no effect on him. Only he, Kit Fox, and the cards existed. The room was hot and Martin was glad that he was stripped to a white shirt with no coat, collar, or cravat. He welcomed every advantage, and like a good diplomat, or gambler, he took every advantage.

"Bet," Fox said, tossing a chip to the center of the table.

"Bet." Martin repeated the gesture.

Both men studied their hands, drawing out the game for a long time, working on each other's nerves.

Fox finally said, "Raise." He threw in more chips.

"Two," Martin said. He discarded the unwanted cards and took the two Strake dealt him. No matter what he held in his hand, he continued to smile slightly. Beneath lowered lids he studied Fox, and noticed the other man's gaze flicker to Harriet—a gambit to distract him by playing on his jealousy.

"Your bet, Fox," Martin said, pretending he'd fallen for the ploy. He did not rearrange his cards, did not discard what he held. Once he was working, nothing jangled Martin Kestrel's nerves. He didn't like to lose.

"One," Fox said after a few moments' consideration, and took the card from Strake.

"Raise," Martin immediately answered, and threw in all his chips.

"Calling me?" Fox asked. "So soon?"

"Call or fold is, I believe, the point we are at in the proceedings, Mr. Fox."

"I'll see you, then," Fox said, and pushed his remaining chips to the center of the table for form's sake.

Martin laid his spread of five cards face up on the table. His smile was quite broad now.

Harriet gasped, and said, "Royal flush? You lucky knave."

Martin tilted his head back and asked, "You play the game, my dear?"

"I don't play any games with you," she spat back.

"Wrong," he answered, rising to his feet. He

hauled her over his shoulder before she had time to argue and kept a firm grip though she pummeled and kicked, as the crowd parted and he carried his prize off to their room.

Chapter 20

❦❦❦

"**P**ut me down!"

This time he did.

"*Ump! Ow!*" He'd expected her to slap his face; the fisted blow to his solar plexus came as a surprise. It took an effort to swiftly put himself between her and the door. For precaution's sake he turned the key in the lock, then pocketed it. "You are not leaving this room," Martin told her.

"I am certainly not staying."

"Don't tell me you want to run to Mr. Fox."

"Don't be ridiculous."

He smiled dangerously. "Then why would you want to leave me?"

"Of all the stupid questions! How could you

293

do that to me?" she demanded. "How *dare* you do that to me?" Tears shone in her eyes as she glared at him, and bright spots of color stained her cheeks. "I have never been so humiliated. I can still hear them laughing and clapping as you carried me away like some barbarian's war prize. You showed me as nothing more to you than sellable property."

"I never intended—"

"You made a fool of me. You treated me like an object."

"Not you," he said, hoping it would help. "Cora Bell. It wasn't *you* they saw carried away."

A tear spilled down her cheek. "Then why do *I* want to die?" She shook her head vehemently as he put a hand out to her. "Don't you dare touch me. Don't even try. I did not deserve that, Martin. No matter how badly you think I treated you, I did not deserve that. You would not have treated Sabine so, and she betrayed you with another man."

Her words cut deeply into his conscience. "Harriet—"

She turned her back on him. Her spine was stiff with angry pride, but he saw the telltale trembling. "You would have given me away just like that." She snapped her fingers.

How could he explain what he'd done, when he wasn't sure how or why he'd behaved so despicably? "I saw you giving your affection to another man and—perhaps it is the atmosphere of this place that lends itself to license and—"

"Oh, no." She had been nearly shouting, with an edge of hysteria in her voice. She paused now and took a few deep breaths. When she continued she was still furious, but a cold calm had entered her voice. "You can't excuse your behavior so easily. I won't believe a day and a half in this hell corrupted your sense of right and wrong."

"It seemed the sort of thing a man jealous of his mistress would do," he flailed around for an excuse. "Perhaps I took the acting too far. I'm not used to playing roles."

"The devil you're not, my lord ambassador. You playact every time you sit down to negotiate. I saw the way you played poker; you were simply being yourself."

"At least you know who I am," he shot back. "You have me at a disadvantage."

"You know me well enough to hurt me, Martin. I hurt your pride, so you found a way to hurt mine. Congratulations, you succeeded admirably."

She was right, to his shame—but only partially. "There's something about seeing you with Fox that infuriated me." *Threatened me*, he admitted to himself. "Seeing you lavish affection on such a scoundrel set my teeth on edge."

"Lavish?" She gave a curt laugh. "How was I lavishing anything on him?"

"Talking to him. Touching him. Laughing with him. You know what he is—"

Another mirthless laugh cut him off. "I do indeed. I know the scamp very well."

Her words reminded Martin of the reason Harriet was at Strake House. He leaned back against the door, and banged his head against it once in frustration. "Please tell me Fox is not the man you came here to meet."

"He's not."

"But you say you know him." She turned to face him as he went on. Her arms were crossed tensely over her waist, yet a slight smile lifted her lips. As usual these days, she completely confused him. "I can't believe you've encountered this American gambler during your spying activities."

"He's not a gambler," she said. "At least not professionally. He's a cat burglar, and—"

"We've known each other practically all our lives," Kit Fox interrupted Harriet's answer.

"My brother," she finished before she whirled to face the man casually leaning in the dressing room doorway, arms crossed and well aware of his insouciant appearance. "Christopher Fox MacLeod, what the devil are you doing here?"

"There's a window in the dressing room," he replied. "You should applaud my ability to climb in without being seen in broad daylight."

"I should box your ears," she answered.

The man who was suddenly no longer Kit Fox—and Martin was getting damned tired of all this cloak-and-dagger business—straightened from his languid pose and strode into the room. Christopher MacLeod did not bother looking at Martin, but Martin was well aware of the man's hostility. "You've been crying," he said, wiping a thumb across Harriet's cheek. "That's something else he has to pay for."

Martin noticed that the man's American accent had disappeared.

"What are you doing here?" she repeated. "Not how, why?"

"I got home after you left. Papa sent me to find Michael."

"Who is Michael?" Martin asked.

"Our brother," Harriet and this other brother said together.

"What are you doing here?" this brother asked Harriet. He jerked a thumb at Martin. "Does Papa know about him?" He glanced at the bed. "And what you've been doing?"

"Mum sent me. She disagreed with Papa about waiting for you. You'd telegraphed you'd be delayed, and we didn't know for how long."

"I see." He flicked a quick look at Martin. "Mum always has been the more ruthless one of that pair."

"You'd be ruthless, too, if you were worried about your child."

"I wouldn't send my daughter off with the likes of him."

"You don't know about the likes of him," Harriet flared.

"He's a cad and ought to be shot."

"How dare you," Martin spoke up for himself, seething with growing annoyance. If the man felt like challenging him this time, Martin wouldn't turn him down. "How dare you break in here and bully Harriet?"

Harriet's brother paid him no mind. "Only question is, do I do it myself or wait for Papa to have a go?"

"Stick to business," Harriet responded. "My personal life is my own."

"Is it rea—"

"I mean it, Christopher."

Martin would have hesitated to argue with that tone. Her brother decided to take the better part of valor himself. He drew his sister into a fierce hug and said, "Lord, it's good to see you again, chit. We've both stayed away from home for too long."

Harriet just as fiercely hugged him back, and in the middle of the embrace she began to sob. Martin took a step forward but stopped at a warning look from her brother. Martin told himself he was not the cause of her distress; she was reacting to seeing a long-lost brother, or perhaps with relief that she could turn her assignment over to more capable, masculine hands.

He did not believe either explanation for a moment.

Two things were becoming clear as Martin tried to apply some balm to his conscience. One was that the situation involving the courier was more complicated and dangerous than he'd been led to believe. The second was . . .

"The card game was a sham, wasn't it?" he demanded, his indignation growing by the moment. "Harriet, you knew all along that you were in no danger of being ravished by this rogue if I lost to him."

Harriet whirled from Christopher's embrace. "*You* didn't know!" she accused. Her contempt scalded Martin to the bone. "You didn't care!"

"Didn't care? Of course I—"

"You made the challenge. You put her up on the auction block," the other man pointed out disdainfully. His look promised Martin that he would pay for it. "You offered your woman to a stranger. The sin's yours, so don't try to get out of it with the excuse that it wasn't real."

Harriet's words had already killed his anger, but he wasn't going to apologize in front of her arrogant sibling. Before he could say something comforting, a hard pounding started on the door at his back.

"Go away!" Martin shouted through the door.

"I don't take my orders from you," an equally angry voice shouted back.

Oh, God, it was Mrs. Swift.

"It's the Legacy!" Christopher slipped past before Martin could block him, and somehow had the locked door opened within several seconds. "Nanny!" he cried, drawing the skinny woman into the room and throwing his arms around her.

For a moment Martin thought Mrs. Swift was actually going to smile, but the moment passed. She pushed away from Christopher and announced, "You smell foreign."

Good, Martin thought. *Someone else for her to complain about.* He smiled at this unkind thought.

Harriet looked his way, and from the faint hint of amusement that lit and died in her eyes, he was sure she knew what he was thinking. He also knew that she wished she didn't share this or any other thought with him. It hurt that he had forfeited her sympathy, though he tried not to let it. The woman had kept him in a state of utter confusion since the day he asked her to marry him, and the machinations and emotions only grew more tangled all the time.

He turned to Mrs. Swift and demanded, "What the devil do you want?"

Mrs. Swift ignored him and approached Harriet instead. "Time to get you changed for dinner."

"We will take dinner in our room," Martin answered instantly.

"No, you won't. There's people you've yet to meet," Mrs. Swift continued to Harriet. "Now that there's two of you, the work'll go faster. Sooner it's done, the sooner we can leave this den of iniquity."

"Are you up to it, Harry?" MacLeod asked his sister. He brushed the hair off her tearstained cheeks. "You game to play Cora Bell one more time?"

Martin couldn't help but feel reluctant pride as he watched her draw her dignity around her and call on some reserve of strength, pride, and sense of duty. She changed before his eyes, and only as she pulled herself together did he truly realize how deeply he'd hurt her this time. Had they been alone, he would have gone to his knee and apologized. One needed privacy for the most delicate of negotiations.

"Mrs. Swift's right," Harriet acknowledged. "We haven't much time. The more of us looking for the courier, the better." She tilted her head sideways and asked hopefully, "I don't suppose Michael's checked in with Aunt Phoebe?"

"Not a word as of yesterday. We have to assume he's been captured and they've learned enough from him to send an agent here on the same business as we're on."

"If I know Michael, he was smart enough to leak the information about the courier," Harriet said.

Her brother nodded. "So we have to spot the courier, but stand back and let the opposition be the one who approaches him." He rubbed his long jaw. "Yes. Good thinking on Michael's part."

Mrs. Swift snorted. "You're assuming the lad's smart enough to think of it. He's the twin that thinks with a part well south of his brain."

Martin was fascinated by what he was hearing, as well as puzzled and concerned. "Why haven't you mentioned this Michael and his dilemma before?" he questioned. "And how many relatives do you have?" It was not a relevant question, but he was intensely curious to find out.

Harriet wished Martin would stop talking, for then she was forced to think about him, and thinking about him caused her intense pain. She did not have time for pain right now. She had to shove it into a compartment in her brain and get on with her assignment. Not only were they racing the clock to help Michael, but the sooner this mission was accomplished, the sooner she could go home and mourn the loss of not only her innocence and her love, but everything she'd respected about Martin Kestrel. She hoped that the intense hatred she felt right now did not last for long, because it was as dangerous as love. If you let yourself hold on to hatred for a person, it, and the person you hated, controlled your life with the same intense passion as love. She'd already let her feelings for Martin control her for four wasted years.

But since she still needed Martin for one more night of the masquerade, she forced herself to look at him and speak to him. "I told you

I was giving you the short version when I explained the assignment to you."

"You might have mentioned someone's life was in danger."

He was frowning at her as though something was once again all her fault. She didn't know if she didn't bother with explanations because they weren't alone, or because she was emotionally spent, or because it was not worth the effort to justify herself to him anymore. She felt so tired and bruised, inside and outside. "Come along," she told Mrs. Swift, then turned and walked into the dressing room.

Martin watched her go, and wasn't surprised when the door was slammed firmly behind the women. That left him alone with Christopher Fox MacLeod, which was distinctly not where he wanted to be. "You've already unlocked the door," he said to the cat burglar brother. "I suggest you use it."

Christopher made no move to go. Instead he walked across the room. He moved silently on the thick carpet, but Martin thought the man would move silently no matter what the surface. Christopher sat on the bed, patted the embroidered satin bedspread, ran a long-fingered thief's hand across a pillow, then looked at Martin coldly and asked, "When's the wedding, my lord?"

Chapter 21

"**W**edding?" Martin, caught on the cusp of outrage and incredulity, matched glares with Harriet's angry brother for a few moments, then decided that he had about all the interference in his life from the clan MacLeod that he was going to put up with. "Get out," he ordered.

"Before you toss me out?" Christopher rubbed his hands together while giving Martin a dangerous smile. "I would love to see you try."

"You have an assignment," Martin reminded him. "Shouldn't you be skulking along the corridors and breaking into people's rooms?"

"That's no way to find what I'm looking for this time." He rose slowly to his feet. "Let's talk about my sister. And the fact that you've been sleeping with her. And the nuptials that follow on that activity."

"The matter is not up for discussion."

"How did you coerce her into becoming your lover?"

"How did I—"

"I know my sister. Unlike men of the world such as you and I, she doesn't take female virtue lightly. Especially her own. Did you make her sleep with you for Michael's sake?"

"I knew nothing about this Michael," Martin replied tightly. Though his conscience writhed, he was very close to striking the man for his accusatory interference. He clasped his hands behind his back and said, "Your sister is also a woman of the world. Her life is her own, as I'm sure she would tell you herself."

"She'd tell me, all right, but that isn't how caring for each other works among the MacLeods."

"I really have no interest in how you people care for each other."

"You certainly don't care for Harriet." Christopher shook his head and sneered contemptuously at Martin. "We've been trying to get her to come home for years, but she insisted you needed her. I see now how you've repaid her care for you." His voice shook with anger as he added, "To think she nearly died saving your worthless life, only to have you put her through this. You don't deserve her."

The world stopped, and a great wave of sickening darkness washed over Martin. Fear such as he'd never known buffeted him, nearly driving him to his knees. When his vision cleared the fear still knotted inside him. "Died?" he asked, barely able to get the word out. "She nearly died."

It was not a question; he remembered. She had not fallen down that mountain where he'd found her. She'd been pushed. But why or how—and who? When he found out who, they were dead.

He would have grabbed MacLeod to shake the answers out of him, but a gentle knock sounded on the bedroom door. Cadwell the valet came in, diffident, polite, firmly intent on preparing his master to go down for dinner. MacLeod sneered at Martin once more and was out the door.

The details would have to wait—and it was better to find them out from Harriet herself.

* * *

"We have something to discuss."

Harriet smoothed the white gloves that covered her arms up to the elbows.

When she did not answer him, he said, "You look lovely."

"I know." Her answer was not in the least bit boastful.

Her gown was peacock-blue, embroidered and beaded in a pattern of peacock feathers. Enamel peacock feather pins decorated her elaborately arranged hair, and she carried a peacock feather fan. Harriet knew she had never looked more attractive, or more like a frivolous ornament. The effect was studied and deliberate. Martin had made her the center of attention that afternoon, so all eyes would be on her when she reappeared. Fine. So be it. She would use the sudden notoriety to keep attention focused on her. She would be bright and alluring and play the coquette. She would make every man want her, and think he could have her. She would make every woman jealous. It was all smoke and mirrors, cloaking Kit's movements.

Once the rendezvous with the courier occurred, retrieving the information could wait.

The most important thing was to find Michael. But first she had to get past the large, intense male blocking her way. She didn't want to deal with him; she didn't know if she'd ever be ready for that. He obviously didn't care.

He came to her and put his large hands on her shoulders. "I want to talk to you."

She made herself meet his eyes. "I've given you quite enough of what you want. As of today, I'm putting paid to any sins I believed I committed against you. Take me down to dinner, then leave me alone."

"I would if I could. I swear."

"I am glad to see that you are as anxious to be rid of me as I am of you."

Her voice had no color in it, not a shred of emotion. She felt like the marble shell of a statue; the heat from his hand was the only heat in her body. She would have to correct that, make herself be bright and vivacious. Weariness must wait.

"There are things you must tell me."

Martin was not asking for a discussion, not suggesting they have a talk when there was more time. He was keeping her away from the bedroom door, a large, formidable man, his square, cleft jaw set, his eyes full of determination. His attitude said there was no getting around him, no putting this off.

Annoyance at his stubborn insistence on having his own way brought some life back to her. "Later," she snapped. "Away from Strake House."

She knew that the suite held no hidden spy holes or secret passages; she and Mrs. Swift had both thoroughly been over every inch of their quarters. She would not put it past Sir Anthony to gather blackmail material on his guests, but she'd found no evidence that the rooms were anything but secure. The doors and walls were thick and solid, and the only servants about were Cadwell and Mrs. Swift, but still, Harriet preferred caution. She could not recall everything that had been said in the heat of the moment and the heat of passion since they'd come there. It was embarrassing; her tongue seemed to have become as loose as her morals, and at the same time. All Martin's fault—not that she'd deny the pleasure that came with the fall, no matter how angry she was at the man she'd made love to.

"I don't want to talk to you," she said.

"Don't pout, my dear. It isn't becoming. And

312

you will talk if you want to ever get out of this room."

"What more do you want me to tell you? About my missing brother? Why I didn't beg you for help in the name of a helpless lad? You would not have given a fig about the safety of another member of my family when I asked you to bring me here. I accept that your anger was justified, but enough is enough. I'm not a martyr, and I won't keep paying for having bruised your pride. It is time for us both to get over it and get on with our lives. Michael needs my help right now. Can we go downstairs?"

"A pretty speech," he said. "But not what we're going to talk about."

Harriet took a deep breath. "I hadn't realized I had that many words left in me." It seemed that she could not break the habit of holding conversations with this man. "Oh, all right," she conceded. "But let's be quick about it. And stop smirking, you cad. You know very well I was not talking about intercourse, quick or otherwise."

He took a hand from her shoulder and touched the spot over his heart. "On my oath, my dear, I was not thinking about intercourse just then. No more than any man thinks of it at all times, that is," he added. "All men are cads that way, especially when alone with the most beautiful woman they know." He grew serious again. "I know this is no time to want to make love to you. For the moment I've forfeited the right to make love to you."

She shrugged away from him. "Stop talking about love."

"For now," he agreed. "I will. Let us talk instead about duty and honor and serving one's country. Let us discuss the dangers of guarding a foolish man who refuses official protection. Let us talk about you, and me, and a mountain in Austria."

She took a step back, her hand came up to cover her mouth, and she felt a flood of heat washing over her face, and then all through her. Suddenly she did not feel like a burned-out, hollow shell of a being. She felt like a girl who . . . whose brother had revealed her most closely guarded secret to the last man in the world she wanted to know about it. "I am going to kill Christopher Fox MacLeod this time," she vowed. "Of all the interfering, intemperate, imbecilic—"

"What happened?" Martin's sharp question

cut her off. He took her hands tightly in his, and his gray eyes searched hers. "Who attacked you? Who tried to get through you to me? Why? Where do I find the bastard?"

He was looking at her as though she were some sort of hero. Better he should be upbraiding her for being a woman who'd tried to do a man's job. She'd upbraided herself for it not long after she'd returned to consciousness in that far-off chalet—as soon as she could think through the pain. The details were still the stuff of frequent nightmares. She didn't want to relive them now; she was afraid she might blurt out the dark truth about herself. But Martin didn't look as though he were going to allow her to do anything but tell him about the incident.

"I did not mean to get involved in a confrontation," she told him. "Truly, I didn't. I discovered someone was on the grounds who did not belong there. I meant only to sound a warning, not get into a skirmish. Really, I'm not brave."

She always carried a derringer in her reticule when she went for the walk around the grounds, but she'd never thought she'd have to use it. She was not as pragmatic as a good spy should be, and prayed she'd never have to use a weapon again.

"But you were attacked. You were gravely injured. You saved my life."

"Actually, you saved *my* life. I wouldn't have lasted out there for long if I hadn't been found."

"You still haven't told me what really happened. Who would want to kill me? That meeting in Austria was a favor for a friend, who was trying to get back some family treasures that had ended up with an Austrian art collector. There was nothing to do with any government."

"The collector was a half-mad prince," she reminded him. "There was touchy national pride to consider, a great deal of money involved, and delicate matters that could have led to family scandals."

"It seemed like a lovely holiday."

"You complained constantly that you were dealing with fools."

"I was enjoying the scenery and the cuisine, until you were hurt."

"There was too much cream in everything, you said. I remember."

He drew her closer. "Tell me what happened, Harriet. Everything. We won't be leaving this room until you do." He led her across the room and drew her down to sit beside him on the bed. A slight smile eased his serious expression when he noticed her glance anxiously toward the door. "Tell me."

"Oh—bother!"

He lifted her chin with a finger, making her look at him. To her surprise he touched his lips to hers, the kiss ever so gentle and fleeting. It sent emotions she did not want to feel through her. Emotions that threatened to soften her heart and weaken her determination. It infuriated her to know how her heart tried to rule her head over this man no matter what he did, and had since he'd opened that door four years ago and snapped at her to come inside and make herself useful. How she wished being useful to him could be enough for her.

"Who, what, why, Harriet," he urged. "I have a right to know."

She supposed he did. Perhaps she would have told him long ago—if she hadn't been wrestling with her own conscience and desperately running from the vivid memories. "It is sordid," she told him, "and you will be angry with yourself when I tell you."

"What?" he asked, only half-serious, "was it the husband of one of my mistresses?"

"It was your wife."

That rocked him back on his heels. "Sabine tried to kill me?"

He certainly didn't look as if he believed it. She didn't blame him; assassination was no way for civilized people to settle marital differences. At least in his world. The safe, secure, civilized world where Martin Kestrel was a paragon, and where Harriet MacLeod, with her bloodied hands, did not belong.

"Sabine entered my world," she told him. "Her lover was a member of a band of spies and assassins headed by a man with many unsavory resources to call upon. Sabine's lover was in trouble with this group for having brought her home rather than the information he was sent to obtain. None of that really touches on what happened in Austria, except that he and Sabine had access to the services of professional killers. Don't look so shocked, Martin. Have you never suspected such people exist?"

He slowly shook his head, and she sighed. She was glad of his innocence, but it was evidence that their worlds were so far apart that she and he could never truly touch.

"Sabine wanted a divorce," she reminded him. "You refused."

"Of course." His indignation was as strong now as it had been when Sabine sent a solicitor to bring up the subject. "I would not put Patricia through the scandal of her mother being publicly declared an adulteress. Sabine had no thought for the child's welfare."

"She did, however, strike upon a more permanent solution. She hired an assassin to end her marriage for her."

Though Martin's head spun with shock, it made horrible sense. Of course fiery, thoughtless, selfish Sabine would seek the easiest answer. *Dear God! I'm even more to blame for Harriet's injuries than I realized. If she had protected me in the line of duty I could almost— almost—have forgiven myself for my stupidity in not seeing her for her true, valiant self. But this . . . this was a curse that fell on her because I married unwisely.* It seemed that he made a habit of falling in love with the wrong women. Or so he'd been thinking for the last several days. He was sure of nothing right now, except—"This was all my fault."

"I knew you'd see it that way." Harriet shook her head.

"Is that why you never told me?"

"Yes. No. The truth is, when I first woke up, I was so befuddled that when you told me I'd fallen from a cliff, I believed you. I didn't recall anything for a few days. When the memories started to surface . . ." She shrugged and looked away. She was faintly trembling, and it twisted his heart. "It was awful, and . . . no . . ." She bit her lip, and a look of annoyance crossed her face.

He knew instantly that she was annoyed with herself for having admitted to fear and horror. He wanted to take her in his arms and hold her in a close, protective embrace. He wanted to tell her how he would never let anything or anyone harm her again. But she would not welcome any emotional advances from the man whose life she'd saved—who was the same man who'd blackmailed her into a sexual liaison and humiliated her in front of a crowd of profligate scum.

"It is not weakness to show frail mortal emotions," was as much as he dared to point out. "Depending on the time and place," he added when she gave him a stern look.

She nodded to this statement. "If word had not reached you about Sabine's death soon afterward, you would have learned about the threat. It seemed . . . kinder . . . not to let you know how despicable she was. She'd hurt you enough," Harriet lifted her chin and declared.

Trying to protect my heart as well as my person, my dear? And protecting Patricia as well, I think, from her mother's folly. Was he starting to think of Harriet as a guardian angel watching over him rather than as a sinister conspirator who used him as her cover?

"The assassin," Martin asked. "What happened to him?"

He could guess, from the way her gaze flicked everywhere but to his. He waited for long, painful seconds for her to answer, but she only shook her head. That would not do. This was a time for truth, painful, ugly truth.

"Dead?" he asked.

"I fell down a mountain," she answered, her voice low and full of anguish. "He fell further."

"There's more, isn't there?"

He stroked the back of his hand across her

cheek, trying to gentle her, to coax with his touch. Though she hid it very well, he thought she was more upset now than she had been earlier. Was knowing the truth worth putting her through such distress? Yes, he decided. For without complete truth between them, they could not move on and—

Move on to what?

"I can't—won't—say anymore about the incident right now," she finally answered. "This is not the time to dwell on it." She put a hand imploringly on his. "Please, I need a clear head tonight, Martin."

Perhaps he was being selfish in forcing the issue. She'd given him plenty to think about for now, and much to regret. "We're not through yet," he told her and rose to his feet. He held his hand out to her. "For now, I look forward to watching you dazzle the masses."

Chapter 22

We're not through yet.

What did he mean by that?

Nothing, Harriet told herself as they proceeded down the hall with her gloved hand delicately resting on his arm. Nothing at all—at least nothing that could be interpreted as meaning that there could be any future for them after tonight. *I do not and will not want it to mean anything,* she thought sternly.

All her confusion faded the moment they met a leering couple as they approached the staircase. The man swept Martin a flamboyant bow, while the woman gave Harriet a look she could only interpret as envious amusement, and fury overtook Harriet at the realization that these people interpreted Martin's behavior as masterful and romantic.

She could imagine very well what they all imagined—that the triumphant Martin had flung his prize down on the bed and claimed the body he'd won with masculine arrogance. If she closed her eyes, her imagination would have supplied all the sensations of the masterful coupling. In fact, for a moment she felt his hands and mouth on her, and more. Worse, excitement flickered deep inside her, stirring a perverse longing for the ravishment to actually have happened. Her knees went weak with combined shame and desire.

This would not do, not at all. Though her lips managed to lift in a parody of a smile, the look she gave Martin was full of venom. Or so she thought. He obviously saw something else, for he laughed and took her in his arms for a long, deep, searing kiss right there on the staircase.

After a few stiff moments her body melted against his and her arms came around his neck. "All the better to strangle you with," she whispered when his lips parted from hers.

His eyes glittered with fierce humor, and equally fierce desire. "I could take you on the stairs right now," he whispered back. He traced her lips, his touch making her head spin. "You don't kiss like a woman who would mind." Then he got himself under control and added, "But that is not in the evening's plans, is it?"

She should have shot back that it was not in the plans ever, but the words would not come, her heart would not let her head rule. "You are a wicked rogue," she said instead, and gently bit his finger when he touched her lips again. "And wrinkling my gown, besides."

"Forgive me," he said, moving to take her by the arm again.

It seemed to her that he put several meanings into those two words, but her analytical abilities were not functioning well where Martin was concerned. She tried to put thoughts of him out of her head, but not thinking about him put her on edge about facing the crowd. She'd been prepared for the ordeal when she first came out of the dressing room. If they'd come down right then everything would have been fine. Now the guilt and dark memories that had been stirred up left her rattled and unsure. This would not do, not at all.

"This is all your fault," she whispered.

"Act like a woman in love," Martin advised as they came arm in arm down the sweeping grand staircase to the main floor. "Smile like a woman who has spent long hours making love. Don't listen to a word they say."

"Be Cora Bell, in other words," she snapped back.

"Precisely." He smiled upon her with a sort of pride that only aggravated Harriet's irritation with him. There had been something particularly gentle in Martin's look. "Just because I'm a rogue doesn't mean I can't give good advice," he added.

"Sometimes rogues give the best advice," she agreed. "Of course, because they are rogues they don't follow it themselves."

"You speak like a woman who knows."

"I come from a large family, my lord. There's many a rogue dangling on my family tree."

That comment reminded Martin of many more things he wanted to learn about Harriet MacLeod. He wanted to know about her family, and her place in it, and why she'd chosen the path that led her to knock on the door of his Italian villa in the exact instant he needed her cool head and helping hands. He *must* be a rogue, he thought, because if he were to listen to his own advice, he would let the woman go and forget they'd ever crossed paths. Anything else was too tangled, complicated, and . . . "Fascinating." He breathed the word like a prayer, remembering the dreadful ennui that settled over him when they were apart.

"What?" she asked, tilting her head curiously at his odd remark.

"Being with you is never boring, I'll grant you that."

Word of their approach raced before them, as did the tale of their kissing on the stairs. The company was already primed for their entrance. Harriet knew all eyes were on them when they appeared in the doorway of the crowded reception room, but she could not manage to take her eyes off Martin. If it looked to the crowd that she gazed upon him with rapt worship and heated need . . . well, sometimes what she truly felt showed raw and open and real. This time Harriet wasn't sure if she could bottle it up again.

Which didn't mean she wasn't still angry with him.

She could almost see the sensual glow surrounding them as they moved into the room. If the masculine eyes were turned to her, then all female gazes settled on the self-assured, deeply masculine figure of Martin Kestrel. There was a fluttering of fans and eyelashes, and bright, enticing smiles turned his way. Harriet almost wished the man wasn't so blasted handsome, but tonight it had its uses.

As they reached the center of the crowded room, they shared a glance and then parted without a word, working like a pair of agents who had been partners for years. Martin spun into the orbit of the obsequious and hearty Sir Anthony, who clapped him on the back and announced loudly, "Well done, my lord! Well done, indeed!"

Harriet allowed her arm to be taken by a balding man in a red and yellow striped vest. She checked his lapels while he made some jocular comment, and moved on as soon as she saw that he wore no lily on his coat. She proceeded to make her way through the crowd, drawing attention to herself with flirtatious laughs, sultry smiles, suggestive comments, and the liquid, languid, tempting movements of a woman who loved to make love.

Tonight's entertainment called for dancing and gaming, with a buffet meal to be served at midnight. Doors had been thrown open between the reception room, dining room, gaming room, and terrace, creating an open and airy setting for the crowd to circulate through. There was altogether too much crystal and gilt and red velvet for Harriet's simple tastes, but the gaudy surroundings had a certain decadent magnificence. Massive arrangements of hot house flowers in huge gold and silver vases decorated every table, lending even brighter color, and their sweet scent perfumed the air. The women were dressed as brightly as butter-flies, and equally beautiful. Every now and then she caught a glimpse of Christopher moving with agile grace among the crowd. His flamboyant dark reddish-brown hair was combed neatly back off his forehead, his formal clothes nondescript. He knew how to make himself inconspicuous, and she did her best to help cover him.

After what seemed like forever of dancing, smiling, and permitting a certain amount of discreet groping, she caught her brother's eye one more time. This time he nodded, and the merest tilt of his chin aimed her gaze in the direction of a rotund man standing in the doorway between the gaming and reception rooms. When the man moved toward the terrace, Christopher followed discreetly.

"Ah," she said. They had their man; now it

remained to see who else would approach him. Her impulse was to grab Martin and follow her brother with him, but she stayed where she was for now. She couldn't stop from turning a triumphant smile Martin's way, though.

So the quarry is spotted at last, Martin thought. He knew even before Harriet turned his way. One moment he was watching a coquette charming a roomful of jaded roués, then, from one heartbeat to the next, he saw her sensual pose change to one of alert, focused attention. While the dark, erotic beauty dressed in peacock finery fascinated his senses and stirred his loins, the woman who turned to him to share her moment of triumph caught his heart.

The end of the chase was near. He smiled in return, happy for her. Inwardly he mourned, though he knew national security and a young man's safety hung in the balance. The bargain was fulfilled; his liaison with Harriet was at an end. So soon? He felt cheated, for he had not made love to her anywhere near enough. She would disappear into her strange, shadowy world—and apparently the loving bosom of her family. He'd be left—with strangers in his bed.

Wasn't that what she was?

Perhaps, but it hadn't felt that way.

It struck him like a bolt of lightning that he could not bear the thought of her ever being touched by any man but himself. He wanted her, body and soul. For days now her masks had been stripped away one by one, and beneath them was no stranger. He'd kept telling himself she was, but that was his wounded pride trying to put all the blame on her for making a fool of him. The woman he'd punished was guilty of no more than protecting him, even saving his life. He was the one who'd wronged her, cursed her, and treated her like a whore. He wanted a chance to hold her, cherish her, protect her, make endless passionate love to her. He didn't know what he could do to gain her forgiveness, to gain her love. He didn't know how to start, and doubted he'd be given the time to try.

His frustration ate at him so hard he mouthed a quiet curse.

He did not think anyone heard, but discovered his mistake when Lady Ellen put a hand on his arm and said, "You're such a moody fellow, I don't know why I'm drawn to you." Before he could react to the impulse to shake her off, she glanced across the room, and a smile played across her lips at the sight of Harriet.

"She's playing you for a fool, my lord. First the American, now every man at Strake House seems to be her prey."

"Play fair, my sweet," Sir Anthony said as he turned from another conversation at the sound of Lady Ellen's voice. "With the exception of intervals hanging on Lord Martin, you've been circulating constantly since you arrived. I'd hoped to have time with you myself when you put in a surprise appearance, but no!" He waggled a finger beneath her pretty, pert nose. "You've led me a merry chase, insisting on meeting every new gentleman the moment he arrived."

"But I haven't taken a fancy to anyone but Lord Martin," she replied. "There are a few people I must meet yet tonight, though," she added, patting Martin's arm as she whirled away from him. "Leave your pretty pet in Sir Anthony's care, Martin," she advised before moving toward the gaming room. "Then come visit me at Hancombe next week. I promise you a lovely time."

"Perhaps I will, my dear," Martin called after her. It was a politeness with no meaning. The thought of any woman but Harriet in his bed left a taste of ashes in his mouth. Even worse, the thought of trying to hold a decent conversation with anyone but the quick-witted, tart, and complicated Miss MacLeod was impossible to imagine.

"Interesting woman, Lady Ellen," Sir Anthony commented when she was gone.

"I find her . . . pallid," was the most polite description Martin could find, when he actually meant that he found her deadly dull.

Sir Anthony chortled. "You've obviously never had her between the sheets. I meant interesting in that she's never been so flighty before. At first she refused my invitation, because she wanted to meet you at the Hazlemoors' party. She informed me that you were the best catch in Britain and she intended to wed you. When she did show up here I assumed that she was so besotted with you that she followed you to become your mistress, for she knows you're not the sort to marry the kind of woman who is on a first-name basis with a man of my reputation. I know I'm looked down on in the clubs and in correct society. If respectable folk occasionally find their way to my country house, and never discuss what goes on here, well, then, the services I provide are tolerated."

Martin was not interested in Strake's whining about being a barely tolerated pimp for the rich and powerful, but he *was* suddenly interested in Lady Ellen's presence at Strake House. "You think Lady Ellen followed me here?"

"So I thought at first," Sir Anthony replied. "But she hasn't put much time into pursuing you. I don't think she expected to see you here."

"She was surprised to see me," Martin agreed. The look on Lady Ellen's face when they met could not have been the wiles of a superb actress; not even Harriet was that good.

"I get the impression she's both besotted with you and distracted by so many men to chose from," Strake went on. "I'd be happy if she'd settle on me, but she's been going from man to man like a bee from flower to flower, not staying long enough to pollinate anyone."

"Looking for something." Martin rubbed his jaw thoughtfully. He remembered how he'd scoffed when Harriet told him that women made excellent spies since no one paid them any mind. Or easily mistook a search for a courier as a hunt for a lover? Lady Ellen wanted him, Martin was sure of that, but she'd invited him to her home next week, not offered to take him to her bed tonight. She could no more afford to let desire rule her tonight than Harriet, could she? "You think Lady Ellen is looking for someone specific?"

"People come and go all the time at my gatherings," Sir Anthony replied. "No doubt the man for her will show up eventually if she waits long enough."

"Yes," Martin said. "I'm sure. Excuse me, Sir Anthony." Lady Ellen was making her way from one group of people to the next, heading for the doors to the terrace. He did not see Harriet's brother in the room. Never mind MacLeod, Harriet's back was to him and he could see the alert tension in her still form, an elegant sighthound straining to be let off the leash now that the game was identified. She was surrounded by avid admirers. The eagerness of so many hungry males set Martin's teeth on edge. He went to retrieve his beauty from the company of beasts.

"Come out on to the garden with me," he said, taking her by the arm and leading her away. "There's some statuary I want you to see."

Harriet could have kissed him then and

there for this timely exit. She waited until they were outside before she pulled him into the shadows beyond the golden light that flooded from the doorway and kissed him there. An hour or two ago she still had been angry enough to think she never wanted to touch him again, but now she realized that this was the last chance she'd ever have, and took full advantage of it.

Martin's arms came around her and his mouth clung to hers with hunger that matched her own. Her hands traced the strong muscles of his back and combed once more through his thick black hair. She breathed in his scent, drew in his warmth, and memorized every nuance of being held by him. It was both bitter and sweet, and it could not last.

Their lips still touched when she sighed. He understood, and moved away. "I've mussed your hair," she said, trying to get her emotions under control.

"And ruffled all my feathers besides," he added with a dimpled smile. He stayed close to her, but he put his hands behind his back. "What now?" he whispered.

Harriet peered past his wide shoulders to have a look around the terrace. Neither Christopher nor the courier was anywhere within sight. "The garden," she answered. "Everyone rendezvous in the garden." He nodded, and went to take her by the hand. Harriet shook her head. "I want to make sure no one is following me. If we can set a trap, so can our opponents. I doubt anyone suspects that our side has found out the rendezvous point, or knows anything about me, but better safe than sorry. If you could wait here for a few minutes and make sure no one follows me into the garden, I'd appreciate it."

He frowned and flicked a finger against her cheek. "You're a suspicious one, but since you ask so nicely, I'll wait and watch. But not too long," he added.

"Thank you." She placed a quick kiss on Martin's cheek, then lifted her heavy skirts and hurried down the marble terrace stairs. Though she hated to retrace her steps through the woods, she knew where she would go if she wanted to meet someone in a very private place. No light came from the grove on the other side of the trees tonight. Perhaps it was too early for an orgy, or perhaps a bacchanal was not a nightly occurrence. What mattered was reaching the grove without being observed. So Harriet bid adieu to the perfection of her lovely gown and stepped off the path to pick her way quietly through the woods, though this route took longer.

She might as well have not bothered with caution, for the grove was empty when she reached it. Or so she thought, until she discerned a deeper lump of shadow in the darkness beneath the trunk of an ancient oak. She moved cautiously, until the lump moaned.

Harriet rushed forward and fell to her knees, helping the man on the ground to sit up. "Oh, Kit," she complained. "What have you done?"

Her brother moaned again and put a hand on his head. After a few seconds he took a deep breath and said, "You could ask if the wound's mortal."

"What happened?" she demanded instead. Her fingers probed gently at the lump on her brother's head while she questioned him. "Who attacked you? Did you find out about Michael? Did you completely destroy all our covers? How many fingers?" she added, holding her hand up before his face.

"It's dark, Harry. Three. No, two. Lord, but I'm dizzy. Ouch! Stop poking me."

"I'm trying to see how you are."

"I'll live. Help me up." When she did he swayed dizzily and leaned on her while he said, "There were two agents, one to make contact, one to keep watch. Thought I'd eluded the second, but no such luck. Came from behind and knocked me on the head. Lucky he didn't finish me off. They didn't suspect me. I remember the first one said I probably came here to meet Kestrel's lover. The courier was skittish, they had to keep him from running off, so they left me alone. Tried to get up, then I passed out."

"So you didn't actually hear anything useful?"

His weight lifted from her shoulders as he stood straighter. He rubbed his head. "That's about it."

"Did you recognize their voices?"

"It was all muffled, far-off sounding."

Harriet rubbed sharply aching temples. She wanted to howl with frustration. Even the best of experienced agents lost a round occasionally, but losing this round might mean their brother's life. Christopher knew that; she had no need to throw it in his face. Not that it wasn't tempting, she was no saint, and the events of the past days had her nerves strung pretty sharply. But what they had to do now was salvage the situation.

"We can forget about the courier; the Russians have his documents. So we have to follow them."

"Aye," Christopher answered. "I doubt they'll be spending the night at Strake House."

"The trouble is, people are in and out of Strake House as if it's a resort hotel. We'll need to trace half a dozen people or more to find the ones we're looking for." They conferred as they made their way from the grove and up the path to the gardens.

"If we hurry, we can catch them in the stables or on the road," Christopher offered.

"Are you in any condition for that?" she countered.

"I'll do what I have to, Harry."

"Admirable." Martin Kestrel came around a bend in the path as Christopher spoke. He looked Christopher over in the dim light. "You are a bit worse for wear, I take it? Does he need a physician?" he asked Harriet.

"We don't have time to find out," she answered. "Did you see anyone come this way?"

340

He shook his head. "Did you notice anyone follow me?"

He shook his head again. "So your brother lost them." It was not a question. "You idiot," he told Christopher. "After all Harriet's done to salvage this operation, you let the Russian agent slip through your fingers?" His outrage was palpable, his voice dripped with contempt.

"Stay out of this." Christopher was equally outraged. "It is no longer any of your affair. It never was. You only aided Harriet to get into her drawers."

"Christopher!"

"True enough," Martin answered. "But I didn't show up at the last minute and wreck her plan, now did I?"

Harriet stepped between them to keep them from coming to blows. "Stop it! We have to find Michael. The longer we spend bickering, the more time they have to get away. We have no idea who they are, we have to—"

"I know exactly who you're looking for," Martin cut her off. "I know the name, and I know where the agent is heading. Don't fear; you can catch them up easily enough. If I choose to help," he shot at Christopher.

"Do you want me to beat it out of you?" Christopher flared back.

Martin only laughed.

Harriet wanted to beat them both. "What do you mean, 'if you choose to help'? What do you know? And how do you know it? Help me, Martin. Please."

"What I know is for sale," he answered, no room for argument in his tone. "How do I know it? I am a diplomat," he reminded her. "I listen. I watch. I ask the right questions at the right time. When I am amiable, people like to talk to me, and I have been very amiable this evening. That is how I came to find out the information all your covert sneaking about could not discern."

"Superior bastard, aren't you?" Christopher asked him. "Tell the woman what she asked for and stop showing off."

Martin's attention stayed steadily on Harriet. She could sense his gaze burning into her, hard and uncompromising. Her response was visceral, instinctively female, kindling a dark burning deep inside her. A wild pang of desire shot through her, and she had to sternly tell herself to keep her mind on business.

342

She grasped his wrist. "What do you want?" she asked. "Name your price."

She saw a gleam of white teeth as he smiled in triumph. His laugh was low, thoroughly arrogant. "I'll name the price in private," he said. "All you have to do right now is unconditionally agree to pay it."

"Carte blanche?" she asked.

"Precisely. What I want, when I ask for it—and I'll name your brother's abductors."

"This is outrageous," Christopher interjected. "Harriet, don't you dare agree to this seducer's demands! We can do this on our own."

"How much time do you have?" Martin asked softly.

Blast him! Once again he held all the cards. He was good at that. "Fine," she sealed the bargain. "What you want, when you want it."

"Done." He kissed her swiftly to seal the pact.

"I'll kill you for this," Christopher declared.

"Later," she said. "We have to go now."

Chapter 23

I had better be right.

This was not the first time the thought crossed Martin's mind on the journey from Strake House. It repeated as steadily in his head as the sound of the horses' hooves and the repetitious rattle of carriage and train wheels as they swiftly made their way south. A young man's life and state secrets both hung in the balance on his guess that Lady Ellen was actually an agent of the Russian government.

He knew full well that if Harriet had called his bluff, he would have unhesitatingly told her what she needed to know. Had she not been distracted by one injured brother and fear for the other, she would not have been fooled for a moment. Or so he hoped. Could she really think he held life so cheap?

Why shouldn't she? he answered himself. He'd already blackmailed her into his bed, why shouldn't she think him capable of even more heinous behavior? Well, if she'd told him about this Michael MacLeod to begin with, perhaps—

No, he'd acted like a cad. She had every right to think him capable of anything. All he'd been trying for with his desperate gamble was to have more time with Harriet. If he'd given her the information then and there the MacLeods would have hared off to the rescue immediately, and Martin's chance to make her his would have been gone.

I had better be right about Lady Ellen's involvement.

He had steadfastly refused to tell them anything but that they needed to head toward London, ensuring that he came with them as guide. Christopher protested, but there was nothing he could do but grudgingly yield to Martin's rules for this engagement. The siblings then swung into action, providing the necessary transport for the quickest possible journey with efficient alacrity. First they stole the three best horses from Sir Anthony's stable, and the chase was on.

Many hours later Martin was tired, grubby, in need of a shave, and sleep even more—but here he was in what the MacLeods called a safe house in a quiet, middle-class enclave on the outskirts of London. He'd asked why they could not simply return to his town house or to their aunt's establishment, but had been told that a neutral base of operations cut down the risk of being compromised. This was all so much jabberwocky to Martin, but he didn't put up any argument.

There had been little conversation on the breakneck journey. Christopher MacLeod as a glaring chaperone was even more daunting than Mrs. Swift. Martin could only be grateful that she had not come along for the ride as well. She and Cadwell had been left to make a more decorous exit from Strake House with their masters' belongings, and Martin fervently hoped never to lay eyes on Harriet's viper-tongued maid again.

He wiped a hand across his face as he looked out a window in the kitchen where Harriet had hastily prepared breakfast for them. Even spies out to mount a daring rescue needed sustenance and some rest, Martin supposed, and he welcomed the hot, strong mug of tea he held in his hands. He must truly be at the end of his energy if his thoughts had turned to Mrs. Swift. He must be dreaming on his feet.

"Nightmares, more likely."

"What did you say?" Harriet asked from where she sat with an empty plate in front of her.

Christopher had wolfed down a hasty meal and then taken himself and his raging headache off for a short nap, giving Martin a hard, warning look before leaving his sister alone with him.

"I said," Martin answered, turning from the window and the view of the gray day, "that I think your sibling expects me to ravish you on the kitchen table."

"Nonsense," she answered. "You are far too tired to ravish anyone at the moment."

"Precisely," he agreed, and yawned to punctuate the truth of it. He noticed that she blushed faintly at mention of ravishment, but didn't tease her about it. He let her fiddle nervously with her teacup and settled for watching while silence drew out between them. She was a tired, bedraggled, anxious woman, but she'd never been more beautiful to him. He wondered if his longing for her was as palpable to her as it was to him. What was she thinking about him? Did she hate him for all the things he'd done, and the threat of more indignities he held over her? Or had she put aside her feelings to concentrate on the job ahead of them?

Before he could ask, she lifted her head and said, "We have to go soon."

"Do we?"

"Christopher and I," she amended. "As soon as you tell us where."

Martin set his cup down on the table and ran a hand though his disheveled hair. "There is no need for you to be involved in anything dangerous." He wanted to slam a fist on the wooden surface and forbid her to put herself in danger, but that would only get him an arch look and a sarcastic comment. "Let Christopher handle whatever needs to be done."

"That's what Christopher will say." Her smile was only slightly sarcastic and arch. "But his arguments will do no more good than yours would."

"I'll save them, then," he agreed. "You are a very difficult woman. I like you that way," he added, "but I wish you'd be reasonable and let me take my information to the authorities who are trained to handle such matters."

"They aren't," she said.

"A young constable named MacQuarrie was assisting me in tracking you down. I could contact him."

"Did he find me?"

"No. But—"

"He wouldn't have. Aunt Phoebe *let* you find me, and only because she decided you were trustworthy enough to deliver the message that set us hunting for Michael."

He frowned. "I delivered a secret message?"

"Yes."

"I see." He concentrated for a few moments, then shook his head. "I'm trying to work up a fit of outrage at being used, but I seem to be too tired to manage it."

"Or you've gotten used to us."

"That might be it. Why don't I call MacQuarrie?"

She shook her head. "Because things aren't done that way."

"A week ago that would not have made sense to me."

"It still doesn't, but instead of discussing police work versus espionage work, why don't you tell me where I'm going and who I have to confront?"

"Are you sure your brother is really in danger?" he persisted. "Perhaps—"

"He's being tortured," she answered. Her jaw tightened with anger and her green eyes flashed. "He knows a great deal, and is handing them information a bit at a time. The longer it takes to find out what he knows, the longer he survives. He's counting on his family finding him from the information that the other side acts upon. That's why knowing who contacted the courier is so important." She stood. "That's why you have to tell me now."

He nodded. "You are right. However, if you are going along on this rescue, so am I."

"Martin!"

He put up a hand. "Before you point out that I am not trained for espionage, let me say that there's no debate on the subject. You're going, your brother is going, and I am going. I know a way I can be of help. I really *want* to be of help," he added.

He didn't know whether she believed him or not, but he saw curiosity and hope in her guarded expression. She bit her lip to keep from arguing while she got herself used to the idea, and finally said, "Fine. It's on your own head if you get hurt."

"I appreciate your concern."

"Just tell me who and where, Martin."

"Lady Ellen Causely," he answered. "Michael will be at Hancombe Manor, her house in Hampstead."

"Lady Ellen?" She was furious, but didn't argue the possibility. "I should have known that weasel-faced tart was up to no good."

"I quite agree. She wants to marry me," he added. "It seems I attract spies."

"The way horse dung attracts flies," said Christopher, who'd come silently into the kitchen.

"Marry you!" Harriet sputtered.

Martin was quite pleased with her indignation. Perhaps there was yet hope. "Lady Ellen says I'm the best catch in Britain."

"Does she indeed?" Harriet had never

looked more dangerous than when she asked this question.

"Oh, yes. She's mad for me—which is why you need me to create the diversion that will get you in and out of Hancombe Manor unnoticed."

After a moment, Christopher said grudgingly, "He's right, Harry. We need him."

"My dear, I know you invited me for next week, but I could not wait so long before seeing you again."

"Martin! I am so happy to see you."

Martin strode across the sitting room and took Lady Ellen's hands in his, drawing her up from her chair. She did not look as if she'd been sitting very long; her gown was not suitable for the time of day, and her hair had the look of having been hastily done up. Her lips were drawn up in the thinnest of smiles, and there was no warmth at all in her bloodshot eyes. Her gaze darted past him nervously when the maid began to shut the sitting room door, and she jumped at the sound of it closing. She was, in point of fact, not happy to see him at all.

"No need to send for tea," he said, bending to kiss the tips of her fingers. He looked up at her from beneath his eyelashes. "Let us take the time to be alone and share pleasant . . . conversation. Or on second thought . . ." He drew Lady Ellen toward the door.

His job was to play the decoy. To make as much noise and fuss as possible, so no one would notice that rescuers were breaking in the back of the house to search for a hidden prisoner. Hancombe Manor was not a large property, but it was secluded behind a high stone wall. The only outbuildings were a small stable and a few storage sheds, not promising places for hiding a prisoner. Christopher claimed Michael was most likely being held in a storeroom belowstairs, so he and Harriet had elected to dispose of any guards at the back of the house and enter there.

Martin had boldly walked in the front door, loudly proclaiming that he must see the fair Ellen, though the butler had at first protested that Her Ladyship was not at home. Though Martin had not had a thing to drink, an aroma of alcohol pervaded his suit. While he had shaved and cleaned up as best he could while at the safe house, he knew he looked like a besotted fool who'd followed a woman home to seduce her. He now paused in urging Lady

Ellen toward the door to kiss his way up her arm and across her throat, making it a long, lingering process. She stood still and let him, but her body remained stiff with taut nerves.

"Please," she said. "I don't think—"

"No need to, my dear," he proclaimed, and brushed his lips across hers. "I'll think for us both. Better yet, let impulse rule." He swung her up into his arms.

"Martin! No!"

He ignored her protest, banged open the door, and carried her out into the entrance hall. "Where's the bedroom?" he shouted at the top of his lungs. Servants came rushing through doorways and paused to goggle as he swung their mistress around, his deep voice booming as loud as he could. "Show me the way to heaven!"

Lady Ellen was a lovely woman, soft and round, a sensual bundle in his arms, and her skin tasted warm and ripe beneath his lips. Martin felt nothing but contempt for her, and would just as happily have walked to the nearest window and thrown her out into the rose bushes. He could not imagine his body responding to any woman but Harriet. His heart and soul could never be touched by anyone but her. Now all he had to do was complete the diversion, so he could rush to Harriet and prove his devotion.

"Put me down!" Lady Ellen cried. "Go away, you fool! I have no time for you now!"

"No time!" He chuckled salaciously. "If you don't want to wait for a featherbed at your back, my dear, we can do it on the stairs!"

There was a gasp of shock from the gaping circle of servants. The affronted butler hastily approached.

"Make him put me down!" Lady Ellen cried as Martin turned toward the stairs, pretending to stumble.

"Have a care, sir," the butler demanded. "Please put my lady down."

Martin swung around to face the butler. Lady Ellen was beating on his chest with her fists, making it a bit hard for him to talk. "P-put h-her down, you s-say? I'm her true love, m-man. She wants me."

"I do not want you!" Ellen shouted in his ear.

"You said I'm the best catch in London!"

"I don't care—put me down this instant!"

"Oh." Martin spread his arms and let her drop to the floor. She hit with a mighty bang on the hardwood.

"My lady!" a maid cried and ran forward.

"Out!" the butler shouted. "Get out this instant."

Martin drew himself up with all the dignity he possessed. "I know when I'm not wanted," he declared and marched regally out the way he'd come, bumping into a doorway for effect.

He could only hope that he'd bought the others enough time by making an utter fool of himself. Making an utter fool of himself was worth it if the price was the safe return of a MacLeod to the bosom of a family Martin believed was very large indeed. He wouldn't know if they'd been successful until they rendezvoused back at the safe house. He would have run if he could, but entered the hackney cab he'd left waiting at the end of the lane and was driven decorously away.

"You're still attracted to him aren't you?"

"Shh." Harriet didn't want to think about it.

She'd just returned from dragging the unconscious guard into a garden shed and making sure he was securely tied and gagged with the restraints and gag she'd brought with her. Christopher had a lockpick out and was working on a side door to the house. A deep, ivy-covered trellis arched over this entrance, providing enough cover to conceal them.

"He's an arrogant swine," Kit went on.

"He has a few good points," she whispered back. He was risking his neck to help them right now, for one. She smiled a little. Martin's action was indeed earning him points with her. Not that she wasn't still furious with him, but . . .

Kit glanced up at her and grinned. "I see. You could do worse, I suppose," he admitted grudgingly. "You're not getting any younger, Harry."

While that might be true, it was no reason to be attracted to a man who'd treated her as Martin had. Still . . . Oh, she didn't know. She needed to think. She hadn't had a moment's peace or a minute alone since he'd tracked her down on Skye. She'd had to concentrate on the assignment, and before she could properly confront Martin she needed to work through what he meant to her, what she wanted, and whether she dared risk telling him the whole truth about herself.

And this was not the time to think about all that. "Are you going to unlock the door or not?" she asked impatiently.

"Already done," he said, and rose gracefully to his feet. The lockpick disappeared up his sleeve, then he produced a tin of thick balm and greased the hinges as a precaution. The door swung open without a sound and they moved cautiously into a small breakfast room. The room had two other doors. One led toward the front of the house. The other let onto a butler's pantry, which led into the kitchen. They waited, listening intently, until shouting started in the front of the house. As soon as Martin's voice rose in the distance, they headed for the deserted kitchen. While the servants were being treated to a show out front, Harriet and Kit rushed down to the basement.

There was indeed a locked storeroom. Harriet held a gun at the ready while Christopher swiftly picked the lock. When he was done they rushed into the room, using surprise to get past any internal guards. Fortunately, all they found in the storeroom was Michael. He was tied to a heavy chair, his mouth gagged. Both his eyes were blackened, but amusement lit them when he saw his siblings.

"They're a small-time operation," was the first thing Michael said when the gag was removed. "I don't think they're part of Rostovich's gang, but freelance brokers who funnel information to the Russians. I met this girl in Paris. Wasn't taken in by her, but let her think I was. Got a coded message off to Aunt Phoebe that the girl might be trying to seduce a MacLeod to their side, and I wanted to let her lead me to her controller. Only she drugged me, and . . . here I am. The controller is named Lady Ellen Causely, by the way."

"Want me to put the gag back in?" Harriet asked Kit as they worked on the ropes.

"Report on how later," Christopher told Michael. "How many in the house, and how well armed?"

"Haven't the faintest idea. I see you figured out that I'd given them the courier drop point so they'd send someone and you'd follow their agent."

"Yes," Christopher agreed.

Harriet could see that her older brother had tensed up at the mention of Rostovich, but Michael wouldn't notice.

"Report later," she repeated Christopher's admonition. "Done here."

"Done here."

Michael sighed. "Can we go now?"

"Can you walk?" Harriet asked, helping him to his feet.

He hugged her and laughed softly. "To get away from here, I'll run."

Chapter 24

"Where is she?" Martin demanded, standing in the middle of Lady Phoebe Gale's sitting room.

The old woman looked at him blandly. "I have no idea."

"That, madam, is a bald-faced lie."

When her brothers had returned to the safe house, Harriet had not been with them. All Martin could get from Christopher was the flat statement that Kestrel wasn't good enough for his sister and ought to be shot. MacLeod had grudgingly thanked him for his help in rescuing Michael, then showed him the door.

Martin had stalked off in a fit of red rage. But after he left, he didn't know where to go or what to do. He had served his purpose; he was no longer welcome in the world of the MacLeods. And Harriet had once again disappeared.

He had shared her company for every hour of the last few incredibly intense days, and for hundreds of hours before that, when he thought her someone else. Even in disguise she had always essentially been herself. He could not imagine a life without her, whatever she cared to call herself.

After hours of roaming the city in devastated shock, he remembered Lady Phoebe Gale and rushed off to confront Harriet's great-aunt. The woman looked at him now as if she barely recognized him, and dared to state that she had no idea where her niece was.

"I won't tolerate any more interference," he threatened. "She belongs to me and I'll have her. You'll tell me where she is right now."

"Belongs to you?" The old lady lifted a delicately shaped silver eyebrow. "Belongs? I see. So you'll have her no matter what she's done or who she is?"

"Of course. I love her."

After he said it, he stood blinking in dumb shock. He'd never said it before, had he? Certainly never told Harriet. Abigail, yes. He'd declared his love to her, when he thought she was—Blast and damn, the two were one and the same! Harriet *knew* he loved her. Except she didn't, did she? How could she believe he loved her, after all he'd said and done in the last several days?

"Never mentioned the word to Harriet, I see," Lady Phoebe concluded. "Well, aren't you the prize fool?"

Martin wiped a hand across his face. He was so tired, so confused. His heart weighed a ton and hurt like boiling lead had been poured into it. "Yes," he agreed. "A fool in love."

"Then you'd best tell Harriet."

"But I don't know where she is!"

Lady Phoebe folded her hands before her and looked calmly up at him. "I am sorry, young man, but for once I am not lying. I have no idea where my great-niece is this time. She should have returned to the safe house with her brothers. If she did not, and didn't tell them where she was going . . ." The old woman gave a slight shrug. "I can't help you." She put a hand on his arm. "Go home. Get some sleep. I'll do what I can to find her. Come back tomorrow, and I'll tell you whatever I find out."

He wanted to search Lady Phoebe's house

from attic to basement, wanted to demand Harriet be produced like a rabbit from a magician's hat. But he believed what the woman told him. She had no knowledge of where her niece was. He swore under his breath, and didn't bother to apologize. She didn't seem to mind.

"Go home," she urged again.

He nodded wearily. "Thank you," he said, and for some reason he did not understand, he kissed her cheek before he left her parlor. Dejected, utterly disheartened, he hailed a hackney and ordered the driver to take him to his town house.

Most of the servants were still away on their summer holiday. Martin was glad. He didn't want company, he didn't want anyone fussing over him. If he didn't have Harriet, he wanted to be alone. He climbed the stairs, but instead of turning down the hallway that led to his bedroom, he turned at the landing and walked up one more flight. His mind was blank but for the pain; his footsteps led him on the familiar path of their own volition. First to his daughter's bedroom, then through the schoolroom, toward the governess's bedroom.

There was a faint light under the door.

His heart stopped. "Harriet?" he called softly, and pushed the door open.

She turned as he entered. She wore a familiar dove-gray gown, and her dark brown hair was tumbled over her shoulders and down her back. She held her silver hairbrush in her hand, and blushed when she saw him.

"Martin?"

He stood frozen in the doorway, unable to move any farther. His heart rammed hard in his chest, coming back to life. It took him a moment to find his voice. "What are you doing here?" he finally asked.

"Well . . ." She put the brush down on the dressing table. "I needed something to wear. And a bath." Her words came out with slow diffidence that made him believe that the simple necessities of life were not the only reason she'd retreated to this spartan room in an empty house.

"You wanted to be alone," he interpreted.

"I—yes." Her shoulders slumped. "Oh, Martin, you have no idea how much I needed to be alone for a while."

"Shall I"—he gestured toward the doorway,

trying to behave like a gentleman, though he ached to rush forward and take her in his arms— "leave you, then?"

"Leave me?" Her voice cracked. "Do you want to?"

He shook his head. "No. Not at all."

"Well . . ." She gestured toward the room's one chair. "Well, then . . ."

"Politeness does not become you. Not when dealing with me," he added.

After a hesitation she said, "Nor you with me." After another pause she asked, "Why is that, do you think?"

"Because we are a great deal alike." He moved closer to her rather than sitting down. He didn't think she noticed moving closer to him, as well. They stopped face to face in the center of the room.

"You think we're alike?" she asked.

He nodded.

Her shoulders tensed, and her hands balled into fists at her sides. "We're not alike," she said. "You're a good man. I'm not a good person at all."

"A good man would not have put you through the last few days," he confessed. "A good man would not have needed to do the things I did to salve his wounded pride. I haven't told you how sorry I am yet, but I am. I know you said we are through. I know you probably can't forgive me for . . . despoiling you like I did."

She looked at the floor. "I did agree—"

"To save your brother. I know it wasn't done out of some secret desire to sleep with me."

"Well—" Her gaze flashed up to his, and she smiled slightly. "I did enjoy the experience." Her voice grew more confident as she added, "I am not the fainting maiden sort, you know."

How he wanted to touch her, to kiss those smiling lips. "I still shouldn't have been so insistent. How can I ever ask you to forgive me?"

She shrugged. "You could try saying, 'Harriet, I'm sorry.' "

He rubbed his jaw. "I was hoping you'd tell me that there was no need for forgiveness."

"Not for the despoiling part. But that card game—"

"I wasn't trying to publicly humiliate you. I see now how you could interpret it that way, considering that I'd been behaving like a bastard to you the whole day. I only acted like that because I was enjoying your company too much."

She considered his words for a moment, then said, "Your logic escapes me."

"It escapes me as well, now. But at the time I was trying to talk myself out of being in love with you."

"Oh. I thought you were doing a very good job of keeping me from being in love with you."

"Oh." He put his hands gently on her shoulders. He was afraid to do more.

She was there, and he wasn't letting her out of his arms again no matter if she wanted to fly or not. He hoped, prayed, that she didn't truly want to fly from him. There was something eating at her, some truth she feared to tell him— but there were other issues to work through first, to smooth the way. He was good at talking, good at diplomacy, and this was the negotiation of a lifetime. It meant a lifetime together or apart—and he wasn't about to lose.

Harriet felt as brittle and fragile as ancient glass. Martin's hands on her shoulders were the only source of warmth in the world; his touch was the only thing steadying her. She felt as though she were going to break apart, or drift away. She felt so full, and yet so empty. So full of the truth she wanted to bring out in the open. The emptiness was a precursor of the hollow shell that would be the rest of her life if he heard the truth and turned away.

Hours away from him had shown her that all she wanted to do was rush back to his side, and stay at his side. Love did not leave room for stiff-necked pride, she'd discovered in the hours she'd spent hidden in this familiar sanctuary. She wanted to be with him, every day, for as long as he wanted. If that meant continuing as his mistress, she'd revel in the role and be the best mistress any man had ever had. She wanted to make love to him, laugh with him, fight with him, make any sort of life she could with him.

But he might not want her, if she told him.

Yet how was she to live with herself, or with him, if she did not? Love had to have truth on both sides, or it really wasn't love at all.

"Did it work?" Martin asked, interrupting her reverie.

She frowned at him. "Did what work?"

"My wretched behavior at Strake House. Did it convince you not to love me? *Do* you love me?"

"Do you love me?" she countered. Then she wished she hadn't asked. She had no right to ask, not when she hadn't yet told him about—

"With all my heart," he answered, and bent forward.

She thought he was going to kiss her on the lips, but he chastely kissed her cheek like a proper suitor, while her heart and her head kept repeating, *With all my heart*. Her knees went weak, and warmth flared deep inside her.

"I love you," she heard herself say. "With more than my heart."

He kissed her other cheek, then her forehead, then her temples, one by one. "More than your heart?" he whispered in her ear. "With your soul, perhaps?"

"That, too," she answered.

His rich, wicked chuckle sent a shiver through her. "With your body, perhaps?" he asked.

Her breath caught. "Yes. With that."

"Ah." His hands brushed across her, not quite touching, as he had seduced her at Strake House, once again kindling a trail of fire in her imagination. "You love me." His voice was like warm honey.

"Yes." She closed her eyes as she sighed. She

370

didn't recall when her body had fitted itself against his, but it felt good and right to press against him like this.

"Since you love me, you won't find fulfilling our latest bargain onerous." Harriet stiffened and pushed away from him. Or would have, if his arms had not been like steel bands around her. "You do recall you promised to do anything I want?" he reminded her.

She searched his face. He was wearing his diplomat's cool mask, but there was a wicked sparkle in his gray eyes. She didn't know what to make of the combination. All she could do was warily acknowledge, "I remember."

"Good. We'll get back to the bargain in a moment. First, my love, my heart, my Harriet, you must tell me what's troubling you." He kissed her on the lips this time, deeply and passionately. "Tell me," he urged again. "And let me help make it better."

Her heart sank. Panic threatened and she wanted to run for the door. *Love demands honesty*, she sternly reminded herself. A minute from now he might not love her, but there was no putting it off any longer.

"I am not like other people, Martin. Not like civilized people. My background is unconventional. I was raised to be self-sufficient. I was also trained to . . . act . . . if need be. I killed a man." She looked Martin in the eye and spoke with the utmost calm. "I put a gun to his head and shot him. Can you love a woman who is capable of doing that?"

Silence reigned between them for a while. He looked very thoughtful but not repulsed. He did not push her away. Finally, he said, "Harriet, my wife tried to have me murdered."

"She did not try to kill you herself. *She* was not personally capable of murder. I am. Do you want a woman who knows how to kill in your bed, at your board, living in the same house with your daughter?"

"Yes," he answered. "Do you have any more questions?"

"Martin! You are not taking me seriously."

He almost grinned. "You know how to kill people—I will always take you seriously. Besides, if you are going to be my bodyguard—"

"I have never been that. That is what the foreign office pays Cadwell for. I work in a supervisory capacity."

"Cadwell?" He did not sound outraged. "I should have thought of that; he was in the army. But *you* saved me from the assassin; that was hardly supervisory. That *is* the man you shot, isn't it? The one who tried to kill me?"

She nodded. "He did fall over the cliff, but not until after I shot him. The gun was knocked out of my hand when he fell. He grabbed me by the wrist as he went over, and I don't recall anything after that. As far as I know, his body was never found."

"But his death still weighs on your conscience."

"I do not approve of killing, Martin. I did what I had to, but—" She suddenly found herself clinging to him, and his coat was wet with her tears. "It was awful. I have nightmares ... still ... I see his face, and the blood—and how could you love me when I ... did ... that ... "

He held her close, and he let her cry. His embrace was like a shield against the night, against the evil of the world. She felt safe with him, and if he could love her, if only a little— maybe she would be all right.

After a while, she sniffed one last time and muttered, "Oh, blast. I can be so pathetic sometimes."

"A little weakness now and then is a good thing," he told her gently.

"Do you hate me?" she asked him. "Should I go now?"

"Woman, I adore you—guns, insane family, and all. Harriet, you saved my life. I can never show you how grateful I am. Never love you enough for what you did, and what you are, and what we can be together."

"Together?" she asked, and dared to let herself hope. "Really?"

He nodded. "I've been an arrogant fool. I hope that you'll someday forgive me for what I put you through. You are a heroine, a shining paragon of honor and duty. I am humble before you—"

"You are going to make us both ill if you don't stop soon," she warned.

"You are also the only sure antidote for my pomposity," he concluded. "How could I possibly live without you?" He put his hands on her shoulders again and moved a little way back from her. "Now," he said, "are you prepared to fulfill our bargain?"

"Actually, I realized you were bluffing about that as soon as I had time to think about it."

"You still agreed—in front of a witness."

"Christopher would swear on a stack of Bibles that he didn't hear a thing."

"You are a very difficult woman." He was grinning like a maniac gargoyle as he said it, and she couldn't help but laugh.

"It takes a difficult woman to deal with a difficult man. All right," she added, fully prepared to plunge into whatever the future offered. "What shall we do?"

"You can't very well remain my mistress, if we live in sin, your father will have my balls on biscuits." He waved a finger under her nose. "You are going to marry me, young woman. You will make an honest man of me, and be a mother to Patricia. And mother to many more sons and daughters before we're done. You've already agreed to it."

She grinned back at him. "I have. I will."

"We have a deal, then?"

She nodded emphatically. "Mr. Ambassador, we do."

They did not seal the bargain with a handshake, but came together like a force of nature, and sealed their bargain with a kiss.

Dear Reader,

If you're like me, once you've finished one book you are already reaching for the next. After all, it's so hard to leave a good love story behind, and it's only the prospect of being swept away on another romantic adventure that keeps me going. Well, you won't have long to wait—next month, look for these spectacular Avon romances.

Connie Mason, *USA TODAY* bestselling author, returns with *A Touch So Wicked*, her newest and most sensuous Avon Romantic Treasure yet! When Damian Stratton arrives in the Scottish Highlands, he seeks to prevent a wedding by kidnapping the defiant bride, Elissa, Maiden of Misterly. Soon, he has little choice but to marry the infuriating woman himself.

Lovers of contemporary romance will be thrilled that *USA TODAY* bestselling author Patti Berg's *Something Wild* is coming next month and it's filled with all the sexy sass that her many readers have come to love. Here, meet Charity Wilde—a Las Vegas showgirl who is not about to let anyone take advantage of her. But she wants to be a star, not a rancher's wife . . . even if the prospective husband is handsome Mike Flynn.

In Malia Martin's *Pride and Prudence*, "the most delectable man in England," James Ashley, wants one woman only—lovely Lady Prudence Farnsworth. But she might just be linked to his despised enemy. Still, when two passionate souls come together it takes more than pride to keep them apart.

And in Denise Hampton's *My Lady's Temptation*, a dashing knight, Josce FitzBaldwin, comes galloping into Knabwell castle in search of a bride. He longs for beautiful Elianne du Hommet, but how can he submit to his desire when Elianne is the daughter of a man he has vowed to destroy?

I know you are going to love these books. Enjoy!

Lucia Macro

Lucia Macro
Executive Editor

REL 0102

Avon Romantic Treasures

*Unforgettable, enthralling love stories,
sparkling with passion and adventure
from Romance's bestselling authors*